"What do you
will be

Nate shrugged one shoulder. "Don't have any idea." He stopped and gazed down at her, his green eyes bright in the daylight. "Don't know how to say this in Spanish, but I'd like to call it 'the place where I hope Susanna settles down.'"

She should answer with something saucy. Should laugh and walk away. Instead, she breathed out, "Oh, Nate, what a lovely thing to say."

She had no idea how long they stood staring at each other. Yet she felt no embarrassment or awkwardness, just very much at home. Distant sounds reached her ears. Birds sang. Cattle bawled. Bess barked. None shattered the wrapped-in-cotton feeling that surrounded her. Against everything Mama had taught her, against her own sense of right and wrong, she longed for him to kiss her right here and now. She also hoped he would not. That was a bridge they must not cross, not now or ever.

Books by Louise M. Gouge

Love Inspired Historical

Love Thine Enemy
The Captain's Lady
At the Captain's Command
*A Proper Companion
*A Suitable Wife
*A Lady of Quality
†Cowboy to the Rescue

*Ladies in Waiting
†Four Stones Ranch

LOUISE M. GOUGE

has been married to her husband, David, for forty-nine years. They have four children and eight grandchildren. Louise always had an active imagination, thinking up stories for her friends, classmates and family but seldom writing them down. At a friend's insistence, she finally began to type up her latest idea. Before trying to find a publisher, Louise returned to college, earning a BA in English/creative writing and a master's degree in liberal studies. She reworked that first novel based on what she had learned and sold it to a major Christian publisher. Louise then worked in television marketing for a short time before becoming a college English/humanities instructor. She has had fifteen novels published, several of which have earned multiple awards, including the Inspirational Reader's Choice Award and the Laurel Wreath Award. Please visit her website at blog.louisemgouge.com.

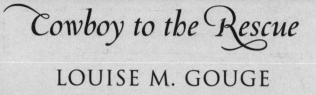

Cowboy to the Rescue

LOUISE M. GOUGE

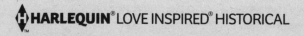

HARLEQUIN® LOVE INSPIRED® HISTORICAL

LOVE INSPIRED BOOKS

ISBN-13: 978-0-373-28279-1

COWBOY TO THE RESCUE

Copyright © 2014 by Louise M. Gouge

www.Harlequin.com

Printed in U.S.A.

Except the Lord build the house,
they labor in vain that build it.
—*Psalms* 127:1

This book is dedicated to the intrepid pioneers
who settled the San Luis Valley of Colorado
in the mid- to late 1800s. They could not have found
a more beautiful place to make their homes than
in this vast 7500 ft. high valley situated between the
majestic Sangre de Cristo and San Juan Mountain
ranges. It has been many years since I lived in the
San Luis Valley, so my thanks go to Pam Williams
of Hooper, Colorado, for her extensive on-site research
on my behalf. With their permission, I named two
of my characters after her and her husband, Charlie.
These dear old friends are every bit as kind
and wise as their namesakes. I also must thank
my dear husband of forty-nine years, David Gouge
(a U.S. Army veteran), for his help in character
development, especially for my military characters.

Chapter One

June 1878

Daddy wouldn't make it through another bitter-cold night. Susanna wasn't even sure how she'd managed not to freeze to death on this Colorado mountainside over the past ten or so hours. Maybe her anger had kept her alive, a real rage like some folks back home in Georgia still felt toward the North and all Yankees. For the first time in all her nineteen years, she understood firsthand how they felt.

The only trouble was that she had no idea whom to hate. Still, if God brought them out of this predicament, she would see to it that justice was meted out on whoever robbed Daddy, beat him almost to death and left him to die amid their scattered belongings. If Susanna hadn't been over the hill fetching water for their supper, she had no doubt those men would have done their worst to her, as well. Always the protector, Daddy had managed to tell her that when the villains had demanded to know who owned the female fripperies in the wagon, he'd told them his wife had been buried on the trail. Such a lie must

have cost her truthful father dearly, but it had saved her
from unknown horrors.

She placed a small log on the fire and used a poker to
stir the flames she had somehow kept alive throughout
the night. The sun had just begun to shed some light on
La Veta Pass, so the day should soon warm up enough
for her to make plans about how to get out of this mess.
Daddy's fever didn't seem too high. Or maybe the cold
just made his clammy skin seem cooler. No matter. She
had to find a way to get them down into the San Luis
Valley to a ranch house or town. One thing was sure. His
silver prospecting would have to wait until he recovered.

A familiar ache smote Susanna's heart, but she quickly
dismissed it. No use reminding herself or Daddy that
if they hadn't left Georgia, they wouldn't be in this fix
now. Oh, how she longed for her safe, comfortable home
back in Marietta. All she had ever wanted was to marry a
good Christian gentleman and raise a family in the hometown she loved so much, just as her parents had. Many
of her friends had already married. Some had children.
She couldn't think of a more satisfying life. But before
Mama died last autumn, she'd made Susanna promise to
take care of Daddy. She didn't regret her promise, but she
was fairly certain Mama never dreamed he'd want to go
prospecting out West. She'd had no choice but to pack up
and go with him, deferring her own dreams for his and
leaving her future to the Lord. After last night's attack,
surely she would have no trouble convincing Daddy to
return to their safe, happy life in Marietta.

"Belle." His raspy voice cut into Susanna's thoughts.

"No, dearest." She swallowed the lump in her throat.
Several times in the night, he'd cried out for Mama. "It's
me, Susanna."

"Ah, yes. Of course." Daddy's eyes cleared and seemed

to focus on her. Then he grimaced in pain and clenched his teeth. After a few moments of clutching his ribs and writhing, during which Susanna dabbed his fevered forehead with a cloth, he shuddered as if to shove away his pain. "Young lady, have you made my morning coffee yet?"

His gruff, teasing tone would have encouraged her if she didn't know the terrible extent of his injuries. The thieving monsters who had attacked him seemed not to have left an inch of his body unbeaten. She knew he had some broken bones, yet he was being brave for her, as he always was. Now she must somehow be brave for him.

"Coffee, is it? I guess I could manage that." She tucked the woolen blankets around him, then gathered her rifle and bucket. "I'll get some water and be back before you can whistle a chorus of 'Dixie.'" She waited a moment for one of his quipped responses, but his eyes were closed and his breathing labored. *Please, Lord, watch over him.*

Trudging up the small, tree-covered rise, Susanna paused to stretch and shake off the stiffness that had crept into her limbs while she'd slept on the cold ground beside Daddy with only a few blankets for cover. She hadn't been able to lift him into the prairie schooner, and she couldn't leave him alone outside.

The thieves hadn't simply stolen their horses, her favorite cast-iron pot and her silver hairbrush; they'd slashed the bedding and dumped out their flour and cornmeal in search of hidden money. Still, they'd found only the paper bills Daddy had kept in his wallet for just such encounters. Even though they'd destroyed just about everything in the wagon, the secret compartment below its floorboards remained secure, as did the gold coins sewn into her skirt. But she'd trade all that gold to be sure Daddy would survive his injuries.

Once over the small hill, she made her way down the shadowed slope to the snowy banks of the rushing creek. Imagine that, snow in June. Back home in Marietta, she reckoned folks were already feeling the summer heat.

Resting her rifle against an aspen, she anchored herself by gripping a budding green branch with one leather-gloved hand, then dipped the metal pail into the surging waters with the other. It filled in seconds, and she hoisted it back to the bank with little effort, snatched up her rifle and began her trek back to the campsite.

What would Mama think of her newfound strength, her growing muscles? Mama had always said that a lady should never be too strong or too capable when it came to physical labors. Such work was for men and servants. But these past months of crossing mountains, rivers and plains had put Susanna through trials harder than any Mama had ever faced.

The moment she thought it, she changed her mind. After all, when those wicked Yankees had gone and burned down the plantation house, Mama had risked her own life to save Susanna and her brother, Edward, Jr. After the war, she'd helped Daddy and Edward build a dry-goods business in Marietta. She'd become a respected society maven, greatly beloved because of her charitable works. Surely, all of that had been harder than walking across America as a pioneer, even considering the rattlesnakes and coyotes Susanna had encountered.

She sniffed back tears. Oh, how she missed Mama. But Mama always said dwelling on the past wouldn't help. That was how she'd managed to go on after the war. Susanna would honor her memory by having that same cheerful attitude. Surely, after Daddy got his fill of searching for silver, he would take her back home to Marietta. But he would have to recover from his beating first. She forced down the fear and doubts that assailed her. Daddy *would* recover. She would take care of him, as she'd promised Mama.

She came over the hill, and her heart seemed to stop at the sight of a man kneeling over Daddy. Had the thieves come back to make sure he was dead? She set down her pail and lifted her rifle.

"Put your hands up and move away from him." Her voice wavered, and fear hammered in her chest, so she leaned against the trunk of a giant evergreen to steady herself. "Do it now, mister, so I don't have to shoot you." She'd shot a coyote on the trail, but faced with killing a person, she wasn't sure she could do it. But this villain didn't have to know about her doubts.

Hands lifted, he stiffened and rose to his feet, turning slowly to face her. Lord, have mercy, how could a murdering thief be so well put together? Maybe twenty-three years old, he was tall and muscular and wore a broad-brimmed hat tilted back to reveal a tanned, clean-shaven complexion and pleasing features—the kind of face that always attracted the ladies and weakened their good sense. But Mama hadn't raised a fool for a daughter. Even as Susanna's knees threatened to buckle, she gritted her teeth and considered what to do next, sparing a glance at Daddy before glaring again at the stranger. If he went for that gun at his side, would she be able to shoot him first?

"Put your gun down, daughter." Daddy croaked out a laugh and paid for it with a painful grimace. "This gentleman has come to help."

Nathaniel Northam wanted to laugh, but with that Winchester cocked and pointed at him, he didn't dare make the lady mad. My, she was a cute little thing, all bundled up in a man's bulky winter coat over her brown wool dress with blond curls peeking out from her straw bonnet. That turned-up nose just about couldn't get any higher, or those puckered lips look any more prim and prissy in her brave attempt to appear menacing. The gal had spunk, that was certain. Fortunately, the old man on the ground spoke out before she took that spunk too far and shot Nate.

Should he lift his hat in greeting or stay frozen with hands uplifted until her father's words got through to her? *Lord, help me now. The Colonel will kill me if I get myself shot before I bring Mother's anniversary present home, not to mention my death would ruin that big anniversary shindig she's planning.*

"To help?" The girl blinked those big blue eyes—at least they looked blue. He couldn't quite tell with her standing up there on that shady rise. To his relief, she lowered the gun, and those puckered lips spread into a pretty smile. "Oh, thank the Lord." Before he could offer to help, she hefted her bucket and hurried down the slope. "You can't imagine how I prayed all night long that the Lord would send help." She swept past him. "And here he is." She set down her bucket with a small splash and knelt beside the old man. "Oh, Daddy, it's going to be all right now. Help has come." She didn't seem to notice the absurdity of her own words.

Daddy? Once again, Nate withheld a grin. That genteel drawl in both of their voices and her way of addressing her father marked them as Southerners, as sure as the sun did shine. Oddly, a funny little tickle in his chest gave evidence that he found everything about the young lady entirely appealing, at least at first glance. Time would tell if there was more to her than beauty and spunk. That was, if they had more time together. Seeing the state her father was in, Nate was pretty certain they would. He'd never go off and leave a wounded man in the wilderness, not when he had the means to help.

"Ma'am?" He put his hands down but didn't doff his hat because she was facing her father and the gesture would be meaningless. "Maybe we ought to get your father up off the ground."

She looked up at him as if he were a two-headed heifer. Then her eyes widened with understanding. "Oh, mercy, yes. Of course."

"Zack." Nate called to his companion. "Get over here and help me."

The short, wiry cowhand jumped down from their low, canvas-covered wagon, secured their lead horses and hurried to Nate's side. "Yeah, boss?" Zack's gray hair stuck out in spikes from beneath his hat, and Nate wished he'd made the scruffy hand clean up a bit more before they started out this morning. But then he hadn't known they'd meet a lady on the trail.

"Let's get this man into his wagon." He wouldn't ask the young miss why she hadn't moved her father there, for it was obvious a little gal like her wouldn't be able to lift him, and the man was in no condition to move himself. But at least he was resting close enough to the brown prairie schooner for it to shield him from the wind, and he had plenty of blankets around him. "Hang on a minute. Let me check inside."

Moving aside the once-white canvas covering, he struggled to calm a belly roiling with anger over what he saw. Just about everything had been destroyed, from the smashed food crocks to the shattered water barrels to the broken trunks. Only a few tools and hardware remained hanging on the outside of the wagon box. Obviously, the thieves had been searching for money and no doubt had left this little family of homesteaders penniless. A strong sense of protectiveness swept through Nate. God had sent him here and, like the Good Samaritan of Scripture, he would not refuse the assignment. If the Colonel got mad, Nate would just have to deal with him later.

He squatted beside the girl, his shoulder brushing hers, and a tiny tremor shot through him. He clamped down on such brutish sensations, which dishonored his mother and sister and all ladies. "Sir, if you'll let me, I'll divide my team, and we'll pull your wagon down to the hotel in Alamosa. They can help you there. Would that be all right?"

He'd offer to take them to Fort Garland just down the road, but a Southerner probably wouldn't like to recuperate among the Buffalo Soldiers stationed there, those soldiers being black and some of them former slaves. Nate ignored the pinch in his conscience suggesting his real motivation was to get better acquainted with this young lady.

"Obliged," the man muttered, giving him a curt nod, but Nate took no offense. Clearly, the old fellow was in pain, and all of his responses would be brief.

"I'm Nate Northam, and this is Zack Wilson." He tilted his head toward his cowhand.

The old man's eyes widened, and his bruised jaw dropped. "Northam, you say?"

"Yessir." Nate stood up. "You know the name?" His father, referred to as the Colonel even by his friends and some of his family, had a powerful reputation from the War Between the States. Maybe this man had met him on some battlefield.

He shook his head and grimaced, almost folding into himself. "No. No. Nothing." He tried to extend his right hand, but it fell to his side. "Anders. Edward Anders."

"Well, Mr. Anders—" Nate reached down and patted the limp hand " you just give Zack and me a few minutes, and we'll get things all fixed up." Nate didn't know how he managed to say all that without choking on the emotions welling up inside, especially with Miss Anders staring up at him as if he was some kind of hero. My, a man could get caught up in those blue eyes and that sweet smile. Those golden curls only added to her appeal. Nate cleared his throat and turned back to deal with the wagon.

Lord, what have You got me into this time?

Susanna forced her eyes away from Mr. Northam to focus on Daddy, her stomach twisting over his lie. This was so unlike Daddy. She understood why it wouldn't be wise to let these strangers know they had money, but his insistence that they make this trip across the country under an assumed name continued to disturb her. And although Daddy had denied it, she could tell the man's last name meant something to him. She wouldn't press him to tell her, at least not until they were alone and maybe when he felt better.

"Daughter, where's my coffee?" The artificial gruffness in his tone further encouraged Susanna. The earlier hopelessness he hadn't quite been able to hide seemed to have disappeared with the arrival of these good men, that and the bright sun now warming the campsite.

While she poured water into the battered tin pot and checked the fire, her own mood remained wary. Not about the men, but about Daddy's health. He always tried to put on a good front, so she would have to watch him carefully to keep him from overdoing.

"Miss?" Mr. Northam gave her an apologetic frown. "If it's coffee you're wanting, I have some in my wagon."

She eyed him as his words sank in. Of course. Their

coffee had been dumped on the ground along with their other supplies. Why hadn't she realized it before? "That would be very kind of you, Mr. Northam."

"Call me Nate, please. Out here, we younger folks mostly use first names." He shrugged in an attractive way and gave her an appealing grin. "Of course, I won't assume—"

"You may call me Susanna." She could just hear Mama's disapproving gasp at her agreement to such informality, especially when it was obvious from their speech that these men were Yankees. But this was not the South, where a strict code of manners ruled the day, accompanied by a strong dose of hatred for all things Northern. She didn't doubt the people out west had a similar code, but maybe not quite as strict, as she'd noticed among the folks in the wagon train from St. Louis. Not once had she heard the war mentioned. Not once had any Southern traveler scowled at or refused to obey their Yankee wagon master, not even Daddy.

In any event, Mama had also taught her that a lady never treated other people as if she were better than they were, even if she was, for kindness never went out of fashion. Susanna hadn't yet figured out this cowboy's social status, but his older friend called him *boss,* and he had a commanding air about him, suggesting he was a landowner. Otherwise, she might have thought twice about granting him that first-name privilege. If he turned out not to be a gentleman, she could always withdraw her permission.

Nate returned from his wagon carrying a cast-iron kettle and coffeepot.

"Thank you." Susanna reached for the items, but he held them back.

"You look after your father." He gave her a brotherly wink. "I'll fix you some breakfast."

Her heart lilted into a playful mood. "Well, as I live and breathe." She shook her head in mock disbelief. "A man who cooks when there's a woman around."

"Yes, ma'am." He chuckled. "Out here, men have to learn to do a lot of things some folks call women's work." He placed the covered kettle over the fire and stirred up the flames. "Otherwise we'd starve and wear the same clothes for a month of Sundays."

In spite of herself, Susanna laughed, and it felt good clear down to her toes. For the first time since she'd returned from the creek the night before, she thought everything might indeed be all right.

"Of course," Nate continued, "you understand that the ladies sometimes have to take on men's work, too." He sent her another teasing wink. "Milking cows, plowing fields, breaking horses, that sort of thing. If you're out here to homestead, you have that to look forward to."

"Well, I never," she huffed, turning away to hide a grin. "The very idea." This was getting entirely too silly. She'd just met this man. But how could she stop when their teasing back and forth encouraged her so much? Should she tell Nate that Daddy was a prospector, not a homesteader?

Nate saved her from the dilemma. "Go look after your father." His soft tone and gentle touch on her arm made her pulse skip in an entirely different way. "I'll bring you something to eat before you know it."

Not trusting herself to answer, she went to tend Daddy, only to discover him watching the whole thing. He said nothing, and his mild expression, marred only by an occasional wince, held no censure. With his strong sense of discernment, he would warn her if her behavior was improper or if Nate did not appear to be a gentleman.

In a short while, Nate brought them each a tin cup of steaming coffee and then a tin plate of beans and bacon, with a wedge of corn bread on the side. Susanna had been eating beans all across the prairies and mountains of this wide land, but never had they tasted so good. Even Daddy grunted his approval. Susanna struggled not to eat too large a portion, but the desire to make up for missing last night's supper almost overwhelmed her. Fortunately, Mr. Northam—Nate—had busied himself dividing his team between the two wagons and had no idea how much she devoured.

In just over an hour, the horses were hitched up and ready to roll. Even the campsite had been cleaned up and the fire doused. Nate and Zack lifted Daddy into the cleaned-up schooner, and Susanna tucked him in. They made him as comfortable as possible on his canvas cot, supplementing the torn ticking and reclaimed straw with evergreen branches and providing pillows from their own bedrolls. Susanna climbed in beside him and settled back to endure the ride. In spite of the bumpy trail and an occasional groan from Daddy, she managed to drift off into a light slumber.

Once Nate's two-horse team got over the initial surprise of pulling the extra weight, they settled into a slow, steady pace. He wouldn't have tried this arrangement if they were on the east side of the mountain pass, because it took all four horses to make it up the many inclines. But the worst of the trip was over, and the valley floor was just another two hundred yards or so downhill. If all went well, they could make half of the journey today and arrive home tomorrow.

Following behind the prairie schooner, he waved away the dust it stirred up, at last resorting to tying on a kerchief over his nose and mouth. Had he made the right decision to tell Zack to drive the schooner? If he were up there right now, maybe he could learn more about Susanna and her father. But the Colonel would be angry enough over this arrangement, so Nate had chosen to drive this specially rigged wagon with its irreplaceable cargo. If anything happened to Mother's anniversary gift, he would need to take the blame, not Zack. What was he thinking? If anything went wrong, the Colonel would blame him regardless of whose fault it was.

As the morning wore on, the sun beat down on Nate's back, so he shed his light woolen jacket. A quarter mile north of the trail, the Denver and Rio Grande train sped along on its daily run, sending up a stream of black smoke that draped behind the engine like mourning crepe.

Up ahead, Susanna poked her head out the back of the schooner and honored him with a wave and a smile. He didn't fault her for her response to his teasing at the campsite, even though they'd just met and hadn't really been properly introduced. Once again, if there was a fault, it was his. From the state her father was in, he figured they both needed all the encouragement they could get. He'd always found that humor lightened a person's load. Fortunately, just like his sister, Susanna cheered up when she was teased and gave back a bit of it herself. Besides, teasing her kept his thoughts in the right place.

He wouldn't put too much into her friendly waves and smiles. After all, she was likely motivated by gratitude. Of course, that didn't keep Nate from hoping to further their acquaintance. They would arrive in Alamosa by midmorning tomorrow and there part company. Somehow he had to figure out a way to have a nice long chat with the young lady to find out whether they had any interests in common. Once he got home, the Colonel would keep him busy for the rest of the summer, and he wouldn't risk his father's anger by coming back for a visit unless he had a good enough reason.

He blew out a sigh of frustration, and his kerchief fluttered in front of his face. Thoughts of his father's controlling ways never failed to ruin his day, and humor rarely worked to cheer him up. The Colonel had it in his mind that Nate would be marrying Maisie Eberly from the ranch next to theirs as soon as she turned eighteen. While Maisie was a nice girl, he'd never felt a desire to court her, nor had she shown any interest in him. The Colonel didn't seem to think that mattered, nor did any of Nate's other opinions.

A familiar anger stirred in his chest. One of these days he would find the courage to take a stand against his father's control, even if it meant he had to leave home and give up his share of the ranch. He didn't like the idea of leaving the land he'd worked so hard to cultivate, the community he'd helped to build, but a man could only take so much and still call himself a man. He would make his decision by mid-July, when the whole community would gather for his parents' anniversary party.

As if a boulder had come to rest inside him, setting that deadline sat heavy on his soul. But what other choice did he have?

Chapter Two

"What do you put into these beans to make them taste so good?" Taking a ladylike bite, Susanna leaned back against the wagon wheel to savor it. Nate had provided a stool for her so she didn't have to sit on the ground, making this meal all the more pleasant. With Daddy fed and taken care of, she could finally eat her own supper— beans again, but wonderfully mouthwatering.

"Now, don't go asking about my cooking, young lady." Seated on the ground, his back against a bedroll, his long legs stretched out in front of him, Nate spoke in that teasing tone so much like her brother's. "Angela—she's our cook and housekeeper—would tan my hide if I gave away any of her secrets."

"Humph." Susanna sniffed with a bit of artificial pique. "As if I didn't have a few secret recipes of my own." Not many, but enough to impress folks back home, especially at church dinners. Like Nate's family, hers had employed a housekeeper who'd taught her some basic cooking skills, which had come in handy on this journey. But she wouldn't mention that they'd had servants, for that would reveal their financial status.

"I'm sure you have some very fine recipes." He chuckled and shoveled in another bite.

On the other side of the campfire, Zack whittled on a stick, his empty plate beside him. He stretched and yawned, then took himself off toward the horses grazing nearby.

Susanna busied herself with finishing her meal before sitting back to relax. After a long, hot afternoon of riding into the sun, they sat facing the trail they had just traversed, taking refuge on the shady side of the prairie schooner. Now as the sun went down behind them, it cast a deep purple hue over the eastern range bordering the San Luis Valley.

"What a wondrous sight," she murmured. "We have our beautiful Appalachian Mountains back home, but these are so much higher. They're truly awe-inspiring."

"They are indeed." Nate pointed his fork toward the tallest peak, which still wore a snowy white crown from last winter's snow. "That's Mount Blanca, and the whole eastern range is called Sangre de Cristo."

"Sangre de Cristo. That's Spanish, isn't it?"

"Yep. Just about every place around here has a Spanish name because Spaniards were the first Europeans to settle here." Nate's soft gaze toward the east bespoke a love of the scene. "*Sangre de Cristo* means *blood of Christ,* an allusion to that deep, rich color."

"Ah." Agreeable warmth filled her. She'd never dreamed she could enjoy the companionship of a Yankee man this way. But Nate hadn't said or done anything that was even slightly improper. "Those Spaniards were people of faith."

"At least the old *padre* who named these mountains was." He shot a curious glance her way. "And you?"

His question confused her for only a moment. "Oh,

yes. My mama always said that after all the South suffered in the war, she didn't know how anyone could go on without the Lord." She instantly regretted bringing up the devastating conflict that had shaped her entire life. But Nate didn't bat an eye, so she hurried on. "I made my decision to follow Christ when I was nine years old, and He's never let me down." His understanding smile invited her to echo his question. "And you?"

"Yep, around that same age. Ten, actually." He stared off as if remembering. "When the Colonel came home safely from the war in answer to our prayers." A frown briefly creased his brow, though Susanna could not guess why. "Of course, lots of fathers came home badly wounded or didn't come home at all. But at ten, I was only concerned about my own. As time went on, praying and trusting God became as natural as breathing." He grunted out a laugh. "Now, don't get the idea I see myself as somebody special. Just the opposite, because I need the Lord's help all the time to do the right thing."

Susanna's heart warmed at his guileless confession. "I believe we all do, Nate." She'd watched Daddy's faith dip after Mama's death, but as they headed west, he seemed to grow more encouraged. Although she would never understand his urge to go digging for silver, anything that gave him a reason to live had her approval, even if she had to be dragged along on his quest. Even if she had to wait to see her own dreams come true. She supposed parents were always a mystery to their children. "Do you always call your father the Colonel?"

"Yep, just like everybody else." Nate grimaced. "If you ever meet him, you'll understand why."

"He's that intimidating?" Susanna knew many former military officers, Daddy included, but they were Southern gentlemen and never made a lady feel uncomfortable. Maybe Northern officers didn't have the same good manners. They'd certainly treated the South badly.

"You could say that." Nate stood and took her empty plate, setting both of them in a metal pail.

"I'll wash the dishes." She rose and brushed dust and twigs from her skirt.

"Nope." Nate held up a hand. "You go see to your father. Maybe you can light a lamp and read to him. I'm sure he'd like to have his mind on something other than…" He shrugged, a charming gesture that conveyed sympathy and understanding.

"Thank you. I'll do that." Tears stung Susanna's eyes, but she managed to keep her voice steady. "We've been reading Charles Dickens's *Bleak House* on our journey. Fortunately, those thieves weren't interested in stealing books. I'm sure hearing another chapter will take his mind off his pain." How kind and thoughtful this man was. Not at all like the Yankee carpetbaggers she'd learned to distrust and avoid. But she quickly shut the door on the warm feelings trying to invade her heart. Mama would turn over in her grave if Susanna even considered finding a Yankee attractive.

"*Bleak House.* That's a good book. My folks sent me back east for a year at Harvard, and that's where I first read Dickens's works."

So Nate had an education and liked to read good books. Now she had something to discuss with him, something that would keep her thoughts off how handsome he was.

She climbed into the back of the wagon to find Daddy staring at her with a slight grin on his dear bruised face. Heat flooded her cheeks. Had he been listening through the canvas to her conversation with Nate? She searched her memory for anything that might have sounded improper but came up with a clear conscience. Why had she worried? Probably because Nate was a Yankee, and Daddy had always said nothing good ever came out of any Yankee. But here he lay with more mischief than censure in his eyes.

"What are you up to?" She would get the upper hand before he could say anything.

He chuckled, then coughed, then grimaced and groaned.

"Oh, dearest, don't laugh." She knelt beside him. "Zack said you probably have some broken ribs and should try not to laugh or cough." She eased him up and gave him a drink of water from a canteen. "Would you like for me to read to you?"

He gave a brief nod. "First take this." He handed her a wrinkled, sealed envelope from the broken remnants of their traveling desk.

"What on earth?" She accepted it only to discover its unusual weight. "Is this one of our gold pieces in here?"

"Shh." He gently clasped her free hand and whispered, "Tomorrow when we reach that hotel, slip this to the manager—before Northam speaks to him, if you can. And don't say anything about it to these cowboys."

"What?" Her mind could conceive of no sensible reason for Daddy's request.

"Shh!" He glanced toward the back opening of the wagon. "Just do as I ask, daughter." He patted her hand. "Will you?"

Susanna swallowed hard. In all her born days, she'd never seen Daddy do anything dishonest. Back home in the dry-goods store, he'd always taken a loss rather than offend a customer. Surely, she could obey this simple order. "Yes, sir, I will."

But an odd foreboding crept into her heart and kept her awake far into the night.

After breakfast the next morning, Nate and Zack hitched up the teams and prepared to head out. As he had several times a day since leaving Pueblo, Nate checked the cargo in his wagon, lifting a silent prayer that they could get it home without any difficulty. So far they'd managed, but they still had the river to cross.

He'd just replaced the canvas cover when Susanna approached and stared up at him with those pretty blue eyes. Without her coat, she appeared much thinner, the mark of most people who had crossed the prairies. This little gal could use a regular diet of steak and potatoes so she could put some meat on those bones.

"Would it be rude of me to ask what's in your wagon?"

He couldn't imagine thinking she was rude. Nor could he imagine denying her any request. He loosened the ropes but paused before lifting the canvas covering. "Can you keep a secret?"

"Pretty much."

Her impish grin tickled his insides and made him chuckle. *Whoa.* He really needed to get a handle on these wayward feelings. "Well…" He drawled out the word. "I guess I'll trust you, anyway." He pulled the canvas back a few feet to reveal one of the four crates. "It's a gift for my mother. My folks will be celebrating their twenty-fifth wedding anniversary, and the whole community plans to take part in the festivities." Tucked around and between the crates were supplies that he'd bought to divert Mother's attention from the real purpose of his trip. "If the Colonel has any say about it, it'll be the biggest party ever given in the San Luis Valley."

Instead of being impressed, Susanna pursed her plump

lips into a silly pout. "You're giving her wooden boxes?" She slid him a sideways glance. "Now, you know I'm going to ask what's inside them."

He laughed out loud. "All right, then, Miss Curious." For the first time in his life, he understood how Samson must have felt when Delilah kept wheedling him to learn the secret of his strength. "It's china. The Colonel had it imported from England." Imagining the joy Mother would feel when she received it come July, Nate felt a kick of anticipation. "Wedgwood," he added for effect, though why he was trying to impress Susanna, he didn't know. "Of course, Mother thinks her present is the new addition to the house."

The wonderment brightening her pretty face gave him the answer, for he had a hard time tamping down the strong urge to give her whatever she wanted. What was wrong with him? They'd just met yesterday. He didn't really know all that much about her. All he knew was that no other lady had ever affected him this way. Certainly not Maisie, who was more like a sister than someone he wanted to court. Not that he wanted to court Susanna, either. Until he settled some serious matters within himself, he couldn't in good conscience court anyone.

"Wedgwood china all the way from England." She breathed out the words in an awe-filled tone, and her blue eyes rounded with unabashed curiosity. "How on earth did you get it here?"

"Let me see, now. Across an ocean." He held up his hands and ticked off on his fingers the legs of the journey this valuable cargo had taken. "Around through the Gulf, up the Mississippi, then the Missouri River to Westport, Kansas. A freight company hauled it over the Santa Fe Trail to Pueblo. They were accompanied by replacement soldiers headed to New Mexico, courtesy of the Colonel's old army friends, so they arrived without incident." He paused to take a breath and to consider whether or not to tell her everything. She probably didn't need to know that the freight drivers had unloaded the cargo at the fort and had taken off for the gold fields outside Denver. Their desertion had meant the Colonel had to send Nate to bring the china home. It also heightened his father's already deep hatred of prospectors.

"And you met them in Pueblo." Susanna grasped the important parts of the story, meaning he didn't have to include the unpleasant side. "Well, Mr. Nate Northam, it remains to be seen whether your Colonel has that intimidating presence we spoke of last night, but I already like him for going to so much trouble to get his wife such a fine gift as this." Her approving smile further melted Nate's insides. "Tell me, how do you keep it from breaking?" She raised herself up on tiptoes and peered down into the wagon bed. "I see. The boxes are suspended on rope webbing." She reached in and pressed down on the ropes, testing their flexibility. "That must keep them from bouncing around as the wagon goes over bumps." She gave him another admiring glance. "Why, Mr. Northam, how extremely clever of you."

Nate lifted his chin and returned a playful smirk. "Clever indeed, if I do say so myself." Even the Colonel had been impressed by his invention. In truth, he'd given a nod and a grunt, the nearest thing to praise he ever dished out to Nate.

"No more compliments for you." She waggled a finger at him and clucked like a scolding schoolmarm. "Pride *goeth* before destruction, and a haughty spirit before a fall."

"Ouch. Guess I'd better repent of my pride." He shuddered comically. "We aren't safely home yet, and I sure don't want any destruction to fall on Mother's china."

Sobering, she touched his hand, sending a pleasant spark up his arm. "I believe God cares about these things, Nate, so I'll be praying all goes well for the rest of your journey."

That promise refocused his emotions, and he placed a hand over hers. "I'll pray the same for you, Susanna. Seems to me you've already had enough things go wrong."

Her eyes brightened with moisture, and his heart warmed. He was doing the right thing to help her and her father, of that he felt certain.

Within two hours, they met their first test of those prayers when they reached the banks of the Rio Grande. Alamosa lay just across the shallow but rapidly flowing river, causing a mixture of emotions in Nate's chest. Soon he would have to say goodbye to Susanna and her father, but first they all had to get across the wide waters. Both would be challenges.

"I don't know, boss." Zack gripped the reins to keep the restless horses from bolting into the water or shying away from it. "Looks like we might need help."

"Maybe." Standing beside the prairie schooner, Nate surveyed the scene. "Let's use all four horses to get this wagon across. Then we can bring them back across for mine." He didn't like the idea of leaving the china unguarded, even though the other wagon would be in view at all times. But they had no choice.

"Can I help with anything?" Susanna poked her head through the front opening of the schooner and peered over Zack's shoulder at Nate. Her gaze dropped to the river, and her eyes widened. "Oh, my. That must be the

Rio Grande River. Not quite the Mississippi, but no easy crossing, I'd guess."

"No, ma'am. It's a good forty feet across these days because of runoff from the mountains." Nate hated to think of the punishing ride her father would have if they took the usual mode of getting to the other side. "How is Mr. Anders doing?"

She disappeared behind the canvas for a moment, then reappeared. "He says not to mind him, just do whatever you have to do." Her usually smooth forehead was creased with concern.

"What do you think?" He could at least give her a chance to decide.

"Do whatever you must." A steely look narrowed her eyes and tightened her jaw. "That's what our wagon master said more than once on the trip out here."

Her courage continued to impress him. Leaving her behind would be all the more difficult in a couple of hours. Maybe he could make it easier with more teasing. "By the way, it's just Rio Grande."

"I beg your pardon?" Her cute little grin appeared.

"You said Rio Grande *River*. That's like saying Big River River."

She laughed in her musical, ladylike way. "Spanish, of course."

"Yep." He could see her mood growing lighter. "And if you really want to get it right, it's Rio Grande del Norte." He used his best Spanish inflections, as Angela had taught him. "Great River of the North."

Susanna put the back of one hand against her forehead in a dramatic pose. "Mercy, mercy. How can little ol' me evah learn all of that?" Her sweet drawl oozed over him like warm honey.

"Poor little thing." He clicked his tongue and shook his head. "I have no idea."

Zack coughed softly, shaking Nate loose from his foolish teasing.

"All right. Let's get this done."

He drove his wagon into the shade of some cottonwoods, then unhitched the two horses and joined them to the team in front of the schooner. Like old friends glad to be together again, the horses nickered and tossed their heads as much as their harnesses permitted.

Nate considered carrying Mr. Anders across the water on foot, but it wouldn't do for the old man to get wet, even in this hot weather. Instead, he instructed Susanna to cushion her father as best she could, then brace him for the crossing.

Taking the reins himself, with Zack beside him to help as needed, he circled the schooner around and away from the water to give the horses a running start. Then he slapped the reins and cried, "Hyah!"

His team didn't let him down. They gamely leaped into their harnesses, built up speed and plunged into the water, their momentum more than matching the current as they angled downriver to conquer the forty-foot expanse. The water covered the wagon's axles but did not breach the box. With a final lunge, the lead horses emerged from the river, then the second pair, at last pulling the wagon onto dry, solid ground. All four animals shook their manes and whinnied almost as if they'd enjoyed the bath.

But Nate had felt every rock and tree branch submerged under the water's surface; he'd heard every clatter of the contents of the prairie schooner, along with a yip or two from Susanna and her father. Now to go back and get his wagon. The prospect made his chest tighten with trepidation.

He'd conveyed Mother's china this far without mishap, but the Great River of the North might just put an end to that. He found it impossible to please the Colonel with his good, hard work, so there was no telling what his father would do if Nate let the china get damaged.

Chapter Three

Susanna's pulse finally slowed enough for her to step down from the prairie schooner. Before climbing out, she checked on Daddy, only to find he'd fared better on the crossing than she had because of the thick padding Nate had put in his bed. Shaking out her wobbly legs, she approached Nate and Zack, who were unhitching the horses so they could go back across for Nate's wagon.

A sudden protectiveness for Mrs. Northam's anniversary gift stirred within her. No matter that she'd never met the lady. If she'd reared this kind gentleman, Susanna already liked her.

"Surely, you don't plan to bring the china across the river that same way." She posted her fists at her waist for emphasis. "Every plate and cup and bowl will be broken." Maybe there was even some crystal glassware in the crates, and that most certainly would not survive no matter how well it was nestled into the straw packing.

Nate shoved his hat back, revealing the tan line on his forehead and giving him a charmingly boyish appearance. He looked down his straight, narrow nose at her. "I suppose you think I haven't thought of that." His tone held a hint of annoyance, but his green eyes held their usual teasing glint. "You have a better idea, Miss Smarty?"

"Humph." She crossed her arms and tapped one foot on the ground. "As a matter of fact, I do." Sliding her gaze northward along the river, she pointed toward the raised railroad trestle. "Have you ever heard of a little thing called a train?" She shook her head. "I can't imagine why you didn't just have the crates shipped that way over the mountains."

Now serious, Nate frowned. "The Colonel didn't trust them to show due care, especially over La Veta Pass. Sometimes trains jump track or run into fallen trees." His tone suggested he didn't quite agree with his father. "He didn't want to risk it."

At the mention of railroad tragedies, Susanna could think only of the stories she'd heard all her life. Sherman's army destroyed the Confederacy's entire rail line, digging up the tracks and wrapping them around trees, burning train stations and cutting telegraph wires. Maybe Colonel Northam participated in that same kind of destruction somewhere in the South. She shook off the memory and forced her thoughts to Mrs. Northam's certain appreciation of her husband's extraordinary gift. After all, Northern ladies hadn't participated in the war, and surely nice things meant as much to them as they did to Southern ladies.

"Maybe he wouldn't mind just for the crossing?" She lifted her eyebrows with the question and smiled at Nate.

He glanced between the bridge and her, and his Adam's apple bobbed. This man liked her, she could tell. But she wouldn't play with him, as she had some of the boys back home. Southern boys understood and even expected flirtation. Yankee boys might get the wrong idea if she behaved as she had back home, and so far their teasing had fallen short of real flirting.

"I wouldn't have you disobey your daddy, Nate, but isn't the most important thing getting the china safely to your mother? That would honor both of them most of all, wouldn't it?"

He grinned in his boyish way. "Yes." He eyed Zack. "Let's unhitch Henry." He nodded toward one of the lead horses. "I'll ride up the tracks a ways and flag down the train to see if they'll carry it over for us."

"It'll cost you, boss."

Nate shrugged. "Broken china will cost me a lot more."

The moment Nate rode away, Susanna heard her father's faint call. Zack gave her a worried look as he helped her climb into the rear of the prairie schooner.

"I'm sure he's all right," she whispered as she gave the cowboy a nod of appreciation. Then she ducked inside. "Yes, Daddy?" She knelt beside him and brushed the back of her hand over his cheek. "You're hot. How do you feel?"

"Don't worry about me, sweet pea." A glint in his eye contradicted the set of his jaw. "While Northam's gone, you walk on up to that hotel and give that note to the desk clerk."

"What? Now?" She retrieved the envelope from beneath her tattered bedding. "Daddy, please tell me what this is all about."

"Now, daughter, you've never been one to question me." He fumed briefly. "Oh, very well. I'm not partial to being laid up in some hotel in a tent city where no one knows or cares about us. I want that proprietor to turn us away. Then Northam won't have any choice but to take us on to his place." He coughed, then held his ribs and groaned with pain. When he recovered, he gave her an apologetic grimace. "Out here in this wild country, it's hard for a man to be so helpless he can't even take care of his own daughter. I trust Northam. He'll do the right thing by us, he and his family."

Susanna studied him for several moments. He'd slept fitfully last night, and no doubt the river crossing had been hard on him. Maybe he wasn't in his right mind. But that didn't give her an excuse for disobeying him. Still, he had never asked her to do anything this close to lying in all her born days. Unless she counted his changing their last name and pretending to be poor. She still hadn't reconciled herself to those ideas.

"Will you go?" He tried to sit up. "If you won't, I will."

"Shh." She gently pushed him back down. "You rest, dearest. I'll do as you asked." Her stomach tightening, she climbed out of the wagon and tied on her bonnet. "Zack, please tell Mr. Northam I'll be on up the road arranging tea and sandwiches for all of us." At least that part wouldn't be a lie.

Nate emerged from the hotel scratching his head over the manager's refusal to take in Mr. Anders. He thought everybody out here in the West knew that when decent folks suffered terrible losses, other good men needed to help them out. But Nate's offer of up-front payment and his promise to return in a day or two to check on them were rebuffed. Even mentioning his father had no effect because the man was new to the area and didn't know the Colonel's position in their burgeoning community to the west.

Granted, the one-story wooden hotel wasn't much to look at, but it was serviceable. New in late May when

Nate and Zack had come through the tent city of Alamosa on their way to Pueblo, it already had a well-worn appearance. Like the other premade wooden structures lining the main street, the six- or seven-room establishment had been transported by train one room at a time and set up in haste. No doubt something more substantial would soon be needed to house the many travelers riding the newly laid Denver and Rio Grande railroad line, which would soon extend both south and west.

Nate glanced across the dusty, rutted street and snorted in disgust. Of course, they'd brought in a building for a saloon to keep the railroad workers happy. There would be none of that over in his as-yet-unnamed community. The Colonel always made it clear up front to everyone who came to his settlement that no liquor would ever be allowed there. Apparently, the founders of Alamosa didn't feel the same way. Even now in midmorning, several disreputable-looking men loitered outside the swinging doors, their posture indicating they'd already had a few drinks. Nate couldn't help but think Mr. Anders and Susanna would have been better off in Fort Garland, Buffalo Soldiers notwithstanding. But he couldn't take them back there now.

Nor could he put off delivering the bad news about the hotel to Mr. Anders. Peering into the back of the prairie schooner, he waited until his eyes adjusted to the dimness before speaking.

"Everything all right, Nate?" the old man croaked.

"Yes, sir. No, sir. I mean—" He couldn't manage to say the words. "Is Susanna back from getting her tea?" Foolish question. Obviously, she wasn't in the wagon. "Maybe I'd better go check on her."

"You do that, son." Mr. Anders lay back with a groan. His belly twisting, Nate turned back to the hotel just as Susanna came up the street carrying a tray laden with a teapot and sandwiches.

"I finally found some refreshments at a cute little tent café down the road." She tilted her head prettily in that direction. "I brought enough for everybody." She held the tray out to Zack, who was eyeing the food like a hungry bear. "Help yourself."

"Much obliged, miss." He tore off one leather glove and snatched up a sandwich with his grimy paw. "A mighty welcome change from all them beans."

At the sight of his dirty hand, Nate cringed, but Susanna didn't seem to notice. Or chose to ignore it, as any lady would.

"Did they give us a room?" Her expression revealed a hint of conflict, almost as if she hoped they hadn't.

Once again, that feeling of protectiveness welled up inside Nate, and his concerns vanished. He knew what he had to do. "No, ma'am, but don't you worry your pretty head about it. It's just a few more hours to my ranch. We'll put you up until your father recuperates."

With some effort, he willed away his anxieties about the Colonel. Mother was hospitality itself, and she would more than make up for his father's reaction. If worse came to worst, Nate could always take the Colonel aside and point out that Susanna was the one who insisted he take the china over the river by train. Otherwise, Nate would tell him, he wouldn't have dared come home, because all the dishes would doubtless have been broken coming across the river's rough bottom in the fast-flowing current. That should convince the Colonel she and her father deserved some help.

For Nate's part, he was grateful for the Denver and Rio Grande engineer and conductor, who had been more than obliging. Once they'd learned the shipment was for the Colonel, they'd ordered their own men to give a hand. And once they'd learned it was imported china, the other men couldn't have been more careful. Seemed every one of them understood a man wanting to do something nice for his mother. When all was said and done, Nate couldn't have been more pleased, and it had only cost him ten dollars for the lot of them.

Nor could he say he was disappointed when the hotel manager turned Mr. Anders away. After all, Nate had wanted more time with Susanna. Now he had it. The Colonel might have ideas about him marrying Maisie Eberly, but he could never feel the attraction for his longtime friend that he already felt after only two days with Susanna.

As they resumed their journey, Susanna noticed how pleased Nate seemed. In spite of the brisk wind whipping up all kinds of dust, he'd left off his kerchief and kept smiling her way. It was plain as the nose on his handsome face that he didn't mind his Good Samaritan role, and she kept thanking the Lord for his kindness.

She really shouldn't be hanging out the back of the wagon, but she couldn't help herself, even with all that dust threatening to choke her. Many weeks ago, she'd resigned herself to landscapes far different from the verdant fields and forests of Georgia. When they had viewed a large area of the San Luis Valley from the mountain pass, she had observed vast expanses of green and several broad lakes glistening in the sunlight. But the valley floor had some stretches of desertlike land, as well, and she wondered how anyone could expect to farm it successfully.

Thank the Lord that Daddy had chosen to be a prospector instead of a homesteader. He was far too old to till unbroken sod, and even his prospecting was more of a hobby than an occupation, at least in her mind. After all, they had enough money to live on. If they hit hard times, Edward would send more. Once Daddy was back on his feet, she'd let him have his fun searching for silver and gold for a little while. Let him find a silver nugget or two, and then she would persuade him to take her back home to Marietta.

Being in the company of a kind, compassionate, educated man like Nate reminded her of her yearning to find a good *Southern* gentleman to marry, someone with whom she could build a home and family in the hometown she loved so much, among the friends she'd known all her life. For now, however, she must set aside those longings and take care of Daddy. She whispered a prayer that the Lord would tell Mama she was keeping her promise.

At last the dust won out, and she pulled her head back inside the schooner and closed the flap. Daddy was bearing up quite well, although he still had moments of incoherence and slept fitfully when he did manage to sleep. She prayed there would be a doctor near Nate's ranch who could help him.

By midafternoon, they had reached a small settlement of several houses, some buildings and a white clapboard church with a high steeple. Nate had said they would take time to stretch their legs and water the horses before going on, and now he hurried to help Susanna out of the wagon.

"Shall we get a bite to eat?" He waved a hand toward another white clapboard building, this one with a sign over the door that read Williams's Café. "Those sandwiches didn't last me very long, and it's a few hours until supper at the ranch."

A sudden nervous flutter in Susanna's stomach extinguished her appetite. Supper at the ranch meant at last meeting that intimidating Union colonel. Would he still be fighting the war, as most Southerners were, if only with words? Habitual animosity filled her chest, but she wouldn't let on to Nate.

"Maybe a piece of pie, if they have some." She nodded her head toward the wagon. "I think it would be good for Daddy, too." As Nate tipped his hat and started toward the building, she touched his arm.

His eyes widened with apparent surprise as he turned back. "Yes, ma'am?"

"Do you suppose there's someplace where I could, um, well…?" She shook her brown skirt, and dust flew in every direction. "I would like to be a bit more presentable before I meet your mother." *And especially your father.* Maybe he would take more kindly to them if they didn't look so bedraggled.

"Now, don't worry about that." Nate grinned. "I'm sure she'll understand that you've been on the road." He glanced toward the building. "But I'll see what I can do."

Mrs. Williams, the café owner, could not have been more accommodating. It seemed that the Northam name held much more power in this unnamed settlement than it did in Alamosa. Miss Pam, as she asked to be called, had a permanent smile etched in the lines of her slender face. She appeared to be around fifty years old, and her warm brown eyes exuded maternal kindness as she invited Susanna into her own quarters at the back of the café.

"Charlie—he's my husband—he'll see what your pa needs." Miss Pam set a pitcher of warm water on her mahogany washstand. "You go ahead and clean up. Is that your fresh dress?"

"Yes, ma'am." Susanna held up the one dress the

thieves had managed to overlook in their destruction. They'd stolen her favorite pink calico, so this green print would have to do.

"It's a pretty one." Miss Pam gave Susanna a critical look up and down, her gaze stopping at her hair. "Do you have a brush?"

"No, ma'am." She tried hard not to sigh, but a little huff escaped her. Almost everything she depended upon to make herself look presentable was gone or ruined.

Miss Pam gave her a sympathetic smile. She reached into her bureau drawer and retrieved a boar-hair brush with a tortoiseshell back, holding it out to Susanna. "You take my spare one."

"Oh, my." Her heart warmed at this woman's generosity. While Susanna could afford to buy her own if she found a mercantile nearby, it seemed best to accept the brush and pay Miss Pam back later. "Thank you."

While she helped Susanna brush her hair and fasten the back buttons on her dress, Miss Pam chatted about the big anniversary party coming up in July. "Out here, we're always looking for something to celebrate, but this one is going to be special. Colonel and Mrs. Northam have done so much for this community, bringing in a preacher and building a church, just generally taking care of everybody. The Colonel says he has a doctor arriving next month. Too bad he's not already here for your pa, but Charlie's pretty good at tending injuries, being a former mountain man. You know how they have to be self-sufficient living out in the mountains by themselves the way they do."

Not giving Susanna a chance to comment, she went on to list various ways Nate's parents had helped folks. Every word and tone suggested only respect and affection for the Northams, especially lauding the Colonel's leadership, but that still did not diminish Susanna's apprehensions about meeting the man.

In less than an hour, Susanna felt sufficiently refreshed, and Miss Pam's husband had taken care of Daddy. Charlie offered his expert opinion that Daddy's left leg was indeed broken, as were several of his ribs. He made a splint for the leg, wrapped torn sheets around Daddy's ribs and gave him a dose of medicine to ease the pain. Nate told Susanna that while the community awaited the doctor's arrival, Charlie was often called upon to help folks out.

After they had enjoyed some of Miss Pam's delicious gooseberry pie with a splash of thick fresh cream over the top, they headed south. Unable to bear riding inside the schooner another minute, Susanna sat beside Zack on the driver's bench watching the beautiful green landscape dotted with occasional farmhouses nestled among the trees.

In less than an hour, the two wagons passed under a majestic stone archway emblazoned with an intricate cattle brand and the name Four Stones Ranch. A long drive between two fenced pastures took them toward the two-story white ranch house built on a stone foundation. To one side were a giant red barn and numerous outbuildings. Susanna noticed the addition Nate had mentioned, also two-storied, on the north end of the main structure. A wide brook ran some fifty yards from the house, and young elm and cottonwood trees grew in clusters around the property.

Nostalgia swept through Susanna at the sight of the beautiful ranch. Back home, magnolias would be in bloom, and maybe a few spring gardenias would still be filling the air with their lovely perfume. Catching a whiff of roses, she searched without success for the source of the fragrance.

As if someone had blown a trumpet to announce their coming, several people poured forth from the barn, while a solitary man emerged from the house.

Nate jumped down from the wagon and gave instructions to his cowhands, who took charge of his wagon and drove it toward the barn. Then he turned toward the other man.

An older version of Nate, and just as tall as his son, the dark-haired Colonel exuded authority before he even spoke a word. Susanna could hardly breathe as she listened to Nate's brief explanation for the presence of the prairie schooner and its inhabitants. All the while, the older man glared at her through narrowed eyes. No one had ever looked at her with such disdain, perhaps even hostility. Yet she didn't dare reveal her own bitter feelings against this Union officer. Maybe it was just those feelings speaking to her mind, but he looked like someone who would chase women and children from their plantation house and burn it to the ground.

"So I thought they would make a fine addition to our community, Colonel." Nate sounded a little breathless, and from the way his right hand twitched, Susanna thought he might salute his formidable father. "Being homesteaders, that is."

The Colonel walked to the back of the schooner and threw open the flap, then returned to face Nate, eyeing his son with obvious disgust. "What's the matter with you, boy? These are no homesteaders. Where's their furniture? Where are their clothes? All I see is a pickax and two gold pans. Can't you tell a money-grubbing prospector when you see one?"

Chapter Four

Nate saw the hurt in Susanna's eyes and the way she cringed almost as if she'd been slapped. He ground his teeth as protectiveness once again roared into his chest. He had long ago learned that arguing with the Colonel was a useless exercise, but he'd never tried to beat some sense into the man. His hands ceased their nervous twitching and bunched into involuntary fists as if they wanted to do that very thing. Only by hooking his thumbs over his gun belt did Nate manage to control the impulse. How would he ever learn to control his temper when his father continued to rile him this way?

"Nathaniel!" Mother bustled out of the house and down the front steps, her fuzzy brown hair streaked with flour and her white cotton apron stained with jam. "You're home at last."

At the sight of her, Nate's anger softened, replaced by the joy her presence always brought him. Spreading his arms, he welcomed her eager embrace. "Mother." He held her tight and savored the aroma of fresh-baked bread that clung to her like perfume. Her nicely rounded form reminded him of Susanna's need to put on a few healthy pounds. But if the Colonel had his way, the An-

ders family wouldn't be enjoying any steaks at the Four
Stones Ranch.

Mother leaned back and brushed a flour-covered hand
over his cheek. "Angela and I have been baking all day,
but I didn't know when to have her cook your favorite—
Oh! What's this?" She broke away and moved toward the
prairie schooner. "Why, Nate, you've brought us a guest."
She glanced at the Colonel. "Frank, help this young lady
down so we can be properly introduced."

Nate gulped back a laugh. His father never tolerated
so much as a grin when Mother took charge this way.

"Of course, my dear." His face a mask, the Colonel
stepped over to the wagon and held out his hand. "Miss?"
Even his offer sounded like an order.

Susanna eyed him with confusion, then gave Nate a
questioning look. He returned a short nod, hoping she
would accept the Colonel's curt invitation. With a grace-
ful elegance Nate hadn't known she possessed, she lifted
her chin like a duchess, then rose and stepped to the edge
of the driver's box to place her hand in his father's.

"Thank you, sir." Her posture stiff, her voice coldly
polite, she permitted him to assist her to the ground beside Mother.

Nate usually waited to be addressed by his father. This
time, however, he approached the little group and said,
"Mother, Colonel, may I present Miss Susanna Anders?
Miss Anders, Colonel and Mrs. Northam."

Her expression filled with warmth and hospitality,
Mother gripped Susanna's hands. "Welcome, Miss Anders. Do come in the house. Supper will be ready shortly,
and I'm sure you would welcome a chance to—" She
started to usher Susanna toward the house, but the young
lady gently resisted and turned back toward the wagon.

"Thank you, ma'am, but my daddy requires my attention."

"Oh." Mother didn't bat an eyelid. "Another guest. Is he ill?" She shot a look at the Colonel. "Frank, my dear, don't just stand there. We must help these people."

The Colonel also didn't bat an eyelid. "Of course, my dear." His expression unchanged, he once again walked to the back of the wagon. "Nate, get over here and help me."

Nate had to turn away and regain his composure before obeying. Mother and the Colonel rarely did battle, but when they did, Mother never lost.

Susanna threw dignity aside and pulled down the tailgate so she could scramble into the back of the schooner. Finding Daddy sound asleep, she lifted a prayer of thanks he hadn't heard that awful Colonel's rude words. Daddy wasn't the slightest bit money-grubbing. He didn't need to be because he already had plenty of money. And what on earth was wrong with being a prospector? Suddenly, camping beside the road they had just traveled seemed a better idea than accepting the hospitality of this Yankee family.

"Dearest." She gently touched Daddy's cheek. "We're here at Nate's house." Only by thinking of it as Nate's could she consider going inside.

"Hmm?" Daddy raised a bruised hand and swept it over his eyes. That medicine Mr. Williams had given him had probably muddled his thinking. He inhaled deeply, then winced. "What?"

Susanna glanced at the three Northams, who were peering into the wagon with varied expressions. She decided to ignore the pity in Nate's eyes and the hostility in his father's, and concentrate on the warm concern beaming from Mrs. Northam's sweet, round face.

As if the older woman realized how the situation appeared from Susanna's viewpoint, she gave Nate a little shove. "Go on inside, son. Tell Angela to get your bed ready. We'll put Mr. Anders in your room. Then come back and help your father."

"Yes, ma'am." He disappeared, and the thumps of his hurried footsteps resounded through the canvas walls of the wagon.

Daddy caught sight of their hosts and tried to rise. "Help me up, daughter. I should greet our company."

A faint growl sounded in the Colonel's throat, and Susanna gulped back sharp words, while Mrs. Northam shushed her husband. As she helped Daddy to a sitting position, Susanna gave a little laugh that sounded a bit too high and a bit too nervous in her own ears. "Actually, dearest, we are the company."

As if he finally grasped the situation, Daddy's eyes cleared. "Ah, yes, of course." He nodded toward the Yankee couple.

Susanna briefly considered presenting Daddy to them, as would be proper, since they were the hosts, but something inside her refused to comply. After all, the prairie schooner *was* her and Daddy's home. "Daddy, may I present Mrs. Northam and Colonel Northam?"

If he noticed her breach of etiquette, he didn't indicate it. "How do, ma'am, sir?" He leaned into Susanna's shoulder. "Edward Anders."

"We're pleased to meet you, Mr. Anders," Mrs. Northam said. "You just rest a minute, and Nate will be back to help you inside." She looked up at her husband and raised one eyebrow.

The Colonel cleared his throat and pursed his lips. His wife elbowed him in the ribs. "So you met up with horse thieves, did you, Anders?"

Daddy coughed out a wry laugh and grimaced. "Indeed we did. Took most of our belongings and supplies and did their best not to leave a witness." He patted Susanna's hand. "The good Lord protected my daughter, as she was off fetching water when they came."

"Oh, my." Mrs. Northam's eyes reddened. "Praise the Lord."

"That I do, ma'am. That I do."

Slightly out of breath, Nate appeared once again beside his parents. "Angela was waiting by the door. She'll have my room ready by the time we get there."

"I don't want to put you out, Nate," Daddy said.

"Not at all, sir. I—" Mrs. Northam began.

"They won't be here long," the Colonel said. "I'm sure Anders is anxious to get on his way to the silver fields." He waved Nate toward the wagon. "Get on in there and help him out."

Instead of the instant obedience Susanna expected to see, Nate fisted his hands at his waist. "He'll need to recuperate for quite a while before he goes anyplace. And they'll need another team of horses." His father started to respond, but Nate hurried on. "We need Mr. Anders to give us a good description of those horse thieves so we can put the word out to everybody. They're a threat to the whole valley. If they get away with what they did, all sorts of criminals will think—"

"You think I don't know that?" The Colonel silenced Nate with a dismissive wave of his hand. "Now, let's get this done."

Despite her outrage over the Colonel's behavior, Susanna could not fail to be impressed by his and Nate's strength as they lifted Daddy's cot from the prairie schooner and carried it toward the house. Daddy was not a small man, so they set him down and summoned two men—she guessed they were called cowboys—to help carry the invalid up to the second floor of the house. Susanna didn't have time to notice much as they entered and climbed the stairs, but what she did see impressed her with its beauty and grandeur, much like the mountains surrounding this high valley. While she wouldn't call it a mansion, it certainly was an imposing domicile.

Within ten minutes, Daddy was resting in a charmingly masculine room, where guns and antlers decorated the walls, and pine furniture and woven rag rugs contributed to the rustic atmosphere. Above Nate's handsome pine secretary, a glassed-in bookcase held several leatherbound books. Susanna didn't take time to read the titles, but she longed to know what he read besides Dickens.

"And now for you, Miss Anders." Mrs. Northam took Susanna's arm and led her down the hallway to another bedroom very different from Nate's. Frilly white curtains fluttered in the breeze wafting through the two windows. A pink-and-blue patchwork quilt covered the four-poster bed, and a blue velvet overstuffed chair sat nearby on a patch of carpet. The scent of roses filled the air, although none were in the cut-glass vase on the bedside table. "This is our daughter Rosamond's room. When she returns from her friend's house, she'll be pleased to learn she has a roommate. Maisie's coming with her to spend the night, but we can bring in an extra mattress."

"You're so very kind, ma'am." Susanna's eyes stung. Would these other girls truly welcome her? Would Rosamond be like her mother or more like her inhospitable father?

Sudden weariness filled her, and she eyed the feather bed with longing. As if reading Susanna's mind, Mrs. Northam gave her a brief hug.

"Why don't you lie down? I'll send our girl Rita up to wake you when it's time to eat."

"How can we ever thank you?" And how could she think any evil of this sweet Yankee lady?

"I will speak to you in my office, Nate. Now." The Colonel didn't grant Mr. Anders so much as the courtesy of a parting word, but strode from the room toward the front staircase. The two cowhands followed after him.

Nate gritted his teeth as he watched his father leave. Pasting on a more pleasant expression, he turned to the bed where Mr. Anders lay, his gaze on Nate.

"You get some rest, sir." Nate bent forward to adjust the quilt. "If you need anything—"

"You've done a lot, young man." The look of approval in his eyes caused a stirring in Nate's chest. How would it feel if his father looked at him that way? "You're a true Good Samaritan, just like the Good Book says."

Nate cleared his throat. He wanted to say *aw, shucks,* like his youngest brother might. Instead, he offered, "Don't mention it, sir. I'm glad to help. We all are."

Mr. Anders coughed out a laugh, then grimaced and clutched his ribs. "I wouldn't say *all,* son, but I'll let it go at that."

Nate took his leave, shutting the door behind him and offering a prayer for the old man's recovery. At the top of the stairs, he hesitated. The Colonel had ordered him down to his office, but Nate couldn't just go off and leave Susanna. He walked to Rosamond's room and tapped on the door just as Mother swung it open.

"Nate." She reached up to give him another welcoming hug. "Oh, it's so good to have you back home. I miss you so much when you make these long trips for supplies. I don't know why your father can't just send some of the hired men." She cast a quick look at Susanna, and her eyebrows arched briefly. She opened and shut her mouth as though she had started to ask him something, then changed her mind. Instead, she patted his cheek. "I'm going downstairs to finish helping Angela and Rita with the baking. Then we'll prepare supper. You may stand right here in the doorway and speak to Miss Anders for two minutes. Then I expect to hear your boots on the downstairs floor fifteen seconds after that."

Nate pursed his lips to suppress a grin. "Mother, Susanna and I have been out on the trail together for two days, with her father looking on the whole time. You don't have to worry about any improper behavior."

"Susanna, is it?" Mother looked at her. "And I suppose you call him Nate?"

"Yes, ma'am." Susanna returned a sweet smile. "That is, if you don't mind."

"Hmm." Mother got a speculative gleam in her eyes. "No, dear, not at all." She swept past Nate, wearing a soft grin and watching him the whole time as she headed for the back stairs that led to her kitchen.

All of a sudden, the kerchief around Nate's neck seemed awfully tight. Mother often teased him about girls. It seemed to him that was what most mothers did to their sons. But she'd never said anything so bold in front of a young lady.

"I hope you don't mind her." He leaned against the doorjamb, crossed his arms and offered Susanna an apologetic grimace.

"Not at all." She untied her bonnet and hung it on the back of Rosamond's desk chair. "She's very kind and hospitable." Now serious, she leveled a steady gaze on him. "I'm afraid your father is not quite so pleased to have us as guests." Biting her lower lip, she stared out the window. "Maybe we should go back to the café. It seems Mr. and Mrs. Williams would be—"

"No." Nate spoke more sharply than he intended, and she blinked. "I mean, they're the salt of the earth, but they run their place without help, so it might be a burden for them. We have servants and cowhands and a big family." He rolled his hat in his hands. "Besides, I feel it's my responsibility to see that your father gets back on his feet." That thought had just come to him. Yet hadn't the biblical Good Samaritan taken responsibility for the beaten merchant even after taking him to the inn? Nate knew he could do no less.

Susanna's blue eyes were rimmed with tears. "I don't know what to say."

He barked out a laugh that didn't sound quite as cheerful as he intended. "I do. We're having steak for supper, and I can't wait to bite into a big juicy one."

Smiling again, she laughed, too. "You mean no beans?"

"Nathaniel Northam!" The Colonel's voice thundered up the staircase.

Nate gave an artificial shudder. She didn't need to know how much he was truly quaking inside over his father's angry summons.

"That's right. No beans."

Her soft feminine laughter followed him all the way down the stairs, and he barely had time to wipe the grin off his face before stepping into the Colonel's office for his scolding—undeserved but nonetheless expected.

Chapter Five

Susanna's laughter died away, and with it her good feelings. Unless she'd missed something, Nate didn't deserve to be yelled at or scolded like a mischievous boy. In her opinion, it was that Yankee colonel who needed a scolding, and she would be glad to give it to him. He had a noble, good-hearted son, and yet he was beating him down for no good reason.

She'd noticed the difference in Nate the minute they arrived at the ranch. For two days, she'd watched a capable, authoritative, helpful man take care of business. But the moment his father stepped out the front door, Nate became an awkward servant trying without success to please an implacable master.

An uncomfortable sensation stirred in her stomach. Back home in Georgia, it wasn't just the carpetbaggers who mistreated people. She'd seen for herself how some Southerners treated their former slaves as if no war had happened, as if no Emancipation Proclamation had freed them. She was thankful Daddy and Mama got rid of the plantation and moved to town. There they didn't have to deal with such things as getting enough people to work in the cotton fields, work they'd always done as slaves but now had to be paid for. The house servants Susanna's parents had employed received a salary and were well treated. She'd never heard Daddy or Mama speak to a servant like the Colonel spoke to his own son. The Southern man she married would need to understand she expected no less for their servants.

Weariness once again overtook her. She untied and slipped off her walking boots and lay on the bed, but could not sleep. Despite Nate's being a Yankee, she must somehow find a way to pay him back for his kindness. Even knowing the trouble he would get into with his father, he had saved Daddy and her from untold grief, perhaps even death. That was worthy of a reward of some kind. But what could she do? The Northams were obviously wealthy ranchers, so he didn't need any material repayment. All she could do was pray and let the Lord work things out.

Her eyelids grew heavy, but she managed to whisper a prayer for Nate to make it through his current scolding without too much difficulty. Even if he was a Yankee...

"Did you check the entire shipment before you loaded it up?" The Colonel stood behind his large oak desk, bracing himself on his fists as he leaned forward in a threatening pose. With him standing, Nate didn't dare sit down, no matter how weary he was from his travels. "Every plate? Every cup?"

An unfamiliar thread of assurance wove briefly through Nate's chest, just before the more familiar anger roared up and closed his throat. Of course he'd checked the shipment before loading it onto the wagon. How stupid did the Colonel think he was that he would have the horses haul home a broken cargo? But a bitter retort never got him anyplace, so he said, "Yessir. Everything was in perfect condition." He made sure he spoke loudly, clearly and respectfully so his father wouldn't have further cause to yell.

Yet he couldn't leave it at that. "It was a good thing Miss Anders was with us."

Snorting, the Colonel straightened and stared at him as if surprised he would offer additional information without being asked.

Nate hurried on. "When we got to the river, she suggested that we take it over on the train. I mean, the water was fast, and when we took their wagon through first, we drove over a lot of rocks and branches. So I flagged down the train and—"

"And you needed someone else to suggest that obvious solution?"

Nate stepped back, and the heel of his boot hit a chair. Somehow he managed not to lose his balance. "W-well, you had it brought by wagon all the way from Westport because you didn't trust the trains, so, no, sir, I didn't think of it."

Again, the Colonel snorted out his disgust, although Nate had no idea what had him so riled. His father ran a hand across his jaw and sat in his leather-covered desk chair. "Now, about those people—"

"Yessir." Nate still wouldn't sit until invited to do so, but the ache in his legs didn't help his temper. "Those people. I know for a fact that you couldn't have driven on past them any more than I could." Where had he gotten the courage to say that? "And you would have been ashamed of me for not stopping to help."

The Colonel's eyes narrowed. "That didn't mean you had to bring them home to burden your mother. You should have left them in Alamosa."

Nate explained the situation at the hotel. "Even your

name didn't affect the proprietor." He offered a sheepish grin.

The Colonel didn't react. "Just make sure your mother doesn't have extra work. And make sure they leave as soon as possible. That Anders fellow seems like the kind of lazy Southerner who will sit around expecting people to wait on him like his slaves used to do."

Nate wouldn't ask how he knew whether Anders had kept slaves. Not everyone in the South had. But his father often spoke disdainfully of Southerners, as if they were all the same, all except Reverend Thomas, the preacher he'd brought from Virginia.

The Colonel snatched up the packing list for the china and thrust it toward Nate. "The first time your mother goes out visiting, you check the shipment again to make sure nothing broke on the way from Pueblo. If it did, I may be able to get a replacement from San Francisco by the time our party rolls around." He waved a dismissive hand. "I expect you back to work on the new addition before dawn tomorrow. Anders and his daughter may get to sit around, but you're back on the job."

Nate started to say he'd been *on the job* during this whole trip to Pueblo, but his father slapped the paper back on the desk, causing him to jump.

"And don't be getting any ideas about that Anders girl. Maisie Eberly will turn eighteen in a few weeks, and George and I expect an announcement from the two of you right after her birthday." The Colonel pulled out a ledger and opened it, scanning the pages as if prospecting for gold, effectively dismissing Nate.

He stared at the top of his father's head. No, he would not be getting any ideas about the lovely Miss Susanna Anders, not her or anybody. He had too many things to work out in his life before taking on a wife or even a sweetheart, not the least of which was whether or not he would keep working like a slave for his father. And he certainly wouldn't be proposing to Maisie. It wasn't fair to either one of them. But George Eberly was as domineering as the Colonel, so avoiding marriage could turn out to be the hardest thing Nate—*and* Maisie—had ever done.

"I'm so grateful to you for sharing your room with me." Rested after her nap, Susanna sat in the blue velvet bedroom chair while Rosamond Northam and her friend Maisie Eberly sat side by side on the bed. Dark-haired and green-eyed like her brother, Rosamond had her father's lean face and her mother's sweet smile. "I'll try real hard not to put you out." She'd never had to share a room and had no idea how this girl would react to such an intrusion.

"Oh, don't worry about that. We'll have a good time." Rosamond nudged her friend. "Won't we, Maisie?"

"You bet we will." Maisie giggled, and her curly red hair bounced as she nodded her agreement. "Just like the Three Musketeers." She leaned toward Susanna. "Have you read Dumas's book?"

Caught up in the younger girl's merriment, Susanna offered a more ladylike laugh. "Yes, but I'm a little rusty with my swordplay." She searched her mind for specific scenes from the exciting tale. "And I doubt we'll find any queens to rescue."

"Maybe just a cowboy or two." The girls giggled and bounced and put their heads together in a familiar way. Despite their differing coloring and features, they were like two peas in a pod.

Susanna's heart warmed. What nice young ladies, although at sixteen and seventeen, they still had some growing up to do. She had no doubt Mrs. Northam was responsible for any measure of decorum her daughter displayed, but the way they had noisily run up the front staircase a while ago revealed that both of them also possessed a bit of Colorado wildness. Someone should establish a finishing school out here. They would probably find many students among ranchers' daughters. Of course, Susanna would never correct them, for that in itself would be a dreadful breach of etiquette. All she could do was set an example of refined behavior.

A soft knock on the door interrupted their merriment, and a dark-eyed girl of perhaps fourteen poked her head in the door. "Miss Rosamond, Mrs. Northam requests your presence in the kitchen."

"Thank you, Rita. Tell her we'll be down soon. And bring us some hot water and towels so we can wash up."

"Yes, miss."

Rita disappeared, and the other two girls continued their discussion of musketeers and scheming cardinals, comparing them to the cowboys they knew. Although they mentioned several names, giggling all the while, not once did they say anything about Nate. Susanna couldn't imagine why she had even thought about that. Clearly, Maisie was too young to be interested in him, at least romantically.

Those few moments revealed much to Susanna. While the Colonel was stern to the point of rudeness, his family was more lighthearted. Further, she was glad to see they treated their servants with courtesy. But she guessed that Rosamond, being the only daughter, was a little bit spoiled. Susanna had never failed to go immediately when her parents called. Indeed, she would gladly answer Mama's summons once again.

She thrust away the grief that tried to engulf her. She

couldn't go back to those days, and until she could get Daddy back to Marietta, she must learn to live as a pioneer woman, whatever that meant. Although she was about two or three years older than these girls, she would open her heart and let them teach her. And maybe she could teach them something in return.

With Maisie on one side of him and Rosamond on the other, Nate could hardly enjoy his steak for all of their chatter and giggling. In contrast, Susanna sat across from him eating her supper with the grace of a duchess. Funny, that was the second time he'd thought of her in that way, yet he'd never even met a duchess. He must have read about one in a book. The thought made him grin. He'd enjoyed their brief chat about books while they were on the trail. Maybe they'd have a chance to do it again.

Guilt wove through him. The Colonel would probably do all he could to keep Nate away from Susanna. He glanced toward the end of the table. His father, watching him with an inscrutable look, bent his head toward Maisie. Nate groaned inwardly. She was a sweet little gal, but still just a child, despite being almost eighteen. How could the Colonel think she was ready for marriage? In Nate's opinion, the way she and Rosamond acted was just plain silly, something that had never bothered him before, but now got on his nerves.

Rebellion kicked up inside him. He looked at Susanna again, determined to talk to her rather than Maisie, and his rebellion turned to—jealousy? Chatting with his middle brother, Rand, on one side and his youngest brother, Tolley, on the other, she hadn't even glanced across the table at him except to give him a smile and a nod before the Colonel said grace and they all sat down.

Rand was yammering on about something, bragging,

really. Until this moment, Nate hadn't given a second thought to a match between the two of them. Even at twenty, his younger brother was about as grown-up as his sister and her friend. Yet here was Rand obviously trying to impress Susanna with some tale about how cattle brands were designed, of all things. As if a refined young lady wanted to hear about that. Yet she focused on him and responded with interest, even including Tolley in the conversation.

Tolley's beaming response earned Susanna another surge of Nate's admiration. Hardly anybody paid attention to fifteen-year-old Tolley, and the boy had begun to show signs of rebellion. Nate was worried but had no idea how to help him.

"But Nate wouldn't want to do that, would you, Nate?" Maisie elbowed him in the ribs and laughed in her schoolgirl way.

"Uh, what?" He glanced at Rosamond, silently quizzing her with a raised eyebrow. Fortunately, she sat adjacent to Mother's place at the end of the table nearest the kitchen door, so the Colonel couldn't see his confusion.

"Of course he would." Rosamond gave him a furtive wink, then leaned around him to address Maisie. "Who else would escort us up into the hills to get flowers for our flower beds?" She lifted her coffee cup and saluted her friend. "Mother agrees with our idea. Columbines will make a beautiful addition to our garden. Being native to Colorado, they sure won't take as much work as Mother's roses. We can fetch home enough to fill that new garden patch, and they'll be all rooted and growing by the anniversary party."

Her foolish chatter gave him all the information he needed, and he offered his sister a grateful nudge. "Girls, I hate to disappoint you, but I'm afraid the Colonel needs

me here at the ranch. I can't run off for a picnic when this
house has a two-story addition I need to finish." He shot
a glance at his father, expecting his agreement, but the
Colonel's expression was surprisingly agreeable.

"I believe a day trip to acquire some columbines for
your mother would be a fine idea." He served himself
another helping of mashed potatoes and ladled on a large
portion of beef gravy. "You three youngsters can go tomorrow. Ride horseback instead of taking a wagon, and
you'll be back in time for milking." He dug into his supper as if that settled the matter.

The girls chirped like baby birds as they made plans
for the upcoming day trip, but Nate could only stare
across the table at Susanna in dismay. No wonder the
Colonel gave his permission for such a trivial excursion,
for it would force him into Maisie's company. Nate should
invite Susanna along, not only for good manners but also
so he would have some intelligent conversation along the
way. But if she didn't know how to ride like his sister
and Maisie, he'd be stuck with two chattering magpies
for a whole day.

Susanna had learned in finishing school that a lady
didn't talk across the table but rather engaged in conversation with those seated beside her. In this case, it wasn't
too difficult. Rand was almost as funny as Nate, and he
could spin a yarn nearly as well as her own brother back
home. But the quieter Tolley touched her heart. His sad
brown eyes made her think of a puppy pleading for approval, and when she turned her attention to him, he all
but jumped around in happy little circles. A glance across
the table from time to time gave her a new perspective
on Nate. Those girls were making him dizzy with their

back-and-forth chatter, but he took it in good spirits, another admirable quality.

She was surprised that Colonel Northam said very little beyond blessing the food and telling poor Nate that he had to take the girls out to pick flowers. If she wasn't so worried about Daddy, she would hint that she'd like to go with them, as she hadn't ridden a horse since they left Marietta four months ago. The girls had been quick to welcome her into their friendship, and she could almost see herself feeling at home here for as long as she had to stay in Colorado.

A glance at the Colonel canceled those thoughts. He was glowering at her as if she were some sort of bug that needed to be squashed. Her own uncharitable thoughts back toward him crowded out all of her good feelings. She and Daddy would never be welcomed even as temporary guests in this community. This Yankee colonel had not ceased to make that very clear to her.

Oh, she couldn't wait for Daddy to get back on his feet so she could take him home where they belonged.

Chapter Six

"You go on, daughter." Daddy's short, shallow breaths seemed an attempt to mask his pain. As always, he was putting on a brave face for her. "After our long journey, you need to have a little fun with other young people."

Seated on the edge of his bed, Susanna raked her fingers through his brown hair to comb it back from his face. In the shadow of the lamplight, she could see he was long overdue for both a haircut and beard trimming. If she left him looking this scruffy and the Colonel saw him, their unwilling host would have all the more reason to despise him, as if his condition was his own fault. Even on the trail, he'd always kept himself well-groomed, quite a feat for a man who all his life had a body servant to tend him.

"Tell you what. I'll clean you up a bit, and if they haven't left, I'll see if they still want me to go with them." Last night after supper as they were preparing for bed, Rosamond and Maisie had insisted that she accompany them to the foothills. They planned to leave at dawn, and soon the sun would rise over the distant Sangre de Cristos. The Colonel's hostility notwithstanding, she longed to accompany them. Yet she was worried sick that something would happen to Daddy in her absence.

A soft knock on the door interrupted his response. "Señor Anders?" A feminine voice with a Mexican accent identified the speaker as Angela, the Northams' cook and housekeeper, whom Susanna had met the night before.

Susanna stared at Daddy. "Isn't it a bit early for breakfast?"

An odd little grin flitted across his lips, and he shrugged. "Get the door, daughter."

Susanna hurried to obey, admitting the servant to the room. Angela brought in a tray holding a pitcher of steaming water and some masculine grooming supplies. Over her arms, she carried several towels and what appeared to be brown trousers and a white shirt. The sturdy, dark-eyed woman, perhaps forty years old, glanced briefly at Susanna, doubt filling her expression.

"Is this time good?" Her question was directed at both of them.

"Well, I—"

"Of course." Daddy coughed and grabbed his ribs. When he recovered, he spoke with effort. "You go on, Susanna. Angela came up last night and offered to help me. She said Mrs. Northam sent her."

"But—" An odd sensation swept over her. Not quite censure, but not quite approval, either.

"Miss Susanna, I am a Christian and a servant." Angela's warm gaze exuded understanding of her confusion. "Nothing improper will happen. On this, you have my word."

"Mine, too." Daddy chuckled and paid for it with another spasm of pain. Again he clutched his ribs, then gave her an artificial glower. "Are you going to obey me, daughter?"

"Oh, very well." She returned to his bedside and kissed

his forehead. "Thank you, Angela." She wagged a finger in Daddy's face. "Now, you behave and get your rest."

Her heart light, she hurried back to her room to don her brown woolen skirt. Rosamond had promised a side-saddle was available for her, as though that was unusual. Then Susanna noticed the other two girls wore skirts that were split to accommodate riding astride. With some difficulty, she hid her shock. On the other hand, their boots appeared to be much more appropriate for riding than her walking shoes. If she rode often, she'd have to get a pair of those boots.

The three of them had talked late into the night until travel weariness had overcome Susanna. Strangely, she woke feeling refreshed, and the younger girls seemed just as energetic. While she'd checked on Daddy, they'd gone downstairs to fix an early breakfast, so she mustn't keep them waiting. Happiness kicked up inside her. Nate would be waiting, too. It took a few moments for her to remind herself that this was a Yankee household. As kind as the children might be, their father's behavior more than negated their generous actions.

Nate drank his second cup of coffee while the girls cleaned up after their breakfast and packed a picnic. Mother had a rule that they had to leave Angela's kitchen the way they found it, so they were taking special care. Still full from last night's steak and potatoes, he'd managed to eat a plate of griddle cakes and eggs so he wouldn't get hungry on the trail. After waking up early to prepare the horses, he couldn't wait to head out.

As restless as he felt, he kept an eye on the kitchen door hoping, even praying, that Susanna would join them. The Colonel had sent him out on chores after supper last night, so he hadn't had a chance to invite her on today's outing. He knew he could count on his little sister to think of their guest, even if it turned out she had to refuse the invitation because of her father's condition.

The door opened, and Susanna peered in almost as if she doubted her welcome. Nate jumped to his feet as relief flooded him. This lady's presence would make today a lot more tolerable. No, make it downright enjoyable.

Before he could speak, both Rosamond and Maisie rushed over and hugged Susanna.

"I'm so glad you decided to come." Rosamond spoke in a hushed tone as befit the early hour.

Maisie retrieved a plate of griddle cakes they'd set back. "You hurry and eat while we finish the cleanup."

She then ushered Susanna to the kitchen table, and Nate held out a chair for her.

"Oh, thank you." Susanna, always the lady, laid her napkin across her lap, bowed her head briefly, poured a dainty amount of chokecherry syrup on her griddle cakes and began to eat.

Nate sat across the table from her and propped his chin on his fists. "How's your father?"

"He had a hard time sleeping last night." Worry skittered across her face, but then she smiled. "Your mother very kindly asked Angela to see to him, and he insisted that I come with you."

"Well, you can see we're all pleased you can go." Nate glanced at the other two girls, who were watching them with identical smiles. He shot them a frown. The last thing he needed was to have them tease about Susanna and him. "I haven't had a chance to ask if you ride, but I put Mother's sidesaddle on a sweet little mare for you, so you'll be all right even if you don't."

"Humph." That playful glint, which he hadn't seen since yesterday at the river, returned to her eyes, sending an odd little thrill through his chest. "La-di-da, Mr. Northam, what must you think of me? We Southern ladies know very well how to ride. But mercy me, where are my manners? I do so appreciate your accommodating me with that sidesaddle."

Her mention of being a Southerner reminded Nate of the Colonel's assumption that she and her father were lazy, which Nate found nothing short of unfounded prejudice. On the other hand, he noticed she didn't seem to hold the bitterness he'd seen in some Southerners. That alone showed real character. He couldn't ask her, of course, for he'd learned long ago not to open discussions about the war with those on the losing side. He could only hope she would overlook the few times he'd slipped.

While he ruminated on that, the other two girls giggled softly, as if they were enjoying this exchange. He needed to take Rosamond aside and tell her to quit it or else. For now he'd stick with teasing Susanna.

"Well, then, if you're an expert rider, maybe I should go put that sidesaddle on our stallion, Malicia." He puckered away a grin. "In case you're wondering, *Malicia* is Spanish for *maliciousness*."

"Don't you dare, Nate Northam." Maisie came over and punched Nate's shoulder. "I wouldn't even ride Malicia, and I've been breaking horses since before I could walk."

"Shh." Rosamond held a finger to her lips. "Don't wake the whole house. Let's get going." She nodded toward the broad window, where sunlight had begun to brighten the eastern hay field. "The sun's crested Mount Blanca, and we have a long way to go."

The group left the kitchen and made their way through the narrow hallway to exit the house through the enclosed back porch. Bringing up the rear, Nate noticed Susanna eyeing the boots lined up by the back door.

"Rosamond, hold on." He touched Susanna's shoulder to stop her, too. "Let's see if a pair of Mother's riding boots will fit."

A quick try-on proved successful, and the group was soon out the door and on their way to the stable.

With no mounting block available, Susanna relied on Nate to help her onto the horse. He gripped her waist to lift her, and a thrill streaked up her spine. One would think she'd never had a gentleman's help to get on a horse before. As he adjusted her left foot in the stirrup and made sure her right knee was comfortably positioned over the pommel, she shushed her irrational feelings and settled into the saddle. As if equally pleased with their arrangement, the pretty little brown mare nodded her head agreeably.

"Her name is Sadie." Nate handed the reins to Susanna. "Her mouth is soft, so a little direction is all you need to give her. Just use the reins, and she'll know what you want her to do."

His frown revealed more than a little apprehension for Susanna, a notion she found altogether appealing. After her long, arduous trek across the country, during which she'd stifled every complaint and worked as hard as any of the other ladies, it felt good to have a gentleman worry about her. If only the gentleman in question weren't a Yankee. Summoning the willpower to dismiss her foolish inclinations, she leaned down to pat Sadie's neck.

"Never you mind, Mr. Nate Northam. Miss Sadie and I will get along just fine."

If his sudden grin was any indication, he rather enjoyed her flippancy. "All right, then." He ambled over to

his own horse and swung into the saddle. "I'll put my
worries to rest."

"If you two are finished jawing, I'd say it's about time
we hit the trail." Maisie reined her horse away from the
stable, dug in her spurs and led out with a whoop.

Rosamond followed, urging her gelding into a slow
gallop. Mindful of her own need to reclaim her riding
skills, Susanna stayed back with Nate. He set a slower
pace as he led the packhorse carrying their picnic baskets and gardening supplies as they rode across verdant
fields toward the low-lying hills ahead.

The early-morning air smelled of fresh grass, with
the pungent odor of cattle occasionally wafting by on
the breeze. Quiet lay over the scene like a cozy blanket
as the sun inched above the horizon to wake up the land.
Sudden birdsong erupted from somewhere nearby in a
marshy ditch, their *chit-chit-chit-terree* stirring Susanna's soul like a welcoming wake-up call. She glanced at
Nate to see if he noticed the sound.

"Redwing blackbirds." He gave her that charming grin
of his, with one side of his upper lip a little higher than
the other, as if he knew something she didn't.

Indeed, how had he known what she was thinking?
She answered his intense gaze with a tilt of her head and
a slight smile. As much as she tried to resist it, a warm
peace settled over and within her. Maybe just for today
she could give herself permission to enjoy the companionship of the handsome young cowboy beside her. The
handsome young *Yankee* cowboy beside her. Somehow
she must rein in this foolishness, but she found her emotions far more difficult to control than the horse she rode.

She glanced westward toward the distant San Juan
Mountains, Daddy's ultimate destination. What dreams
had drawn him to those silver fields? He possessed all

the money he'd ever need. Unlike some former plantation owners, he'd made a successful new life for himself after the war, and the family had never wanted for anything. Maybe prospecting had been a boyhood dream, and only after Mama died was he free to pursue it. The thought stung so much that Susanna quickly dismissed it. Mama's death had made a gaping hole in Daddy's heart, so he'd had to fill it with something. If prospecting made him happy, Susanna wouldn't fault him for it.

Unlike the Colonel.

The thought brought her up short, and she unconsciously pulled on Sadie's reins, bringing the little mare to a halt.

"What is it?" Nate stopped and turned back to face her. "You all right?"

There he went again, showing that gracious concern. This time his worried frown didn't sway her emotions in the slightest. Yesterday when the Colonel had spoken of prospectors as if they were just the same as horse thieves, Nate hadn't disagreed, hadn't defended Daddy *or* her. But what had she expected? After all, an apple didn't fall too far from its tree. In fact, if she'd told him right away that she and Daddy were headed to the silver fields, he probably wouldn't have helped them.

That wasn't fair, and she knew it. He'd never asked any nosy questions about them, just helped. But she couldn't let that sway her feelings.

"I'm fine." She nudged Sadie with her left heel and loosened the reins.

The mare resumed her pace, even prancing a little bit as if eager to catch up with the other horses. Susanna held her back, and after a while, Sadie settled back into a steady pace beside Nate's mount.

They rode in silence for some time, following an irregular trail toward the rolling green hills where Rosamond had promised they would find a field of columbines. Susanna could see in the corner of her eye that Nate kept glancing at her, but she refused to acknowledge him. It just wouldn't do any good to let her heart go. In fact, she should make herself as unappealing to him as she could so he would stop being so nice.

"Just what does your father have against prospectors?" She watched with satisfaction as dismay swept over his fine features.

For a short time, he just looked away from her across the open field. At last he turned back, his eyes full of regret. "I'm sorry you had to hear him say those things yesterday. It wasn't much of a welcome, was it?"

She doubted she was supposed to answer, so she kept her gaze on the trail. Some hundred yards ahead, Rosamond and Maisie had slowed to a walk and appeared to be chattering in their usual sisterly style. Once in a while, they'd glance back and wave. Susanna couldn't resist returning the gesture. After all, she'd found no fault in the girls other than their lack of social graces. Manners could always be learned, but prejudices were rooted deep in the soul. She'd seen plenty of that back home when some of the men had taken to wearing white sheets to scare former slaves out of trying to make something of their lives. Mama had forbidden Daddy to take part, and it spoke well of him that he'd honored his wife's wishes. Any man Susanna married would have to respect her opinions that same way. She had to admit even the Colonel had acquiesced to Mrs. Northam's will yesterday.

"The Colonel is pretty free with his opinions, isn't he?" Nate's question broke into Susanna's thoughts, but again she doubted she was supposed to answer. "But sometimes his anger is justified."

Susanna offered him a questioning look, both eyebrows raised, but no smile.

"That shipment of china? It was supposed to be delivered all the way to the ranch. The freight drivers left it at the trading post in Pueblo and headed out to the gold fields near Denver." He huffed out a sigh edged with frustration. "That's why Zack and I had to go get it."

Susanna stifled a gasp. If Nate hadn't gone to the fort, he wouldn't have been on La Veta Pass, wouldn't have been there to save Daddy's life. Why, he'd been an answer to prayer, and the Lord set it all in motion long before those thieves stole their horses. She started to mention that important fact, but Nate kept talking.

"'Course, the Colonel never did think much of prospectors, even before that." Nate grimaced as if he knew it was rude to say so. "You see, he's trying to build a decent community out here, a Christian community where everybody works hard and helps his neighbor."

"Unless that neighbor is a prospector?" Susanna couldn't keep the crossness from her voice.

Nate shrugged. "Most prospectors are out for one thing, finding a fortune, sometimes at a terrible cost to themselves or others."

Susanna held her peace. What good would it do to tell him Daddy already had a small fortune? That prospecting was only a pastime, an enjoyment in his old age?

"'Course, you and Mr. Anders aren't typical prospectors." Nate offered one of his charming smiles, and Susanna had to look away to keep from smiling back. "It'll take some time for your father to heal up so you can continue your journey. I'm sure by the time you head out, the Colonel will see you're decent Christian folks."

His statement, so simply spoken, sent another one of those pleasant but traitorous feelings through Susanna's chest. At his core, Nate Northam was an upstanding man, one who gave people a chance to prove themselves beyond appearances. Her heart reached out to attach itself to him, and she could think of only one way to stop it. *Yankee! Yankee! Yankee!* she shouted in her mind. Yet somehow that epithet failed to engender the usual sense of anger and dismissal.

How could she hate a man who had saved Daddy's life and showed her only kindness?

Chapter Seven

The Colonel would change his opinion of Mr. Anders? Nate had no right to advance such a notion. His father was as unpredictable as a San Luis Valley winter and often just as cold and bitter. But Nate couldn't let Susanna go on feeling bad about the Colonel's remarks. Maybe with Rosamond's and Maisie's help, he could cheer her up, at least for today. This brave little lady had a lot weighing on those slender shoulders, and he longed to lighten her load.

"How was your father this morning?" The moment the words came out of his mouth, he wanted to kick himself. He'd asked the same question back in the kitchen and learned the old man hadn't slept well.

He could see she caught his mistake, because she grinned and looked the other way, ducking behind the brim of her bonnet. When she turned back at him, the smile was gone and her eyes had a misty look. "Brave, as always. Trying to hide his pain from me."

Brave would fit Susanna, too. "Don't let it worry you. Charlie told me yesterday that broken ribs are just about the most painful injury a man can have, sometimes even worse than a broken leg. But he'll heal." At her doubtful expression, he added, "Angela has a real gift for taking care of people. She'll make him comfortable."

Susanna favored him with a slight nod.

He'd let her be for a while. She needed healing, too—heart healing. After almost losing her father to murderous thieves, she could do with a little bit of happiness and security. Rosamond and Maisie, for all of their immaturity, had welcomed her like a long-lost sister. And of course, Mother had relished the rare chance to show hospitality. He'd leave it to the ladies to take care of the happiness. As for the security, Nate would have to keep her away from the Colonel as much as possible. Susanna didn't need to wonder whether he would throw her and Mr. Anders out before the old man was well enough to stand on his own two feet and provide for the two of them. Not that Mother would allow such a thing to happen. The dear woman loved everybody and never let anyone leave her house hungry or in need.

As often before, Nate pondered his father's disposition and the way it differed so completely from Mother's. The Colonel made quick judgments about people and seldom changed his mind. Yet he had an uncommon ability to inspire loyalty and to gather good people to himself, a trait that no doubt came in handy during the war and never left him. To a person, everyone in the community thought the sun rose and set in the Colonel and looked to him for leadership. No wonder everyone was eager to make the upcoming anniversary celebration an event that no one would ever forget.

Nate knew his father rose early every day and went to his study to pray and read the large, leather-bound family Bible. He had observed the Colonel's faith many times in the ten years since they had come to the San Luis Valley. But he often seemed to Nate like an angry Old Testamont prophet rather than a man saved by the grace of Jesus Christ. His favorite target to preach at? Nate himself. And it wearied him into the very depths of his soul.

He could leave. The thought was never far from his mind. But then he would remember these past ten years. The long journey from Boston, mostly by wagon. Helping the Colonel with the hard jobs. Helping his brothers and sister when things got tough. Coming over the mountains. Finding the right acreage. Building the house. Nate could remember every board, every nail, every stone cleared from the fields and laid for the foundation. He had more skin in the house, the barn, the stable and the church up the road than a man of his age had a right to claim. That alone gave him a reason to stay in the community. He must not let his father drive him away.

"How much farther?" Susanna's question was a welcome relief from Nate's dismal musings.

"You getting tired?" He challenged her with a smirk, hoping to lighten her mood and his own.

"La-di-da, Mr. Northam, not in the slightest."

When she spoke in that sassy way of hers, how could he not cheer up?

"Well, I was just checking. Wouldn't want you to wilt away in the summer heat."

"Now, there you go again." She stuck her pert little nose in the air. "We Southern ladies may look delicate, but we're made of steel. You'll see." She sniffed with artificial haughtiness, adding a little lift of one shoulder. "Besides, I can't seem to locate this summer heat you're so busy talking about. Have you evah been to Georgia in August? That's a heat you'll never forget. Why, it gets so hot, the chickens lay hard-boiled eggs. It gets so hot, our candles melt into little puddles before they're even lit."

Nate threw back his head and guffawed. He hadn't

laughed this hard in he didn't know how long. "That's pretty hot."

They rode in silence while their horses waded through the fast-flowing Cat Creek. Once they reached the opposite side, Susanna gave Nate a saucy look. "Go on, now. Try to outdo me."

It took him about four seconds to understand what she meant, another ten to come up with a retort. "I don't suppose I can beat you for hot weather, but I'll give you a warning about the cold."

"I'm waiting." Susanna looked so pretty sitting up straight and proper on Sadie, just like a duchess. Oh, mercy, there he went again.

Remembering how Zack told tall tales in the bunkhouse on a winter's night, Nate got a faraway look in his eyes. "Well," he drawled, "it was nigh on five years ago I learned a mighty hard lesson about Colorado winters." This was harder than he'd thought. His quip wasn't that complicated. A glance at Susanna revealed her interest... and amusement. He had to come up with something fast.

The thunder of hooves broke into his panicked thoughts. Rosamond and Maisie were racing back to join them, each one bent low on her mount's neck, determined to win the spur-of-the-moment contest. Rosamond won, pulling her horse to a stop as if she was set to rope a calf for branding. Nate wouldn't be surprised if she jumped off and lassoed something, maybe that jackrabbit that just took off running from the thicket a few yards away. Despite being a little embarrassed by his sister's rowdy ways, he couldn't complain about the reprieve he'd just been handed. Maybe Susanna would forget the subject of their banter. Or maybe he could use the interruption to come up with some clever yarn about the cold.

* * *

"Hurry up." Maisie pulled up beside Rosamond. "We found the columbines just over that hill." She tipped her head in that direction, knocking her wide-brimmed hat askew. She didn't seem to notice.

"What's the hurry?" Nate looked mighty relieved over being interrupted.

Doubting he actually had a cold-weather story, Susanna laughed to herself. But guilt quickly swept away her amusement. What was the matter with her? Against everything she'd ever been taught, she'd been flirting with this Yankee boy. Mama had taught her never, ever to flirt with a man she didn't think she could marry. *Forgive me, Mama.*

"Let's go." Nate urged his horse to a brisk trot, with the packhorse trailing behind.

Instead of pulling up beside him, Susanna held Sadie to a slower pace. Nate sent her a questioning look over his shoulder.

"I want to enjoy the scenery." She used that excuse to avoid resuming their teasing conversation, but it was also the truth.

The past four months had been constant motion, yet as slowly as she and Daddy had traveled west, they always seemed to be in a hurry. Hurry to catch one train then another on their way to St. Louis. Hurry to purchase a wagon and supplies so they could make it across the plains in good weather. She wanted, no, *needed* to relax and enjoy this beautiful country.

She drew in a deep breath and let it out. The air smelled clean and fresh, with a hint of alfalfa. Above her, the sky was a deeper, richer blue than she'd ever seen. A pleasant breeze brushed over her with a featherlike caress. An occasional deer appeared in the distance, then danced away into the cottonwoods, while numerous long-eared rabbits scurried around in the tall grass. Every sight, every smell, seemed to call out to her to surrender to the happiness trying to invade her soul. Oh, how she longed for the freedom to enjoy this place, this day. These people.

Nate slowed his pace but remained ahead of her, checking back often and waving or touching his hat brim in a salute. No one could say he wasn't a considerate man. But she'd known that from the moment she met him.

She must remember who she was and where she came from. Georgia had its fields and flowers and beautiful skies. That was where her friends and relatives lived. That was where she belonged. Somehow she must guard her tongue, her heart, her mind and not let these Yankees invade her soul as their soldiers had invaded her beloved homeland. She must not lose hold of all she'd ever been taught.

As depression threatened to overshadow her, she reached the top of the hill where Nate awaited her. The instant she pulled up beside him, all sadness vanished at the breathtaking sight. Below in the shallow valley lay a carpet of blue columbines, their rich, sweet perfume rising on the breeze to fill her senses.

"Ohhh," she breathed out on a sigh. "How beautiful." In all her life, the only flower fragrance to rival this came from the gardenias in Mama's garden. She glanced at Nate to find him studying her, and her foolish heart skipped. "Yes? You have something to say?"

He grinned in his charming way, with one side of his upper lip higher than the other. Did he give that same smile to all the girls?

"No, ma'am. I'm just enjoying the look in your eyes."

He gazed down into the valley. "It truly is something, isn't it?"

Rosamond and Maisie had already dismounted and were studying the flowers. Rosamond beckoned to them. "Come on down."

Instead of answering Nate, Susanna moved the reins on Sadie's neck, and the mare began to pick her way down the slope, zigzagging until she reached her friends. The other two horses nickered and tossed their heads as if to say *What took you so long?* If only Susanna could enjoy the similar welcome Rosamond and Maisie offered her.

"Come take a look." Rosamond held Sadie's reins so Susanna could dismount.

Not waiting for Nate's help, Susanna freed her right knee from the pommel and her left foot from the stirrup, then jumped to the ground. Her landing on the hard ground sent a sharp pain through each of her feet and up her ankles and calves, causing her to yelp in a most unladylike way. She never should have worn Mrs. Northam's boots, for they weren't really a good fit.

Nate jumped down from his horse and hurried to her side. "Why didn't you wait for me? I'd have helped you down."

"I'm fine." Pride forced a smile to her lips, even as the other two girls voiced their sympathy. Even as the balls of her feet continued to sting. "What have you found?"

The girls appeared to accept her quick recovery, but Nate didn't dismiss it so lightly.

"Are you sure you're all right?" He gently gripped her elbow, and a pleasant sensation swept up her arm, clear to her neck.

She shook it off as best she could without jerking away from him. "Yes. Don't give it another thought."

He released her but held her gaze, his green eyes bor-
ing into hers with a commanding intensity. "Next time,
you wait for me. Your father doesn't need for you to be
injured." How could a man's tone of voice be so stern
and gentle at the same time?

Susanna felt the wind go out of her attempt at aloof-
ness. She could not dislike this man, for he showed nothing but concern for Daddy and her. "You're right, of
course. Thank you."

With considerable difficulty, she broke away and
limped over to the girls. "Tell me about your plans to
transplant these." Mama had taught her how to move
flowers about the garden, but she wouldn't show off her
knowledge unless asked.

"I dunno." Maisie at last straightened her wide-
brimmed hat, a boyish creation that resembled Nate's and
Rosamond's. "Just dig 'em up, I suppose, and put 'em in
a sack." She indicated the burlap bags on the packhorse.

"Do you have any ideas?" Rosamond asked.

Susanna took a minute to kneel and study the plants
and dig a gloved finger around the base of one cluster. "Well, I don't know about columbines, but I would
suppose they're not too much different from jonquils or
Johnny-jump-ups." She brushed the dirt from her leather
gloves and stood. "Do you have a small spade?"

The girls retrieved their equipment from the packhorse, and Susanna set about teaching them how to dig
up the flowers. She wasn't sure this was the best time of
year for transplanting, being that the columbines were
in full bloom. But here they were, so she would make
the best of it.

Kneeling back down, she dug into the ground with
the spade Rosamond had given her. "If you come across
runners, don't worry about cutting them. I can tell these

are hardy flowers, surviving out here in this climate, so they'll be fine. Just be sure you keep enough soil around each cluster of roots. We'll wait to separate the roots until we're ready to plant them in Mrs. Northam's garden."

Maisie dug into the ground with enthusiasm, while Rosamond proceeded with more care. Susanna reasoned it was because the flowers were for her mother. Nate situated himself on a rough woolen blanket on a patch of grass, propped himself back on his elbows and chewed on a green blade. When Susanna glanced over at him, he grinned in that dangerous way of his and touched the brim of his hat. She wanted to say *Stop that!* But that would only reveal the effect his smiles had on her and encourage him to keep it up.

After an hour or more of digging up the plants, wrapping the roots in burlap squares and dousing them with water from their canteens, the girls joined Nate on the blanket. They removed their gloves and splashed more water over their hands, then unpacked sandwiches, cold chicken and potato salad, a jar of pickled vegetables and another jar filled with cold coffee.

Once they'd finished their picnic, the other girls wandered off, chatting in their usual way. Susanna knew she should go with them, but her feet still ached, the pain made worse by the narrow boots she never should have borrowed.

"My, just look at those puffy little clouds." Nate tipped his hat back and stared upward. "Looks like a flock of sheep."

"Humph." Susanna eyed the same clouds. "I'd say they look more like a field of cotton bolls ready for picking." Oh, would she never learn to stop teasing? Why hadn't she simply agreed with him?

He chuckled, a deep sound that rumbled in his broad

chest. "Well, seeing as how I've never seen a cotton field, I wouldn't know." He held out the coffee jar, silently offering to pour more into her tin cup, but she shook her head. "Did your father grow cotton in Georgia?" A strange little frown flitted across his brow, almost as if he wished he hadn't asked the question.

For a moment, she considered her answer. Maybe if she mentioned how General Sherman's troops had destroyed their cotton plantation, how they'd very nearly destroyed her family, it would expose the unbridgeable gulf between them. To gather her thoughts, she looked off to the southern hills, and a gasp escaped her.

Several Indians on horseback were staring down at them, and if their threatening demeanor was any indication, they were not at all pleased to see Nate and Susanna.

Fear shot through her. *Dear Lord, please help us!* Had she made it all the way across the country without a serious encounter with Indians only to die by their hands in this remote mountain valley?

Chapter Eight

Nate stood and pulled Susanna to her feet. "Get behind me." He tried to keep the tension from his voice. "I'm sure they don't want trouble. They'll ride away shortly." He doubted that, but no need to alarm her.

He glanced in the direction Rosamond and Maisie had gone. They were running back through the columbines, determination on both of their faces. If he didn't stop Maisie, she might shoot first and ask questions later. At least Susanna had the good sense to obey his order to move behind him. But as the Indians rode down the hill toward them, his chest tightened.

The girls reached him just as the Indians—Utes, more accurately—rode into the edges of the columbine field.

"Keep you gun in your holster, Maisie," he said. "Let me handle this." He understood why her father insisted she carry it, but along with teaching her how to shoot, he should have taught her to control her temper. "You girls help Susanna mount Sadie, then mount up."

To his relief, all three girls obeyed without argument or comment. He would stay on the ground so as not to appear combative to the approaching men. Lifting his empty gun hand to wave—and to show good faith—he called out, "Greetings. It's a fine day." *Lord, please let one of them speak English or Spanish.*

As they drew closer, he noticed they were leading extra horses, and cautious hope sprang up in his chest. This was a trading party, not a war party. In fact, the Utes had peacefully settled in the southwest corner of the San Luis Valley a few years back. But a man could never be sure younger men like these might not go on a tear over something or other, just as the Plains Indians did.

"Greetings." One man returned Nate's wave, but all of them were focused on the girls.

The hair on Nate's neck stood up. Could he defend them against four men? Maisie would be some help, and Rosamond had a rifle on her saddle.

"We're just headed home, so help yourself." He gestured toward the columbines. Angela had told him that Indians used these flowers to spice up their food, but she wouldn't have them in her kitchen because parts of the plant were poisonous.

"Wait." The man who seemed to be the leader rode closer to Nate. "We had a fever last winter. Lost our wives." He nodded toward the girls and held up the reins of the two horses he was leading. "You trade?"

Nate could feel the heat rising up his neck, but anger would only create problems. Besides, this was an honorable custom for these men. They meant no insult. Behind him, however, he'd heard Susanna gasp and Maisie snort. He could imagine Rosamond clapping a hand on her rifle, but he dared not look around to be sure.

"Now, friend, you know we don't do that." He decided to end the matter as quickly as possible. "Colonel Northam won't appreciate your coming our way looking for wives. Why don't you head down toward Santa Fe or the pueblos?"

The instant he'd mentioned the Colonel, all four men stiffened. Conferring among themselves, they turned their horses southward and rode away without a word. Nate heaved out a sigh, then turned to check on the girls.

Rosamond and Maisie continued to glare at the men, but Susanna's face was as white as those clouds they'd talked about a few minutes ago.

"We'd best head back to the ranch." Nate mounted up and gave Susanna what he hoped was a reassuring smile. "Gotta get those flowers in the ground before supper. Go on, now." He would stay at the rear, just in case.

The other girls led out, with Rosamond taking charge of the packhorse, but Susanna stuck close to Nate. He didn't mind that at all, especially since his pride had suffered a pinch over having to use the Colonel's name to close the matter with the Utes. But on second thought, he was grateful to be the son of a man whose name meant something to folks, at least in these parts. In times like this, he doubted he could ever leave the community, no matter how harshly the Colonel treated him.

He looked over at Susanna, whose face was hidden by her bonnet brim. "You doing all right?"

She cast a sassy little glance his way. "Now, Mr. Nate Northam, you were saying something about how cold it can get in Colorado? Did you ever come up with something clever, seeing you've had all this time?"

He laughed so hard, he almost choked, but part of that was probably pent-up feelings of relief over the safe ending to their encounter. As for Susanna, well, she was an amazing lady to recover so quickly from her fright and return to their earlier teasing. Fortunately, he had figured out a response. "I sure did. That winter, it was so cold that when I went to milk the cow, she gave me ice cream instead."

* * *

Susanna rewarded him with a soft laugh and a tight smile. "I guess that'll do, since you can't come up with anything better." She turned away from him to hide behind her bonnet again. If she said anything more or tried to control her quivering lips, she might burst into tears. She'd had enough trouble saying those few sentences, hoping to divert Nate's attention from her terrified reaction to the Indians.

Never in all her life had anyone looked at her as those men had. But she'd seen that expression before. Back home, men studied horses or dogs or items in Daddy's mercantile with that same speculative look as they considered whether or not to make a purchase. Sometimes she'd even seen men, not gentlemen, of course, but others, studying women that way. But she had never been the object of such bold stares. Even Colonel Northam's rude looks had acknowledged her as a person, no matter how unwanted a guest she was in his home. And now she could not even begin to describe the feelings churning about inside her. She was not a piece of merchandise, not something to be bought and sold at the whim of other people.

Something nagged at the back of her mind, but she couldn't pull it forward into her conscious thoughts. Something that happened a long time ago when she was very small, before the Yankees came and destroyed the South and her family's way of life. A slave auction, that was what it was. She wasn't supposed to see it, but she'd wandered away from Mama on a shopping trip to Atlanta and come face-to-face with another little girl, a dark-skinned one, on sale just like a horse. For the first time in her life, she understood the terror in that child's eyes.

And not for the first time, she was grateful slavery had been abolished, especially for the sake of that little girl.

"Say, Susanna." Nate's overly cheerful voice cut into her thoughts. "I think Angela's cooking up some of her excellent chili for supper tonight. Have you ever eaten chili?"

Using a trick Mama had taught her, she took several quiet, deep breaths to steady her nerves before she answered him. "My, my, is food all you think about? First ice cream, then chili?"

He laughed, again sounding a bit too cheerful. Her brother had used that same tone when she'd confided her fears about the trip west and he'd done his best to calm her worries. Bless Nate for showing such brotherly concern for her. "After eating Angela's chili, I think we'll all agree that ice cream is just the thing to cool us off."

Susanna surrendered to a real laugh, and it felt good deep inside. They were all safe, and just as some of the dangerous incidents that happened during the trip west, this one needed to be put behind her. If it could.

After tending to the horses, Nate wandered over to the flower bed to see how the transplanting had progressed. Both Rosamond and Maisie appeared to be covered with dirt from head to toe, but Susanna didn't have so much as a smudge on her cheeks. Once again, her characteristic elegance brought the word *duchess* to his mind. One of these days, he was going to slip and call her that. Such a blunder would reveal how tender his heart was growing toward her, which would be a big mistake. He just couldn't afford to fall in love, not until he had matters settled in his own life, especially his anger toward the Colonel. Maybe the only way to avoid trouble was to tease Susanna some more.

"You girls about got this job done?" He plopped himself down on a nearby cottonwood stump and pulled out his folding knife to whittle on a stick. "I just unsaddled and brushed down five horses all by myself, got 'em fed and watered and sent out to pasture. Seems like the three of you could manage to stick a few flowers in the ground in all that time."

Rosamond and Maisie traded a look, and he knew he was in trouble. He didn't know which one lobbed the first handful of mud at him, but before he could put away his knife and take off running, he found himself being bombarded with wet dirt from both sides by giggling girls. No matter which way he tried to escape, they cut him off like cow ponies corralling a calf and rubbed soil into his hair and down his shirt.

"Help me, Susanna." He managed a glance in her direction, only to find her backing away from the scene, her expression going from dismay to amusement and back to dismay again. She'd probably never in her life been in a mud fight. Before he could stop himself, he snagged up a handful of wet dirt and slung it at her.

She nimbly sidestepped. "Ha. Missed. Now, Nate Northam, don't you dare—"

Splat! A wad of mud struck her cheek. She stared in disbelief at a blissfully guilty-looking Maisie. The shock on Susanna's pretty, *dirty* face was a sight to behold. Nate almost fell over laughing, but he thought it best to stay upright to defend himself.

"Well, I never!" Susanna's indignant tone matched her regal bearing. "The very idea!"

Everyone else froze, while disappointment pinched at Nate. Surely, a little mud couldn't offend her that badly.

"Oh, dear." Maisie looked stricken. "I'm so sorry."

Rosamond hurried to Susanna's side. "Here, let me

help you." She pulled a handkerchief from her pocket and started to dab away the offending dirt.

"Never you mind." Susanna politely took the white cloth and scrubbed it across her cheek, leaving a streak of gray. "Now, if you'll excuse me, I have flowers to finish planting."

She walked slowly to the flower bed, where about half of the columbines had been planted and the rest of the separated clumps lay awaiting their new home. Something in her ambling gait dispelled Nate's disappointment, but he held his peace and watched. Sure enough, Susanna knelt down and made a mud ball, and before he could blink, she sent it hurling through the air to land smack on Maisie's chin.

Maisie shrieked louder than Nate had ever heard her, and then all three girls fell into a fit of laughter. He allowed himself to sit back down on the stump as they all looked around at each other and enjoyed the moment.

"You know, I thought for a bit that Nate was going to take those horses." Rosamond wiped her sleeve across her face, causing more damage than repair. "But I couldn't figure out which one of us he was going to trade for 'em."

Both she and Maisie guffawed like cowpokes, and neither seemed to notice the horror on Susanna's face.

"Now, girls, you know I wouldn't—"

"Oh, my, what a mess." Mother emerged from the side door and studied the scene, her hands fisted at her waist.

"Yes, ma'am." Nate gave his sister a wicked grin. "These girls have been impossible to control all day long, and now look what they've done."

Mother gave him one of her no-nonsense glares. "And of course, you're entirely innocent. Well, I won't have any of you leave the cleanup to Angela or Rita or any of the hands. You'll clean up this yard, and you'll do your own laundry." The lilt in her voice belied her stern words. She started back toward the door, then stopped to study the flowers. "These columbines look lovely, girls. I'm sure they'll recover from the shock of moving by the time we have our party." Her voice softened, as it always did when she spoke about the big anniversary event. Nate couldn't wait to see her face when the Colonel gave her the china. "Now, don't forget tomorrow is Sunday, and we're all going to church, so everyone will need a bath. Nate, you'd better get busy pumping and heating water and bringing it to the back porch." She went back inside, shaking her head, but Nate had no doubt she was laughing to herself.

As for Susanna, he hoped this bit of tomfoolery had lifted her spirits after this afternoon's fright. Once they cleaned up and sat down to supper, he could count on the Colonel to ruin any feelings of inclusion he and the girls had conveyed to Susanna.

Chapter Nine

Wrapped in a borrowed robe, Susanna hurried up the back stairs to Rosamond's room. As the least dirty of the girls, she had taken the first bath and now had time to visit with Daddy while the other girls bathed. She couldn't imagine what had gotten into her, participating in such a brawl.

Well, no, she really did know. Her first instinct had been to flee the scene when the girls started throwing mud at Nate. But when Maisie had impulsively included her in the fight, then looked so stricken by her own behavior, Susanna could not bring herself to add to the girl's chagrin. In finishing school, Mrs. Sweetwater had taught that all good manners should be motivated by a desire to make the other person feel comfortable and to save him or her from embarrassment, no matter how awkward the situation.

The only way to save Maisie from humiliation had been to serve her a dose of her own medicine. Susanna was fairly certain Mrs. Sweetwater would have been shocked by the entire affair, but it certainly worked out well. Even Mrs. Northam found the whole scene amusing. And all of that foolishness showed Susanna that the

other girls were as unnerved by the incident with the Indians as she was. They'd all had a good laugh, the best
antidote to any fright, the best first step to any recovery.

As she entered Rosamond's room, another memory
of finishing school surfaced. In spite of all the manners
taught there, the girls always had to initiate newcomers.
Susanna's initiation had included sugar in her reticule,
which of course drew hordes of ants. By laughing it off,
she'd won many friends. The same had happened today,
and it felt good deep inside her. Even though the girls
were Yankees.

Rita had laid out several of Rosamond's outgrown
dresses for Susanna to choose from. Her hostess was a
few inches taller and a bit broader, but by no means too
large. If anything, Mama would say Susanna was entirely too thin. She'd lost the last of her childhood chub-
biness on the trail, and while she wouldn't wish it back,
she could afford to gain another pound or two in order
to feel at her best.

She selected a blue print dress, then thoroughly brushed
her windblown hair. Fortunately, no mud had lodged
there, so she hadn't had to wash it. Soon she was dressed,
groomed and ready to visit Daddy. She found him propped
up in the bed reading *Bleak House.*

"You were asleep when I peeked in a while ago." She
pulled a chair up beside him. "Did you have a good day?"
His clean-shaven cheeks had lost their gray cast, and his
newly trimmed hair had restored his handsome appearance. Susanna could only be encouraged.

"Fair to middling." He offered a weak smile, but his
eyes exuded peace and a hint of amusement. "How was
your day?"

Susanna hesitated. He appeared recovered enough
to hear the truth, so she told him about the entire trip

to the columbine field and back. No, not the entire trip. She could talk about the lovely flower field and the nice little mare she rode. She could minimize the dangers of the encounter with the Indians and her fright, though she could see the situation troubled him. She could even describe the mud fight, which gave him a good laugh that resulted in some pain in his ribs.

But she dared not tell him what a fine man Nate Northam was turning out to be. Not that he needed any further proof after Nate's Good Samaritan actions in bringing them here. But she must not speak of her struggle to keep from caring too much for him. Daddy had been teasing her about beaux since she was born, but never about any of the young Yankee men who'd come around their prairie schooner in the wagon train. A few cold words had been sufficient to drive away their interest in her, so she could not, *would* not, dishonor him by forming an attachment to Nate.

"And what about your day?" Best to deflect any possible questions he might have. "What did you do?"

"As you can see, I'm in a bit better shape than when we arrived. It's remarkable how much better a bath can make a man feel."

Susanna gasped. "Angela gave you a bath?"

"Of course not." He lowered his chin and gave her a chiding look. "You know my stance on such matters. Have you ever seen me do anything improper with a female servant?"

"No, sir." Susanna held back a laugh. My, he looked indignant—a good sign his old self was returning. "But don't tell me you did all this yourself." She waved a hand over his clean presence.

"When Miss Angela saw the task was bigger than she'd thought, that cowboy Zack brought up the tub and water, then helped me." He went on to explain how the process had wearied him, and he'd slept most of the day.

Susanna barely heard the rest of his remarks. *Miss* Angela? Since when did a servant merit that courtesy title used in the South?

Voices and footsteps down the hall indicated Rosamond and Maisie had come upstairs, and Susanna glanced toward the door. Maybe she should offer to help with supper.

Daddy patted her hand. "You go on, daughter. I know you want to be with your new friends. I'll be fine."

"All right, dearest. You rest now." She bent down to kiss him and caught a whiff of a woody cologne. Seemed Zack and *Miss* Angela had made an extra effort in their care of Daddy. That wouldn't entirely make up for the Colonel's attitude, but it surely would make things easier as long as they had to stay here.

The girls were busy combing out tangles from their freshly washed hair, but rather than stay and chat, Susanna felt compelled to go downstairs and see if she could help with supper. Perhaps if she made herself useful, the Colonel wouldn't object so much to Daddy's recuperating in his home.

Two steps before she reached the landing where the back staircase made a right turn, she stopped at the sound of the Colonel's voice just below.

"Monday morning, when Mrs. Northam is away visiting, you slip away just like we planned. I've made all the arrangements for you to ride one of the horses." His soft tone held an unmistakable note of affection.

"*Sí,* Señor Colonel." Rita's voice!

A sick feeling churned in Susanna's stomach. What kind of wickedness was this? Obviously, this man did not hold the same moral convictions as Daddy regarding female servants. And to think this girl was younger than his own children. What would poor Angela think if she knew her employer had designs on her daughter?

Hearing Rita's light footfalls ascending the steps, Susanna backed up as quietly as she could and hurried through the hallway to descend the front staircase. To her chagrin, on her way down the center hall to the kitchen, she encountered the Colonel. Fighting the urge to back up against the wall to let him pass, fighting the urge to tell him what she thought of his character, she forced a smile Mama and Mrs. Sweetwater would have been proud of.

"Good evening, Colonel Northam. Did you have a chance to see the columbines we planted?"

Instead of bowing politely as any Southern gentleman would, he stopped short and stared at her as if trying to remember who she was. A scowl quickly replaced his confusion. "I trust your father will be back on his feet soon." It sounded more like an order than a friendly inquiry.

"Never you mind, Colonel." Susanna put on her sweetest voice. He might not be a gentleman, but she was still a lady. "Once he can walk, we'll be out of your house faster than a jackrabbit running from a coyote. You can count on that." She punctuated her words with a perky smile, picturing him as that coyote she'd shot out in Kansas. "Now, if you'll excuse me, I should go peel some potatoes or something."

She brushed past him and made her way to the kitchen. While the welcome Mrs. Northam and Angela gave her didn't entirely make up for his inhospitable behavior, it went a long way to soothing her disquieted soul.

"Did you get their names?" The Colonel sat behind his desk grilling Nate about the Indian encounter. At least this time, he didn't stand in his usual intimidating way.

"No, sir. The only name mentioned was yours, and they took off as soon as I said it." Flattery had never worked with the Colonel, and it didn't this time, either.

"Humph." He brushed away the idea as one would a bothersome fly. "I doubt they meant any harm. But just to be sure they don't come up here again, I'll send a message to the commandant over at Fort Garland." He waved a hand toward a chair, wordlessly ordering Nate to sit. "Now, about that china. On Monday morning, your mother and Rosamond are driving up to Swede Lane to deliver some food to those folks during their convalescence. That's when I want you to check for any broken pieces. You think you can get it done in a few hours?"

"Yessir." Nate started to say Susanna could help him, but it probably would be best just to have her do it and tell him later.

"You be careful with it."

"Yessir." In spite of his resolve not to get angry at his father, Nate felt heat rising up his neck. "Of course I'm careful with Mother's gift."

The Colonel sent him a scowl. "After that, you can work on the addition." He grunted in his usual dissatisfied way. "That carpenter from Denver had better show up to complete the woodwork." He seemed to be speaking to himself, as if making a mental list of all the things that needed to be finished before the anniversary party. "All right, you can go." Again he waved his hand, this time in a dismissive gesture toward the door. "And check on that Anders fellow. Make sure he's not faking his injuries so he can loaf around here at my expense."

"Yessir." Nate stood and stretched. It had been a long, tiring day, especially coming right after his trip to Pueblo. These were the times when it was hardest not to respond to his father in anger. "He could be faking the broken ribs, but it's kind of hard to fake a broken leg." He hurried from the room before his father could holler at him for talking back.

One thing was sure. His stomach was hollering at him right now. Drawn by the mouthwatering aroma of Angela's chili, he ambled down the hall to the kitchen to see if he could find something to hold him until supper. When he opened the door, Susanna's lovely face was the first thing he saw, and his heart skipped. What was the matter with him? It hadn't been two hours since they parted company to go clean up, yet he felt as if he'd been away from her for two days. And that was just short of how long he'd known her. The smile she gave him seemed a little strained. If the Colonel did something to hurt her feelings, he'd go right back to the office and give him what for.

"Nathaniel." Mother looked up from her work over a large crockery bowl. "Just the man I wanted to see. Come over here and stir this cookie dough. It's so stiff I can't manage to blend all the ingredients together."

"Yes, ma'am." He grabbed the wooden spoon and took a turn at mixing the heavy dough, which contained candied fruit, nuts, spices and molasses. "You know I'll do anything to have some of my favorite cookies." Once he'd blended everything to Mother's satisfaction, he pinched off a piece of the dark brown substance and popped it into his mouth. "Mmm. Just right."

"You'd better leave some for baking." Mother sprinkled a little flour on the kitchen table, then spooned out a chunk of dough and began to flatten it with her rolling pin. "This recipe has to go a long way if all the hands are going to get some."

"Yes, ma'am." Turning a chair around and straddling it, he propped his chin on his hands to watch Susanna cut carrots and other vegetables. This was where they'd started the day some twelve hours ago, yet she still had enough energy and the good manners to help in the kitchen. That spoke well of her. So much for the Colonel's talk of lazy Southerners.

"May I help you do that?" He hoped she'd give him one of those *la-di-da* answers he found so appealing.

Instead, she shook her head and gave him a tight smile. "No, thank you. I believe I can manage." She scooped up the vegetables and set them in a bowl, then carried it to Angela, who was stirring the chili in a large cast-iron pot on the stove. "Is there anything else I can do? I could start washing those dishes." She nodded toward a collection of items by the dishpan.

"No, *gracias, señorita.* That is Rita's responsibility. She will do it soon." She put the vegetables in a pot, then moved to the side table and began to assemble the ingredients for tortillas.

Watching the ladies cook had always been one of Nate's favorite pastimes, but usually he was busy with his own chores at this time of day. He noticed the disappointment on Susanna's face when Angela refused her offer, and tried to think of some way to divert her.

As if reading his mind, she glanced in his direction, and he felt the little jolt in his chest that was getting all too familiar.

"If it's not too much bother," she said to Angela, "could you teach me how to make tortillas?"

"*Sí, señorita.*" Always accommodating, Angela made room on the table for Susanna to work beside her and began her instructions.

Susanna's persistence in wanting to help deepened Nate's admiration for her. He glanced toward Mother, hoping she would appreciate their guest's good manners, too, and found her watching him. The sly smile on her face cut short his enjoyment of the moment. He frowned and shook his head, but her smile merely broadened. He wanted her to like Susanna to make up for the Colonel's rudeness, but he didn't need her to play matchmaker.

He stood and headed for the back hallway. "Guess I'll go check on those columbines."

Mother chuckled. "You do that, son."

Susanna said nothing. Didn't even look his way. Nate was surprised at how disappointed that made him.

Susanna tried to concentrate on Angela's instructions, but Nate's presence made it impossible. She was glad when he left. No, not glad at all. Just plain sad. In any other time or place, regarding any Southern gentleman with the same depth of character, she could let her heart lead her. But here and now, these feelings just would not do. Even if she and Nate did fall in love, they had no future together. But she mustn't even entertain the word *if.* She would not love this man. Would not! To distract herself, she pictured the house in Marietta she loved so much and her dreams of having her own children growing up and playing on that same grassy lawn, as she and Edward Jr. used to do. She must never lose sight of those dreams.

"No, no, Miss Susanna, too much water." Angela laughed as she reached over to add more finely ground cornmeal to the bowl she'd given Susanna. "Make the dough like this." She held up a round lump that appeared pliable enough to flatten without falling apart.

"Oh, dear." That was what she got for not paying attention. "Have I ruined it?"

"Do not worry, Miss Susanna." Rita had entered the room moments ago and begun washing the dishes. "I still cannot make tortillas like *madre mia.*" She reached to place a glass jar in the rinse pan, but it slipped from her fingers and crashed to the floor. "Oh, no."

"Be careful," Angela and Mrs. Northam chorused.

Rita grabbed for the shattered jar too quickly, then gasped and pulled back her hand. Trying not to cry, she gripped her injured palm with the other hand, but blood seeped through her fingers. "Mama," she whimpered.

With a worried gaze on her daughter, Angela rinsed her hands, while Mrs. Northam left her cookie-making to come help. Susanna waited until they moved to the center table to tend the wound before finding a broom to sweep up the shards. She could not help but wonder how this would affect the poor girl's assignation with Colonel Northam.

She soon found out. Once the hand was bandaged, they all went to work again and within a half hour had supper ready. As Susanna and Rita set plates and silverware around the table, the Colonel entered the room, spied the wounded hand and demanded to know what happened. After hearing Rita's explanation, he summoned Angela and Mrs. Northam.

"This child is not to wash dishes again. Is that clear?" Both women appeared surprised by the vehemence of his order, but both agreed to obey him.

But Susanna wasn't the least bit surprised. The Colonel would likely do anything to protect the girl who was the object of his favor.

Chapter Ten

The moment Reverend Thomas opened his mouth to speak, Susanna felt as if she'd come home. His Southern pronunciations varied slightly from hers and Daddy's, but it was clear the man was no Yankee. She couldn't imagine why the Colonel had let this Southerner take such a prominent place in his community, but she expected to enjoy his sermon. Maybe the minister would visit Daddy, who'd insisted that Susanna must attend church with the Northams.

After a few words of welcome to Susanna and two other visitors, Reverend Thomas announced the Scripture verses he would address in his sermon. Seated beside Susanna, Nate held his Bible up so she could look on, just as he had the hymnbook at the beginning of the service. When they'd begun singing, she could barely hold back a giggle. Nate was no singer, but what he lacked in pitch, he made up for in enthusiasm. From the light in his eyes as he sang "When I Survey the Wondrous Cross," she could see that he held deeply the faith he'd spoken about on the trail. She might as well admit, if only to herself, that a Yankee could be a true and decent Christian, despite what his people did to the South during the war. Despite what his father said in the back hall of their house.

Before they'd left the ranch, Nate had gone out of his way to make sure she was comfortable in the family carriage with Mrs. Northam, Rosamond and Maisie. Everything he did prompted warm sentiments in Susanna's heart. Somehow she must find a way to cool that warmth before it blazed up and burned her.

She quieted her thoughts and settled back to enjoy the sermon. The verses they'd just read in Hebrews 11 might be the very thing to help her. All those Bible folks had acted in faith in the midst of serious difficulties, and most had suffered terribly for it. While staying in the home of a Yankee colonel wasn't exactly perilous, spending time with the man's son could well be dangerous to her heart.

As it turned out, the minister focused his message on the faith these congregants had in building this new community in such a harsh land. In faith, they had all left their comfortable homes back east at the invitation of Colonel Northam. His purpose? To build a Christian community where all would be welcomed with the love of Christ.

The moment the pastor mentioned the Colonel and the Lord in the same sentence, Susanna stopped listening as Rita's sweet, innocent face came to mind. Oh, the deeds done in secret! Wasn't there a passage of Scripture about how those deeds would be brought to light? If it wouldn't cause a scene, she'd grab Nate's Bible and hunt that verse right here and now.

Figuring he should dodge Mother's matchmaking efforts outside of church, Nate didn't mind when she put him next to Susanna in the pew. Susanna was wearing

Rosamond's Sunday dress from last summer, so he would just think of her as a sister.

Who was he fooling? No man in his right mind could lightly dismiss the effects this beautiful lady had on him. When she'd worn that blue dress yesterday afternoon, her eyes had sparkled like the rare gems in Mother's sapphire necklace. And now in this frilly pink gown, her ivory complexion glowed like one of Mother's alabaster vases, the ones painted with roses like the soft blush on Susanna's fair cheeks. How had she managed to cross the entire continent without turning brown? Or freckled like Maisie. Maisie, whom the Colonel had seated on Nate's other side.

He forced his thoughts away from his woman troubles and tried to concentrate on Reverend Thomas's sermon. Faith. That was what he needed. Faith that the Lord would continue to build this community. Faith that in spite of the Colonel's domineering ways, Nate could stay and make a contribution worthy of the Northam name. Faith that one day he would earn his father's approval.

With that thought, his spirits sank. The only way for him to get the Colonel's approval would be to become Rand. And there at the other end of the pew sat his middle brother, dozing after his late-night doing who knew what with Seamus and Wes, two of the Northam cowhands. They'd probably been gambling, something the Colonel had made clear he wouldn't permit in his community. Yet he refused to come down hard on Rand when he did it.

The familiar resentment against his brother crowded out Nate's attempts at worship. Yes, those Bible heroes had great faith, but right now, he just wasn't up to joining their ranks.

After the sermon, Nate listened halfheartedly to the announcements. The fever that had spread through the

Swedish community was now under control, thanks to
Charlie Williams and his herbal remedies learned from
the Indians. With the plan Mother already had in place,
meals would be delivered to those folks until they could
stand on their own feet again. Finally, Reverend Thomas
commended the congregation for their donations to the
charity fund, for several needy families had been helped.

As usual, the congregants lingered in the church-
yard, chatting and catching up on news and innocent
gossip. Then hunger sent them scattering to their respec-
tive homes. The Northams parted company with Maisie
with a promise to send Rosamond for a return visit in a
few weeks.

Nate couldn't help but notice that Susanna had been
very quiet. Other than brief chats with Pam Williams and
Reverend Thomas, she had stood by the carriage waiting to go home.

Except she didn't have a home. And Nate didn't have
one of his own to offer her.

Susanna spent part of Sunday afternoon reading to
Daddy and the remainder of the day alone in Rosamond's
room. The Northams took the Sabbath seriously, resting
after church just as her family had back home in Marietta, so no one came looking for her. She'd wanted to take
Daddy out into the sunshine, but he wouldn't be able to
go down the long staircase for some time. An upstairs
veranda opened out from Colonel and Mrs. Northam's
suite, but she wouldn't go anywhere near that end of the
upstairs hallway.

Rosamond had told her that even Sunday supper was
quiet and simple, with Angela and Rita away visiting
family in a small Spanish settlement to the southeast. Susanna wondered if Rita would find a confidante, maybe a

grandmother to whom she could expose the Colonel's reprehensible behavior. Obviously, she had not been able to tell her mother, probably because she feared they would lose their employment.

Not wanting to encounter either Nate or his father, Susanna waited to fetch supper until she observed through the bedroom window that the two men had walked toward the stables, no doubt to tend to chores. In the kitchen, she found a tray laden with food and a note for her to take all that she and Daddy needed.

As they ate in the bedroom, Daddy seemed to grow more cheerful, while Susanna's heart grew heavier. How long must they stay in this place? After only two days of bed rest, Daddy's leg hadn't healed enough for him to find new horses, much less hitch them up and drive the wagon. She certainly didn't have the strength to manage all the work required for traveling.

After church, she'd thought about asking Miss Pam if they could stay with her and Charlie, maybe camp out behind the café. Before she could say a word, however, Miss Pam had told her how fortunate she and Daddy were to be in the care of such good people as the Northams. When Susanna thought to make her plea for other accommodations to Reverend Thomas, the young minister had gone on and on about what a good man the Colonel was.

In this small, developing community, no hotel had been built, and none of the homes had been made into boardinghouses. Susanna found it more than frustrating to have plenty of money to move out of the Northams' house, yet to have no place to go and no means to get there. All she could do was remember Mama's everlasting optimism and try to make it her own.

The next morning as she sat again beside Daddy's bed as he ate breakfast, Nate came to the half-open door and gave them both a big smile. That cute smile of his, with one side of his upper lip higher than the other. Despite her determination to shield herself from his charms, her traitorous heart skipped.

"Susanna, would you be able to help me with something?" The twinkle in his green eyes did nothing to fortify her resolve.

"Well…" Having left Daddy alone too much these past two days, she'd turned down the invitation to go with Rosamond and her mother to deliver food to the needy. "I planned to read to Daddy—"

"Nonsense, daughter." Daddy gave her arm a little nudge. "You go on. I'll be fine."

Her heart tried to pull her out of the chair, while her mind refused to budge. "Exactly what do you need help with?" In spite of herself, she couldn't keep the sassiness out of her voice.

He glanced back down the hallway, then ducked into the room and closed the door. "The Colonel wants me to make sure none of the china is broken. Mother and Rosamond are going out calling all morning, so this is the perfect chance to go through the boxes. I figure it'll take two of us."

His eager expression added to his charm. Here was a man who loved his mother and delighted in doing things for her. As for the china, Susanna wondered how the Colonel could worry about it being broken when it was his wife's heart that would be broken if his actions with Rita were discovered. Still, Mrs. Northam had been kind to Susanna and Daddy, so this was one small way she could pay the lady back.

"Just exactly where do you plan to do this operation?" She pictured bringing the crates into the house and spreading the china out on the long dining room table. They would need to add the extra leaves, and there would be a mess to clean up afterward with all of that straw packing—

"In the barn. We don't want anybody to know about it. My brothers and all the hands will be out herding cattle or working in the fields all morning, but we'll still have to be quick about it."

"Harrumph." Daddy glared at Nate. "Young man, do you mean to say you're going to be in the barn behind closed doors alone with my daughter?"

Surprised by his concerns, Susanna held back a laugh. "But, Daddy—"

"Oh." Nate's face turned red beneath his tan. "I didn't even think how that would look. Would you approve if Zack worked with us? He's the only person who knows the secret other than the Colonel and me." His eagerness to do the job added to his already dangerous appeal. He was nothing if not persistent, another admirable quality to add to the list Susanna was trying not to compose in her mind.

Daddy's expression changed from a scowl to a smile quicker than a blink. "Why, that would do just fine, Nate. You have my approval."

Nate's grin broadened. "Thank you, sir." He focused on Susanna. "Will you help?"

She couldn't keep from smiling at his boyish enthusiasm. "Of course I will."

An hour later, after Rosamond and Mrs. Northam had left, she followed Nate's instructions on going to the barn. She left the house by the front door and meandered around the grassy yard smelling the roses and checking on the columbines. Some of the transplanted flowers had wilted or lost blooms, but none looked as if they wouldn't make it. She next wandered toward one

of the corrals, where several horses munched on a pile
of hay. Several barn cats called out to her, and she took
a moment to pet them. Then, following Nate's instructions on how to avoid being seen from the kitchen window, just in case Angela looked out, she found a door on
the far side of the barn and quickly entered.

A medium-size black-and-white dog wandered out
of a stall and eyed her curiously, tail wagging. Susanna
bent down to pet her and noticed a litter of four or more
puppies amid the straw and burlap on the stall floor. Her
heart melting at the adorable creatures, she rubbed behind
the mother's ears. "Hello, little girl. What's your name?"

"That's Bess." Nate sauntered over. "She's been keeping to the barn since having her pups, but I expect her to
get out more as time goes on."

"Will she let me hold one?" Despite a strong urge to
cuddle a puppy, she didn't want to upset the mother.

"Sure." Speaking to Bess in soothing tones, Nate
picked up one of the pups and set it in Susanna's waiting
arms. "This little girl is the runt of the litter, but she's
pretty healthy.

"Oh, how sweet." Susanna held her up to one cheek
and received a good lick. "My, you're friendly."

Bess danced around as if worried, so Susanna set the
puppy back among the others. "I must have one of them,
Nate, unless they're all promised."

"I think we can work that out once they're weaned."
Nate walked toward the specially rigged wagon where
Zack stood awaiting orders. "Let's get started." He
grabbed a crowbar and started to pry open one of the
crates.

"Now, you just hold on a minute, Mr. Nate Northam."
Susanna marched over to the wagon, suddenly feeling
the weight of responsibility for this endeavor. "Just ex-

actly where do you plan to lay out the pieces as you unpack them?"

The two men exchanged a look.

"Um…" Nate looked around the barn as if he'd never seen it before.

Zack pushed his hat back and scratched his head. "Well, I'll be. Hadn't thought of that."

"What did you do when you inspected the shipment at Pueblo?" She glanced around, not sure what she was looking for. All she saw were stalls, bales of hay, harnesses and other items used for the care of horses.

"The trading post owner's wife let us use her dining room." He and Zack traded a look and a laugh. "I think that man's going to have a hard time when his next anniversary comes around."

"Well, he should." Susanna fully understood the lady's feelings. Mama had always expected something special to celebrate her wedding anniversary and always gave Daddy something special in return. "Do you have some blankets we can lay out?"

The two men scrambled to pull out several large blankets used for horses in the winter. After shaking out the dust, they laid them on the flat dirt floor.

"Don't know what we would have done without you." Nate gave Susanna that charming grin of his, and she couldn't help but smile back.

He opened one crate, removed a handful of straw and lifted out a plain oak chest. "As you can see, it's all in smaller boxes." Inside the box were four crystal goblets, each safely nestled in its own flannel-lined compartment.

"This is like a treasure hunt." Susanna couldn't wait to see what the next box held. "My brother and I used to hunt pretend treasures." She wished back the words as soon as she said them. Would Nate think she was a "money-grubbing prospector," as his father had accused?

"My brothers and I did, too." Nate winked at her as he pulled out another box, and her heart warmed. Not for the first time did she consider how different he was from his father.

The box he held contained plates separated by flexible, flannel-covered dividers. All in all, they counted twenty-four place settings, plus numerous serving pieces. Platters, serving bowls, finger bowls, creamers, sugar bowls, all in the same blue, silver-rimmed Wedgwood pattern.

As they began to repack the items, Susanna felt close to tears. Not one piece was broken. Mrs. Northam would be so pleased, and she deserved this wonderful gift. Susanna could only pray that she would never know how her gift was tainted by an unfaithful husband.

"I can hardly believe nothing's broken. That's answered prayer." Nate tucked the inventory list into his shirt in case Mother returned early and asked about the fancy parchment paper he was carrying. "And once again, I have you to thank." He eyed Susanna, who was daintily dabbing her face with a handkerchief. "Sorry you had to work up a sweat, but this barn gets mighty hot during the summer." He tried to think of a clever comparison as to how hot it got, but nothing came to mind.

"Mr. Nate Northam!" She glared at him in that cute way of hers. "Ladies do not sweat. We perspire." She sniffed with mock indignation. "And you're very welcome about the china."

Zack snorted out a laugh at the lady's remark. "I should go, boss. The boys will wonder why I'm not out there working alongside 'em."

"The boys can wait. I need you here another minute." Nate wouldn't give Mr. Anders any cause to worry about his daughter's reputation. "Susanna, do you give your stamp of approval on the way we stored the boxes?"

"Now, wouldn't I have said so if I didn't?"

"Yes, indeed, I'm sure you would have." He loved it when she got sassy. It showed spirit and optimism, maybe even faith in the midst of her difficulties. Yet one small thing nagged at him. As they'd opened each of the boxes, she hadn't viewed their contents with the same covetous glint he'd seen in the eyes of the trading post owner's wife. In fact, Susanna had inspected the dishes with a critical, even knowledgeable approach, searching for possible blemishes. She appeared to be familiar with Wedgwood and named other china patterns made by the company.

Were the Anderses truly poor, as he'd assumed? Had they fallen from wealth into hard times? Was a patrician background the reason Susanna carried herself with such dignity? Did Mr. Anders want to seek his fortune in the San Juan silver fields so they could return to some former social status? Nate didn't dare ask Susanna these questions, for that would be the worst side of rude. Maybe it was time he got better acquainted with her father so he could disguise his questions as friendly interest.

He sent Susanna out first, then waited a few minutes while Zack shuffled his feet impatiently.

"Good work handling that china, Zack. You've been a big help with it all along."

The old cowboy grinned and shrugged. "My ma never had anything that fancy, but she did teach me how to treat nice things."

"Good, because I want you to meet me in the addition tomorrow morning first thing. There's nobody I can trust to help me finish it."

As expected, the other man rebuffed his praise. "I'll be glad to, boss. Now, I'd better head out."

As Zack left, Nate gave one last appraising look at the stall where he'd stored the boxes of china. The men, and even his brothers, knew better than to go poking around the barn, and the dust- and straw-covered canvas on top of the boxes would keep anyone from prying.

He ambled out of the barn and headed toward the house to take the inventory list to the Colonel's office. He didn't particularly want to see his father, but if he was in, Nate would have a chance to tell him how much Susanna had helped with the china…again.

Entering the house through the back door, he followed his nose to the kitchen. There he found Susanna up to her elbows in dishwater and Angela pulling bread pans from the oven.

"I sure did come in at the right time, didn't I?" Nate swallowed hard at the overwhelming aroma of the freshly baked bread.

Always accommodating, Angela dumped a loaf onto a cloth on the table and cut a large slice for him. "Butter, Señor Nate?" She brought a crock from the side table, then went back to her work.

Nate slathered butter on the slice and started to take a bite, then paused. Susanna hadn't spoken to him or even looked his way since he came into the room. That was taking their secret a bit too far. If she'd just look at him, he could give her a surreptitious wink. Since she didn't seem inclined to do so, he broke off a bite of bread, stepped over to her and put it up to her lips.

"Want a bite?"

She pulled back from him. "From those dirty hands?" She sniffed in her haughty way. "No, thank you."

Laughing, he popped the bite into his own mouth. This

little gal got under his skin in the worst—or the best—
way. What he wouldn't give to just consider courting her.

He whistled as he strode up the hall to the Colonel's
office at the front of the house. Maybe his father would be
out in the fields, although this summer he was spending
less time working side by side with the hands than in pre-
vious years. If he wasn't in, Nate would tuck the inventory list in his desk drawer, where Mother never looked.

At his knock, the Colonel called, "Enter," in his gruff,
commanding voice.

A sigh of disappointment escaped Nate as he obeyed
the order. He crossed the room, removing the inventory
paper from inside his shirt. "All there and in perfect condition."

"Hmm." The Colonel didn't look up from his ledger.
"That was fast. You sure you didn't break anything?"

Clenching his teeth, Nate placed the paper on the desk.
"If it hadn't been for Miss Anders, I could well have broken some. She made suggestions on how to go about it,
then on how to store everything until the party."

At the mention of Susanna's name, the Colonel's head
snapped up, and he glared at Nate. "She helped you, did
she?"

"Yessir, she and Zack." Better get that information
out there right away so the Colonel didn't assume they'd
been alone. Yet at his father's harsh expression, rebellion
kicked up inside Nate. "And by the way, I promised her
one of Bess's pups."

The Colonel placed his knuckles on his desk, stood
and leaned toward Nate. "They are not yours to promise.
You know very well we're going to raise those dogs to
herd cattle, and we need every one of them. Why do you
think I sent for an expert dog handler all the way from
Scotland? To train them, that's why."

Nate glared back at his father while a half dozen retorts came to mind. In the end, he just spun on his heel and strode from the room, not bothering to shut the door. He stormed out of the house and across the yard back to the barn. Up in the loft, he grabbed a pitchfork and started tossing down hay. Lots of hay. And when he'd tossed down more than the horses would need that evening, he climbed down and tossed some of it out the door into the attached corral, where the horses already had plenty to eat. Then he kicked a fence post. Which only served to send pain shooting up his leg. Now he had to move the extra hay back to the loft so the horses wouldn't overeat and get sick.

Court Susanna? What was he thinking? Two unchangeable things kept him from it. His father's vise grip on his life, and his own inability to manage his temper. That last one worried him most. He didn't really want to use that pitchfork on the Colonel, but someday he might just give in to the temptation to land a punch on his father's square, stubborn jaw.

Chapter Eleven

"Before coming here, I never ate anything made from chokecherries." Susanna stirred a bite of pancake into the dark red puddle on her plate. "This syrup is delicious."

"Just don't eat the berries raw." Nate sat across the kitchen table from her, his teasing smirk not getting in the way of his polishing off his griddle cakes. "There's a reason they're called *choke*cherries. Right, Angela?"

Working as usual at the stove, Angela nodded her agreement. "*Sí.* Never eat them without sugar or honey, or you will be sorry."

Seated next to Susanna, Rosamond ate her breakfast with the same enthusiasm as her brother. "Maybe you'll still be here in September when we gather the berries and help Angela put them up. Won't that be fun?"

"Oh, yes. I always loved—" she stopped before blurting out that she'd helped the family's cook put up jelly "—making blackberry jelly. I'm sure this will be just as enjoyable."

His mouth too full for speaking, Nate nodded and arched his eyebrows, as if he was saying he also hoped she would still be here. If it wasn't for the Colonel, Susanna could almost wish for the same thing.

As these few days had passed, it had become harder to remember all the reasons she'd been taught to hate Yankees. She found this family not just tolerable, but worthy of her friendship. Except for the Colonel, of course. A lady couldn't be expected to sit at the supper table every evening under his angry looks without feeling a bit uncharitable in return, especially knowing what she did about his treatment of young Rita. But otherwise, Susanna's days had been fairly pleasant as she basked in the hospitality of the rest of the family.

Still, she must keep Nate at arm's length and not let their friendship go any deeper. She'd always had her heart set on marrying a Southern gentleman just like Daddy and Edward Jr., and she must not lose sight of that dream. The South was her world, the place where she belonged, where she was welcomed by everyone. This small community could not compare to all she'd left behind.

But then there was Nate. No Southern gentleman had ever dug into her heart as he had begun to do. Perhaps the only way to keep a hold on her emotions was to treat all the Northam brothers the same. "Where are Rand and Tolley? I never see them except at supper."

Nate's brief scowl surprised her, but she had no time to examine his reaction.

"My brothers and I are out early for chores every day. They grab a bite to eat in the bunkhouse, then head out with the hands."

"But you don't?"

"Usually I do. Right now I'm building the addition." He shoveled in another bite.

"Oh, yes." She remembered what he'd said about the structure. "Your father's gift to your mother for their anniversary." She would wink at him if such a gesture wasn't unladylike.

"Yep." He kept his expression neutral.

"I must say I'm impressed to learn you're a builder." She was rewarded with his most attractive smile, and her uncontrollable emotions did somersaults inside her. Such feelings would not help her reach her dream of going home.

"Nate's had a hand in just about every building on this property." Rosamond's voice was filled with sisterly pride. "Not to mention the church and several barns for our neighbors."

"My, my." Susanna could not imagine her own brother doing such hard labor, but she'd grown very proud of Daddy for learning many manual skills on the trek west.

Nate stood and carried his plate to the dishpan by the sink. "Can't sit around jawing. Gotta get to work. What are you girls doing today?" He directed his question to Susanna, but Rosamond didn't seem to notice.

"Mother suggested that I take Susanna on a tour of the ranch." She began to clear the table but paused. "That is, if you'd like to go."

"I would indeed. That is, after I wash these dishes." Since Rita had been relieved of the duty, Susanna tried to step in as often as she could. She actually enjoyed the chore. She'd been surprised to see the indoor pump and sink like the one her family had back home. A pipe in the sink drained the water out through the floor and all the way to the kitchen garden.

"No, no, *señorita*." Angela clicked her tongue in a maternal fashion. "You wash dishes yesterday. Today you go along with Señorita Rosamond." She set her stirring spoon on the table beside the stove and stepped toward the dishpan. "I will wash them."

"Please let me." Susanna blocked her as graciously as

she could. "You all work so hard, and it would be silly for me to sit around with my hands folded in my lap."

Her words brought an approving smile from both Nate and Rosamond.

"Let her help, Angela." Nate spoke with a hint of gentle authority, and the housekeeper nodded her acceptance.

"*Sí,* Señor Nate."

"I'll help, too." Rosamond tied on an apron and offered one to Susanna.

"You ladies have a nice time." Nate disappeared through the kitchen door.

With some difficulty, Susanna turned her attention to the task at hand. Too bad Nate couldn't go with them on the tour of the ranch.

Once the chore was completed and she had checked to make sure Daddy had everything he needed, Susanna joined her hostess outside the back door. "Is Mrs. Northam well? I wondered why she wasn't in the kitchen for breakfast."

"She's very well, thank you." Rosamond beckoned to Susanna, and they began their walk toward the outbuildings. "This morning she's working on Father's anniversary present. It's a surprise, of course, so she always has to wait to work on it until he goes off on business or out to see how the men are managing things. Today he went to Alamosa and will be there overnight, so she'll have all day and evening."

"I see." Despite her dislike of the Colonel, Susanna felt that funny little tickle inside over helping to keep a secret. "Do you know what she's giving him?"

"Yes." Rosamond giggled. "And I know what he *thinks* she's giving him. She's making a quilt from scraps of all our clothes since we came to Colorado. It's for him to take on trail drives or other such trips. She has a Singer, so she should get much of it done today." She snickered. "Father knows about the quilt, but makes a big show of pretending not to know."

Fondly remembering her own parents' secrets at gift-giving time, Susanna laughed. "But that's not the real present?"

"Nope." Rosamond looped an arm around Susanna's and leaned close. "She's having a set of silver-and-turquoise spurs made for him by our blacksmith. Just the three of us know about it." Another giggle. "And now four. I can trust you not to tell Father, can't I?"

Susanna could barely keep from choking. No, she would not tell the Colonel about the spurs or anything else. She could hardly look at him without feeling a little sick. Forcing herself to recall his generous gift of china now hidden in the barn, she managed a smile. "Of course. I didn't realize your family employed a blacksmith. And to think he's a silversmith, too."

"Bert's like everyone else around here. He has to do more than one job." She waved a hand in the direction of an outbuilding near the stable. "That's his workshop." Above the weatherworn wooden structure, a gray stream of smoke drifted into the air. "We'll go there in a minute, but first I have something else to show you."

They had crossed the wide backyard to the barn, and Susanna surveyed the place with interest as if she'd never seen it before. When they went inside, she studiously kept from looking toward the stall where a deceptively dusty canvas covered the china crates. Fortunately, Rosamond's attention was on Bess, who bounded over to them, her tail wagging furiously.

Kneeling down, Susanna pretended not to have met the dog. As uncomfortable as it made her feel, she decided not telling all she knew was not the same as lying, especially when the secrets she was keeping were not hers to divulge.

"What a sweet dog." Susanna suffered Bess's affectionate licks with good grace. "And what adorable puppies." Which one would Nate give to her? Maybe the chubby little one who was pouncing boldly through the straw to join them. No, she'd much prefer the little runt she'd held on Monday. Right now the little female stayed in the back corner of the stall whimpering for her mother and melting Susanna's heart. She'd always felt a special affection for the underdog.

"Father and Mr. Eberly brought a trainer from Scotland to teach them how to herd cattle." Rosamond picked up the brave puppy and cuddled it. "Maisie gets to take care of the puppies' father. It's an experiment, so we'll see how it works out." She held it up with its nose to hers and murmured, "You're going to tell those great big steers what to do, aren't you?"

As Susanna tickled the runt's tummy, she noticed it had one underdeveloped rear paw. The puppy settled comfortably into her arms and promptly fell asleep. Susanna decided she would call her Lazy Daisy. "When do you think they'll be weaned?" She could hardly wait to make this little one her own.

"Usually before they're two months old, but we won't rush it. Father wants to be sure they're happy and healthy before their training begins." Rosamond spoke of the Colonel with great affection, but never called him by his rank, as Nate did. Susanna hadn't noticed how Rand and Tolley referred to him.

After they had their fill of puppy affection, Rosamond took Susanna to the blacksmith shop and introduced her to Bert, a former slave. He showed them his handiwork, large silver plates fashioned to fit over the boot tops. Each was adorned with turquoise stones and delicate scroll-work. Even the leather bands and the spiked rowels had attractive etchings.

"Of course, Father won't wear them for work, just for dressing up," Rosamond said as they left the blacksmith to his work.

Susanna's mind spun with the contradictions she was seeing. So the Colonel employed a former slave, entrusting him with such an important job as blacksmithing. Many Southerners, including Daddy, had often condemned the North for freeing the slaves and then not providing a livelihood for them. Once off the plantation, countless former slaves wandered the South with no way to earn a living. For all of his evil ways, this former officer had at least given a job to one such freedman.

When her family had sold their plantation, Susanna had been too young to have learned much about the day-to-day operation of producing a cotton crop. Now with Rosamond as her guide, she could observe the many and varied activities on a ranch, and she began to comprehend all the work that went into producing any sellable product, whether cotton or beef.

"Until we get more businesses in the area, Four Stones Ranch has to be self-sustaining." Rosamond pointed to another structure beyond the blacksmith shop. "Besides Bert, we have Joe, who tans leather and makes anything from saddles to belts to boots. We won't go over there because it really stinks when he's tanning."

Susanna had noticed the pungent smell and wondered what it was. Today a warm breeze carried most of the stench away.

Rosamond now indicated a distant field, where green, knee-high alfalfa waved in the breeze. "Of course, we grow our own feed for the animals."

"And your own food," Susanna said. "I certainly do admire that kitchen garden."

"I noticed you liked the squash." Rosamond wrinkled her nose. "You and Nate are the only ones who do, other than Mother and Father."

Susanna felt another one of those emotional somersaults near her heart. As silly as it seemed, she was pleased to learn she and Nate liked some of the same things.

A high-pitched whinny sounded from a corral some distance from the barn, and both girls turned to investigate.

"Now, that's exciting," Rosamond said. "Looks like Rand's planning to teach Tolley how to break a new horse." She grabbed Susanna's hand and rushed her toward the scene. "Let's watch."

Her excitement was catching, so Susanna ran along beside her and copied her as she climbed on the lower rail of the corral and hung over the upper rail to get a better view.

Rand was as tall as Nate and their father, but not as broad in the chest. He still gave the impression of being able to handle any of the varied duties of a cowboy. Right now he was murmuring instructions to his younger, shorter, thinner brother, who stood beside a restless horse. Susanna couldn't hear their exact words, but Tolley seemed to chafe under Rand's cautionary tone.

"If you can do it, I can." Tolley turned away from his brother, slung a blanket on the horse's back and transferred a saddle from the fence to the animal.

Before he could reach under and grab the cinch, the horse sidestepped and bucked, throwing the saddle to the ground.

"Whoa." Rand, holding the bridle and reins, tried to

apply a soothing touch, but the horse tossed its head and snorted angrily.

At least it sounded angry to Susanna. She glanced at Rosamond, who was chewing her lip. Sudden protectiveness for young Tolley filled Susanna's heart. She'd noticed a bit of acrimony among the brothers, but this was certainly not the time for these two to argue. Lifting a silent prayer for both to be safe, she tightened her grip on the rail.

"Hey!" Nate appeared on the scene and entered the corral through a gate. "What do you think you're doing?"

At his take-charge tone, relief swept through Susanna. She couldn't stand it if anything happened to young Tolley. Like her little puppy, he almost seemed like the runt of the litter.

Rand rolled his eyes, but Tolley appeared relieved to see his oldest brother.

"Rand keeps treating me like a kid." Tolley shot a glance toward Susanna and Rosamond, and his face reddened. "Why don't you two go make a cake or something?"

Rosamond laughed, clearly not concerned about her little brother. "Or I could break that horse for you."

Susanna had already stepped down from the fence, but she couldn't walk away until she saw how Nate handled the situation.

"Rand, you know the Colonel put me in charge of breaking these horses." Although his hands were bunched into fists, his voice was surprisingly calm.

His hands also fisted, Rand cast a quick glance toward Susanna, and the scowl he had aimed at Nate softened. "I know he did. He also told you to go all the way to Pueblo for supplies and build that addition and make sure the hands were kept busy." He shrugged and gave

Nate a smirking grin. "With all you've got to do, I'm just trying to help you out, big brother."

"So you think Tolley getting his neck broken is helping?"

"Hey—" Tolley now scowled at Nate.

Nate waved a hand to silence him. "Both of you ride out and help Seamus and Wes check the fencing, especially in the south pasture. You know it needs to be checked every day." The brothers exchanged glowering looks all around. "Now!"

Tolley jumped at his command and hurried to exit the corral.

Rand lifted his hands in surrender. "All right. All right. Ladies." He tipped his hat to Susanna and Rosamond and sauntered toward the gate. Then he jerked his head toward the horse and gave Nate another smirk. "I'll leave you to take care of Spike."

"No." Nate took a step toward him. "You'll take care of him and put away this saddle." He paused as if waiting to see whether Rand would obey him.

Rand glared, then shrugged and moved toward Spike. "Come on, you dumb beast. Back you go to your friends till the big boss here makes time for you in his busy schedule."

"And about tonight," Nate said, "just because the Colonel is away, don't get any ideas about going over to Del Norte with Seamus."

Spike snorted, and Rand laughed. "That about sums up what I think of that order."

As he led the horse out of the corral, Nate didn't respond. Susanna couldn't help but admire his self-control, even as she failed to comprehend why he and his brothers, especially Rand, seemed to have some sort of rivalry. She and Edward had always gotten along so well, despite his being six years older. A sudden ache to see her dear, protective brother swept through her. All the more reason to go back home.

"Did you ladies finish your tour?" Nate spoke so pleasantly one would never know he'd almost come to blows with his brother.

"Yep." Rosamond stepped down from the railing. "I guess it's about time to help Angela fix supper."

Nate came out of the corral, and the three of them walked toward the house.

"What did you like best, Susanna?"

Hoping to ignite some playful banter, she gave him a saucy smile. "Why, the puppies, of course. I fell in love with one in particular."

His responding frown sent a shard of worry through her. "Yep, they're heartbreakers. That's for sure." He kicked a stone in his path with unusual force.

Susanna's heart sank. Had he changed his mind about giving her the puppy? Or had she made a mistake by hinting at his promise while they were in Rosamond's company?

No matter the cause of his displeasure, one thing seemed apparent. She would not be getting Lazy Daisy for a pet. And that hurt more than she could have imagined.

Chapter Twelve

The next morning, Susanna approached the breakfast table with great hesitation. Nate's pleasant but subdued greeting confirmed her fears. He'd changed when she'd mentioned the puppies, so something had happened between his promise and that moment. From the cheerful way Mrs. Northam and Rosamond greeted her, she knew they were not the cause. It had to be the Colonel. While the three family members carried on their usual morning chitchat, she considered her options. Maybe the mean old bear of a colonel would sell her Lazy Daisy. She'd hand him a solid five-dollar gold piece and enjoy the shock on his face. That would show him she wasn't a poor little nobody who didn't even deserve common courtesy.

Having cheered herself, she looked across the table at Nate, trying to think of something clever to cheer him up, too. He chose that second to rise from the table and gather his plate and silver.

"Well, those rooms won't get finished if I sit here jawing." Now he gave Susanna a warm smile that held no reservations and punctuated it with a wink. "You ladies have a nice day."

As disappointed as she was that he was leaving, her

Get 2 Books FREE!

Harlequin Reader Service,
a leading publisher of inspirational fiction, presents

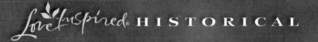

Love Inspired HISTORICAL

A series of historical love stories that will lift your spirits and warm your soul!

GET 2 BOOKS

WE'D LIKE TO SEND YOU TWO FREE books from the series you are enjoying now. Your two books have a combined cover price of over $10, but are yours to keep absolutely FREE! We'll even send you two wonderful surprise gifts. You can't lose!

Each of your FREE books is filled with joy, faith and traditional values as men and women open their hearts to each other and join together on a spiritual journey.

HOW TO GET YOUR
2 FREE BOOKS AND 2 FREE GIFTS

1. Return the reply card today, and we'll send you two novels, absolutely free! We'll even pay the postage!
2. Accepting free books places you under no obligation to buy anything, ever. The two books have combined cover prices of over $10, but they're yours to keep, free!
3. We hope that after receiving your free books you'll want to remain a subscriber, but the choice is yours—to continue or cancel, any time at all!

EXTRA BONUS

You'll also get two free mystery gifts!
(worth about $10)

FREE!

Return this card
today to get **2 FREE BOOKS**
and **2 FREE GIFTS!**

YES! Please send me 2 FREE novels,
and 2 FREE mystery gifts as well. I understand I am
under no obligation to purchase anything, as
explained on the back of this insert.

102/302 IDL GGDS

Please Print

FIRST NAME	LAST NAME

ADDRESS

APT.#	CITY

STATE/PROV.	ZIP/POSTAL CODE

EMAIL

Visit us at
www.ReaderService.com

LIH-914-2F-13

HARLEQUIN® READER SERVICE—Here's How It Works:

Accepting your 2 free Love Inspired® Historical books and 2 free gifts (gifts valued at approximately $10.00) places you under no obligation to buy anything. You may keep the books and gifts and return the shipping statement marked "cancel." If you do not cancel, about a month later we'll send you 4 additional books and bill you just $4.74 each in the U.S. or $5.24 each in Canada. That is a savings of at least 21% off the cover price. It's quite a bargain! Shipping and handling is just 50¢ per book in the U.S. and 75¢ per book in Canada.* You may cancel at any time, but if you choose to continue, every month we'll send you 4 more books, which you may either purchase at the discount price or return to us and cancel your subscription. *Terms and prices subject to change without notice. Prices do not include applicable taxes. Sales tax applicable in N.Y. Canadian residents will be charged applicable taxes. Offer not valid in Quebec. Books received may not be as shown. All orders subject to credit approval. Credit or debit balances in a customer's account(s) may be offset by any other outstanding balance owed by or to the customer. Please allow 4 to 6 weeks for delivery. Offer available while quantities last.

heart still skipped pleasantly. Until she slushed it up with a reminder that he was not the Southern gentleman of her dreams, and Four Stones Ranch was not the home she'd always wanted.

"Rosamond, you may use the Singer today." Mrs. Northam stood and straightened her apron. "Angela and I will clean up the kitchen so you can get started on those shirts right away."

"Yes, ma'am." Rosamond finished her glass of milk. "Susanna, would you like to help?"

"Indeed, I would. For whom are you making shirts?"

"Just about every man on this ranch." Rosamond beckoned to her, and they proceeded up the back stairs.

"Oh, my. How many will that be?" The more, the better to Susanna's way of thinking. She loved to sew and should have brought Mama's Singer on the trip west. Of course, the horse thieves probably would have stolen or destroyed that, too.

"About eighteen or twenty." Rosamond headed toward her parents' bedroom at the far end of the hall. "Give or take a few. Some hands aren't as reliable as others, so Father and Mother aren't as eager to provide for them."

"That makes sense." She hesitated at the bedroom door, hoping they wouldn't be sewing in there.

"It'll take both of us to carry the machine downstairs." Rosamond's words set her mind at ease.

"Of course. Just a moment." After a quick hello to Daddy and reporting the happy news that she would be sewing today, she joined Rosamond in carrying the Singer downstairs to the sunny dining room. The heavy treadle machine, housed in an oak sewing cabinet, gave them more of a challenge than either one had expected. As usual, Susanna knew Mama would be shocked at how strong she had grown over these past months.

After they set the machine in front of the two wide windows, Rosamond stood back and breathed out a hearty, "Whoosh! Next time we'll get the men to move it."

Susanna laughed as she tried to catch her breath. "Sounds like a good idea."

The time had come for her to revise her opinion of Rosamond as a spoiled girl. She was as hardworking as her parents and brothers. Now she sorted through the heavy bolts of fabric Nate had brought over the mountains nestled among and cushioning the boxes of china.

"This green plaid will make a nice shirt for Nate, don't you think?" Rosamond nodded toward a bolt of bright cotton she'd set on the dining table. "Of course, there's enough to make shirts for Rand and Tolley, too. What do you think?"

Susanna guessed that her friend was baiting her, but she refused to bite. "I suppose. Do your brothers mind dressing like triplets?"

They both laughed, but Susanna did wonder how the three men—well, one boy and two men—would appreciate having that connection, considering their quarrels.

"They don't have much choice." Rosamond sat in front of the Singer and started pumping the treadle to wind thread onto a bobbin. "We girls often run into a twin at church because we can't let the material go to waste. Oh, here's Nate now."

"What about Nate?" As he entered the room, he gave his sister a suspicious frown. "What are you two up to?"

"Oh, nothing." Rosamond kept her eyes on the machine. "Susanna, would you hold that material up to him and see what you think? If it doesn't suit him, we'll use it for the cowpokes. Most of them don't care what color they wear."

Susanna did as she was told and was not in the least surprised when Nate's green eyes lit up like emeralds. This was a good color on him, all right, and her pulse started to race when he gazed down at her. Gracious, what was wrong with her?

"It'll do." She set the bolt back on the table and took up the sleeve pattern they had made earlier from newspaper. "Stick out your arm."

"Yes, ma'am." As he obeyed, he grinned at her with mischief in those green eyes. All of his reserve had disappeared, so maybe she was wrong about the puppy.

That happy thought swept away her fears. Or was it his increasingly intense gaze? She avoided looking at his eyes and concentrated on measuring the length of his arm. His very muscular arm. Trying not to touch him, she felt her insides shake like aspen leaves in the wind. No sense in denying that he was an attractive man, but she must not let him affect her this way.

"So, Mr. Nate Northam, what have you been up to the past hour?" She kept her tone as light as possible but still could hear her own breathiness. She gave his shoulder a shove so he'd turn his back to her for measuring.

"Like I said at breakfast, working on the addition." As he turned, he tilted his head toward the double sliding doors he'd just come through. "Just a few more finishing touches, then the carpenter can come in to do the fancy woodwork. That's going to be one very fine ballroom, not to mention the additional bedrooms upstairs."

"A ballroom!" Susanna couldn't have been more surprised. "My, my." She held a piece of newspaper and marked his size on it with a stubby pencil, then used a tape measure to double-check her work. Gracious, what a broad back. She wrote down the measurements with a shaking hand. "Just imagine having a ballroom way out here in the country." She laid the paper on the table and took a deep, quiet breath to calm her nerves while she cut it to shape.

"Mother loves to entertain." Rosamond's voice held a hint of defensiveness. "Other than barns, nobody has enough room for the whole community to come together, and she didn't want to leave anyone out of the anniversary party."

Having intended her teasing remark for Nate, Susanna was appalled that she'd wounded Rosamond. "Well, I think it's just grand. All the plantation houses back home have ballrooms for entertaining." She shouldn't have said that. Daddy wanted her to keep their social prominence a secret. "I attended a ball once." More than once, of course. Oh, she was making a muddle of it all. "I think I hear Daddy calling." She left the pattern pieces spread across the table and fled the room, using the back stairs to avoid any possible encounter with the Colonel.

Nate stared after Susanna until he noticed Rosamond watching him. "Wonder what got into her." He shrugged for effect before heading for the door.

"Yes. I wonder." Rosamond's laughter followed him all the way into the kitchen.

She and Mother were getting a little obnoxious in their subtle teasing about their houseguest. Didn't they know the Colonel had other marriage plans for him? Not that he'd go along with those plans, even if Susanna weren't here. But he sure wished they'd all leave him alone to decide what to do with his own life.

One thing he'd decided overnight was that he would keep his promise to Susanna about the puppy. He would tell the Colonel not to pay him next month's wages in exchange for it. That should impress his father with how serious he was. There would be other litters, but a promise was a promise, no matter what the Colonel thought about either Mr. Anders or Susanna. Nate would have to find out which one she'd fallen for so he could give it to her as a surprise, maybe with a big red bow around its neck.

Other than trying to figure out how she knew so much about Wedgwood china, he hadn't been too concerned about her past, but that comment about attending a ball rang true. While not one item he'd seen in the prairie schooner indicated Mr. Anders came from money, Nate got the impression they'd once been wealthy, maybe before the war. Of course, Susanna would have been a small child when the war ended, so that didn't answer his questions about her fine manners. He'd never known a poor person who behaved with such grace nor one with such knowledge of fine china.

He didn't care whether the Anderses had been poor. He just wanted, *needed,* to know more about them. If he decided to go to war with the Colonel over letting them stay until Mr. Anders healed, he didn't want any unpleasant surprises about them to come up later. Of course, his father would misunderstand his intentions and assume he was interested in Susanna, a luxury Nate couldn't afford until he'd settled on his own future. If she turned out not to be what she seemed, that would be the last straw in losing what little respect his father had for him. Not to mention the heartache he would bring upon himself, maybe even Mother and Rosamond. He'd visit Mr. Anders this afternoon and check up on him. If a few personal questions slipped out, all the better.

After dinner, he left Zack to finish painting the ballroom ceiling and made his way upstairs. Last week when he'd brought Susanna and her father to the ranch, he'd been more than willing to surrender his own bedroom

to the injured man. Now seeing Mr. Anders's pale face
and sunken cheeks reinforced his determination to keep
him here until he regained his strength. He must make
certain the Colonel didn't turn the old man out.

"How's it going?" Nate kept his tone cheerful as he
pulled a chair up beside the bed.

"Can't complain." Mr. Anders tried to sit up but fell
back with a grimace. "Not much, anyway." His deep
chuckle brought another pained expression.

"Hush, now." Nate already felt guilty over his plans
to interrogate the man, and now he'd caused him pain.
"Have Angela and Zack been keeping you comfortable?"
The room smelled surprisingly fresh for a sickroom.

"They have indeed." Gratitude shone from the invalid's eyes. "I just hope we're not putting you out too
much."

"Not at all, sir." Nate waved a dismissive hand. "In
fact, Susanna's been a big help around the house. She's
helped with everything from cooking to sewing, not to
mention working in the kitchen garden."

"That's good." The older man gave an approving nod.
"She's like her mama, not wanting to sit idly by while
others do the housework."

Nate scrambled to decipher that comment. Had her
mother been able to choose whether or not to perform
household chores?

Mr. Anders stared at him. "You want to ask me something?"

Feeling foolish over his suspicions, Nate shrugged.
"Nothing in particular." Maybe Mr. Anders was one of
those people a man could talk to with candor. Not like the
Colonel, whose anger Nate was always trying to dodge.
"Just thought it was about time we got better acquainted.
Mind you, I don't mean to be nosy."

"Of course not." Mr. Anders's doubtful expression belied his words. "I understand your father doesn't think much of prospectors."

"Yessir." Nate appreciated the way this man took the bull by the horns. "And if Susanna told you that, she probably told you it's because of the freight drivers who left our cargo at Pueblo so they could go off prospecting." He didn't need to add that the Colonel didn't want prospectors to settle in the community because of their generally unreliable character.

"She did. That was downright dishonest of those men, especially if your father paid them in advance." He pressed a hand against his ribs and took a deep, raspy breath. "But I can't say I'm sorry they did quit the job. No telling how long we would have been up on that pass without help if you hadn't come along."

Nate chuckled. "And I wouldn't have come along if I hadn't gone to Pueblo. Yessir, I've thought of that." Probably wouldn't have met Susanna, either, an idea he didn't care to dwell on because it made his heart sink clear down to his belly. He really needed to stop that nonsense.

"Then rest your mind about it, Nate. It was God's plan all along." Mr. Anders stared at the wall, but didn't really focus. "The Lord's been leading me across the entire continent, so I have to trust that the robbery was part of His plan." His eyes closed briefly, then he gazed at Nate again. "About my prospecting, I'll know what I'm looking for when I find it." His eyes briefly flared with some emotion Nate couldn't define. Rage? Lust for riches? It sure was different from Susanna's detached viewing of the china.

Mr. Anders's face softened into a more peaceful expression, so much so that Nate wondered if he'd been mistaken. "After I find it, I'll go home." The old man's voice grew even raspier as he closed his eyes again and shuddered, as if the warm breeze coming through the window had chilled him.

"Yessir." Worry for Mr. Anders threaded through Nate, so he tugged the patchwork quilt up to the old man's chin. Lying still like this could give the man ague, so he'd better consult with Angela or Charlie Williams about the situation. "I'm praying you'll be back on your feet soon so you can start your search."

Not that he was in a hurry for them to leave. After this short talk, Nate felt certain Mr. Anders was a man of integrity, whatever his past, just as he was a man of faith. If he needed to restore his lost fortune for his family's sake, then that made him all the more admirable. And it made Nate all the more determined to get closer to Susanna before she left Four Stones.

Giving her the puppy would be just the beginning of what he would do for her.

Chapter Thirteen

Susanna helped the other ladies pack the large picnic baskets with sandwiches, cold coffee and baked goods. After three days of sewing, she was eager for a change, especially one that would take her out of doors. Today Mrs. Northam insisted she must help Rosamond carry the noon meal out to the men working in the field. While she endeavored to ignore the older lady's obvious matchmaking, she did look forward to seeing Nate. Having finished his work on the ballroom, he now worked with the men every day and took his breakfast in the bunkhouse. Susanna missed seeing him.

With their horses saddled and the packhorse laden with the baskets, they began their trek at a slow pace. Once again, Susanna rode sidesaddle on the agreeable little mare, Sadie, while Rosamond rode her bay gelding astride.

"How far do we have to go?" Better to ask that simple question rather than ask whether or not they might encounter the Indians again.

"Just under a mile, over in that field." Rosamond indicated the uncultivated land to the west. With her hat hanging on its strings down her back, she tossed her long, dark brown hair in the breeze. "Too far for the men to walk back to the house to eat, then walk back out to work."

"That makes sense." Not to mention it gave her a chance to see Nate.

With the sun beating down on her, Susanna longed to go bareheaded like her companion. But this worn straw bonnet had saved her complexion on the long journey west, so she must not toss it aside. With her lighter coloring, she might not fare as well as Rosamond, whose sun-browned skin looked surprisingly attractive, especially with her green eyes, so much like Nate's, sparkling like jewels in the bright day.

"There they are." Rosamond waved toward the men some fifty yards away. "They're digging irrigation ditches and… Oh, dear." She pulled her horses to a stop, and Susanna came up beside her. "Let's just wait here until they notice us."

"Why?" Susanna focused on the men briefly before quickly looking back at her friend. "'Oh, dear' indeed." Heat rushed to her cheeks.

"We mustn't blame them." Rosamond giggled. "Ditch digging can make a man terribly hot, not to mention ruin a good shirt."

Susanna bit her lower lip to keep from laughing. Mama had taught her all about modesty, and Mrs. Sweetwater had reemphasized those lessons. But on the wagon train, privacy had sometimes given way to expediency, leading to some awkward situations. Today, Susanna thanked the Lord they had not ridden closer to the working men and embarrassed them all.

A sharp whistle split the air, and they saw Nate with his shirt back on and waving his brown hat. The other four men were also properly clothed.

"Let's go." Rosamond urged her horse forward using her knees, as Susanna had observed before. While she couldn't imagine riding astride, she could see how practical it was for this life. She gave Sadie a little tap with her riding crop, and the mare followed the other horse.

They neared the work party, and her heart began to race. Yes, indeed, it had been entirely too long since she'd seen Nate, and the sight of him made her happier than she could have imagined. My, he looked healthy. Due to his outdoor work, his cheeks had tanned even darker than before. Beneath his hat, his green eyes glinted in the sunlight, just like Rosamond's.

"It's about time." He wiped a red handkerchief over his face. "I hope you brought plenty."

The men crowded around the packhorse and wasted no time in removing the baskets.

Nate sauntered over to Susanna and tilted his hat back. "Will you girls join us?" He gave her that charmingly crooked grin of his, and her heart did its usual somersault, despite his smelling of hard work.

"Of course." Rosamond jumped down from her horse and hurried to the grassy spot where the men were laying out blankets and digging into the food. "Don't you men ever wash your hands?" One hand fisted at her waist, she pointed with the other to the nearby stream they were working to connect with the ditch. "Wash. Now."

Tolley was the first to obey, then Rand and the other two men joined him at the water. While they were occupied, Nate gripped Susanna's waist and helped her down from Sadie, and pleasant shivers shot up to her neck. "Will you stay and eat with us?" His hands still on her waist, he gazed down at her, not seeming to realize he'd already asked that question.

She had to take a deep breath before offering him a

shaky "Yes, thank you." Gracious, would she ever feel this way about a Southern gentleman? Did that nice young minister from Virginia have a wife? Susanna hadn't noticed a lady at his side last Sunday.

"Why, Mr. Nate Northam." She stepped back to break his grip, but her breathiness refused to subside. Nor could she manage to inject the slightest bit of sassiness into her voice. "Shouldn't you go wash up? And pay particular attention to that dirt smudge on your nose or it just might end up in your dinner."

"Yes, ma'am." With a laugh, he wiped his handkerchief over his face again, then headed toward the stream.

Watching him walk away, Susanna could only admire his fine, manly form. In fact, she couldn't think of a single thing not to admire about either his physical presence or his character. *Oh, Mama, this is one thing you never taught me. I'm trying so hard not to fall in love with this Yankee, but my heart refuses to mind me. What am I supposed to do now?*

As he'd stared down into Susanna's sky-blue eyes, Nate had felt his pulse hammer wildly. He was glad to have an excuse to walk away from her before he did something foolish. Like tuck those loose blond curls back under her bonnet. Or tell her how pretty she looked. Or tell the boys he was taking the afternoon off so he could spend it with her. Now wouldn't that be something for the Colonel to hear about? And Rand might just be the one to tell him.

Just this morning, Nate had come to the decision that he would quit feeling so partial toward her. Oh, he'd still work a month to give her the puppy of her choice. He wouldn't break that promise. But until he could control his temper and get over his anger at the Colonel, it wouldn't be fair to her or any other lady to seek anything more than friendship.

Even so, he silently thanked Rosamond for bringing Susanna along to deliver dinner. He'd missed seeing her these past couple of days, missed her sassy, teasing ways. Now that his part of building the ballroom was finished, he had to leave the house every day before daylight and ride herd on his brothers and the hands. That meant he saw Susanna only at supper under the Colonel's watchful eyes. In fact, they hadn't had a private conversation in three days, if he could count that bit of teasing in front of Rosamond private.

Settling down on one of the blankets the girls had brought, he fished a ham sandwich out of the basket and took a bite. Just as Susanna finished setting out items on the other blanket, Seamus gave her an appraising look Nate didn't care for in the slightest.

"Will you join us, miss?" The Irishman spoke with that foreign brogue some women found so appealing.

"Well…" she began.

Nate felt heat rushing up his neck. "She's already accepted my invitation." He waved her over. "I've saved you a spot, Miss Anders." That should put Seamus in his place. Nate might not be able to court Susanna, but he wasn't about to let just any cowpoke sweet-talk her. He had an obligation before the Lord to take care of her while her father was laid up.

"I was going to say—" walking over to his blanket, Susanna wore that cute, scolding look on her face "—someone should say grace before anyone eats."

Nate felt a pinch of shame. As the foreman in charge, he should have set an example for the men, especially his brothers. "You're right. Let's pray." He offered up a spoken prayer of gratitude for the food, for the hands that prepared and brought it out to them, and for good progress as they continued to work on the ditch that afternoon. Once he said "amen," he silently prayed for the Lord to give him guidance about Susanna. After his hot reaction to Seamus's friendly invitation to her, something any cowboy might say to a pretty girl, Nate could not deny he was beginning to care deeply for her. But it just wouldn't work out.

Now, if he could just make his foolish emotions accept that painful fact.

Susanna sat cross-legged on the blanket, one folded knee only a foot away from Nate's. Mama would be shocked by her posture, but Susanna had learned early on the trip west that for the noon meal, it was either sit like this or stand. She could tolerate the temporary ache in her back so she could be near Nate. She'd appreciated the way he'd set Seamus straight about where she was going to eat. On the other hand, his protectiveness had stirred up some unruly emotions she couldn't seem to silence. She tried to think of some way to tease him, but finally settled on a neutral topic.

"The ballroom is beautiful, Nate. You and Zack did a fine job. The wallpaper is exquisite, and there's not a wrinkle in it." She picked at the bread crumbs that had fallen on the blanket to avoid looking into those appealing eyes.

"You saw it? Nobody was supposed to go in there." He scowled at his sister. "The Colonel wants Mother to be the first one to see the finished room."

Rosamond returned a haughty sniff. "And just how are we supposed to make those velvet drapes if we don't go in and measure the windows?"

"Oh." He gave Susanna a sheepish grin. "You're helping make the curtains? That's real nice, but you don't have to do it."

Warmth spread through her chest at his appreciative gaze. "I enjoy sewing."

"Susanna is very good with velvet," Rosamond said. "It always slips for me, and I end up with puckers or uneven seams. And she refuses to give me her secret." She laughed along with her complaint, so it didn't give Susanna cause for worry.

"Can't give away family secrets, now, can I?"

"Well, I still say it's real nice."

As he gazed at her, Nate's expression softened in a way Susanna had never seen before, almost to a glow. With difficulty, she looked away, fighting the pleasant bonding of her heart to him. Did he feel the same way? Were his friendly feelings toward her growing into something more, as hers were toward him? And if they were, what could they do about it? She just couldn't marry a Yankee. If she did, she'd never be able to go home to Marietta. And surely Nate could never get his father's approval, for the Colonel not only disliked her, he obviously hated her.

"Have you and Mr. Anders had time to read any more of *Bleak House?*"

Lost in thought, Susanna jumped at Nate's question. "A little, yes." She scrambled to remember where they'd left off last night, but she'd fallen asleep right in the middle of reading. Daddy'd had to wake her up and send her off to bed. "I must say, there are so many characters and story lines, it's difficult to keep track. I was making a chart on our trip, but the horse thieves must have thrown it in the fire, because it's not anyplace in our wagon."

His eyes darkened a little at the mention of the thieves, but then he grinned. "A chart, eh? Have you figured out who the villain is yet?"

"Daddy and I disagree, so we're having a little contest to see who's right. It makes our traveling more fun. If he wins, I'll have to shine his shoes, and if I win, he'll have to wash dishes. That is, once we're back on the trail."

"That's a nice way to pass the time." Nate's soft gaze lingered on her, making it hard for her to swallow. Was he hoping, as she was, that it would be some time before she and Daddy would be back on the trail?

After all those months of traveling, surely she could rest for a while longer and enjoy the fellowship of this community. In spite of the Colonel, she really wanted to attend the anniversary party. Or any party, for that matter, if anyone happened to throw one.

Her hopes were realized two days later when Maisie rode over from the Eberly ranch with an invitation to her family's barn raising the following week. Joining the ladies in the kitchen, she announced, "After the work's done, we're having a big shindig to celebrate Independence Day." Shrugging, she added, "And my birthday."

"You don't have to tell me twice." Rosamond gave her a sly smile. "We already have your present." She winked at Susanna. The two of them had made a new shirtwaist for Maisie, and both looked forward to giving it to her. At Susanna's insistence, it had many more frills than Maisie's usual shirts.

"Why, Maisie," Mrs. Northam said, "I'd forgotten that you share your birthday with our United States. Of course we'll be there. What can we bring?"

"Cook's gonna roast a side of beef and a whole pig over open pits, so any side fixings will be good. And Ma said to tell you to bring your special lemon cake."

While the other ladies discussed what their neighbors might bring, Susanna scrambled to think of something she could prepare. Not that they would need her efforts, but she'd still like to participate. If Angela had the right ingredients, Susanna could impress Nate…well, *everyone,* with her special dessert.

Maisie chuckled. "Anybody want to make a guess what Mrs. Halstead will bring?"

"No need to guess." Rosamond pinched her nose as if smelling something bad. "Sauerkraut."

As Mrs. Northam laughed at their banter, Susanna glanced around the kitchen searching for the ingredients for her special recipe. Her heart skipped when she located molasses, pecans and even vanilla. She couldn't wait to ask Angela to help her. Yet even as she planned, she chided herself. Her growing desire to please Nate in every way only added to her slippery hold on her heart.

Chapter Fourteen

"Don't forget the barn raising at the Eberly place this coming Thursday," Reverend Thomas announced as he stepped down from the podium after his sermon. "Not that I think any of you will." Chuckling, he walked up the aisle toward the door. "Some people will do any kind of work to chow down at one of Joe's barbecue feasts."

Nate laughed along with the rest of the congregation as they all stood to leave the church. Although he didn't think any cook in the San Luis Valley could compete with Angela, he did agree that Joe ranked right near Pam Williams as second best. Remembering his discussion with Susanna while they were out on the trail, he leaned against her lightly in the pew.

"Maybe you'll fix one of your family recipes." He gave her his most charming grin and wiggled his eyebrows. "I seem to recall your bragging about them."

"Nate Northam." She sniffed with artificial haughtiness. "I never did any such thing." Her pretty face creased into a cute, teasing smirk. "But you just wait and see. You're the one who'll be bragging that you know me." She peered around him, and her smile vanished as she scooted out of the pew.

Nate didn't have to turn to know the Colonel was responsible for the change in her. As much as he didn't want to look at his father, his head swiveled involuntarily. He lifted his hat from the pew and gave the Colonel a curt nod. "Nice sermon."

"Glad you were listening." His father's eyes darted briefly toward the door, where Susanna stood in line waiting to chat with Reverend Thomas. "Maybe you'll take heed."

For a moment, Nate couldn't grasp his meaning. Then some of the passages the preacher read from Proverbs came to mind, and he could barely resist slamming his fist into his father's stubborn jaw. If Susanna heard his insulting remark, the Colonel deserved nothing less.

Lord, forgive me. Here I am in Your house, and I'm thinking such sinful thoughts. But what am I supposed to do, to feel, *when the Colonel is so unfair and judgmental against someone so sweet and innocent? Someone I can't help but care for? Help me, Lord, 'cause it's a sure thing I can't help myself.*

He moved out of the pew and followed the rest of the congregation toward the door. Susanna had stepped out onto the front stoop and stood shaking hands with the preacher.

"Daddy would be so pleased if you could come visit, Reverend Thomas." She gazed up at the preacher with a sweet, guileless smile that would charm a grizzly bear.

A wave of jealously swept over Nate, almost knocking him off his feet. Reverend Thomas was a bachelor, just like Seamus, who'd flirted with Susanna earlier in the week. Only the minister wasn't some free-ranging cowpoke, but a godly, upright man. Rebellion kicked up inside Nate. Maybe the preacher could marry Maisie. That would show the Colonel. It would also set Nate free to court Susanna. *Court!* There was that word again, one that increasingly sprang up in his mind like the pesky cowlick on the back of his head.

Conviction struck hard on the heels of those thoughts. Anger. Jealousy. Rebellion. Right here in God's house. Nate mentally slammed a fist into his own square jaw, a replica of his father's he stared at every morning when he shaved. Until he dealt with those faults, those *sins,* he wasn't fit to court—or marry—anybody.

After overhearing the Colonel's insulting words, clearly aimed at her, Susanna appreciated the warm firmness of Reverend Thomas's grip as he shook her hand. She thrust aside all unpleasant thoughts and gave her full attention to the minister. In his eyes, she noticed a brief spark that hinted at something beyond pastoral interest. Nothing improper, of course. Merely the look of an unmarried gentleman appraising an unmarried lady. A Southern gentleman, she reminded herself, and therefore a prime candidate for the fulfillment of her lifelong dreams. But she doubted he would want to leave his church and go back to the South. And as she returned his gaze, no emotions somersaulted through her chest. No giddy sentiments caused her hand to tremble. Instead, she felt just plain comfortable, as she did with her kindly old minister back home.

"I'll be happy to visit your father, Miss Anders," Reverend Thomas said. "You just name the day and time."

"Why not today, Reverend?" Mrs. Northam came up beside Susanna and put her arm around her waist. "It's been too long since you've been out to the ranch for Sunday dinner, and we'd be delighted if you'd come. It would give us an excuse to cook something special on a Sunday instead of eating leftovers. I know my boys would appreciate it."

The joy that surged through Susanna and brought tears to her eyes had nothing to do with romantic feelings. Mrs. Northam's kind touch reminded her of Mama's loving embraces. More than that, her hospitality to this fine minister would mean he could talk with Daddy this very day, maybe encourage him and help them find another place to live.

If the Colonel thought she hadn't heard his despicable comment to Nate, he was sadly mistaken. Or perhaps he'd meant for her to hear. Either way, she just had to get away from his wicked judgments.

She might not be a perfect Christian, but she wasn't like the immoral woman in Proverbs, not in any way. All her life, Mama had set an example of being a godly Proverbs 31 woman. And all Susanna's life, that was exactly what she'd also striven to be, as did every Southern lady she knew. But what would a Yankee colonel know of such things? The way General Sherman and his troops had swept through the South, murdering and pillaging as they went, they'd never honored Southern women nor cared whether they lived or died. How hypocritical of the Colonel to cast aspersions on her character when his own moral behavior was reprehensible.

Once they all arrived at the ranch, Susanna offered to help in the kitchen because it was Angela and Rita's day off. Last week, the family had eaten sandwiches and spent the day resting. With Reverend Thomas as their guest, however, Mrs. Northam insisted upon a more formal meal. While the ladies cooked, Nate kindly offered to take the minister upstairs to meet Daddy.

"I don't know what I'd do without you." Mrs. Northam patted Susanna's arm as she peeled potatoes. "On the rare

Sunday when we have company, Rosamond and I always have to rush around to get the meal on the table. It's so nice to have an extra pair of helping hands."

"You're very welcome, ma'am." Susanna put on her best, brightest smile, but her heart ached. Was this dear lady so blind to her husband's faults that she couldn't see how he treated their unwilling guest?

Rosamond stoked the fire in the cast-iron stove, placed a large skillet on top and lay flour-covered pieces of chicken into the bacon grease left from breakfast. Soon the aromas mingled into a mouthwatering scent that filled the room and probably the rest of the house.

Trying to ignore her growling stomach, Susanna decided she would take her own dinner upstairs to eat with Daddy so she could avoid the Colonel. Maybe Reverend Thomas would eat with them. No, of course not. He'd accepted Mrs. Northam's invitation, so he would dine with the family. At least the minister was with Daddy now. She would pray Daddy would inquire about another place to live, but last night he seemed more than content to stay at Four Stones. Of course, hidden away in Nate's bedroom, he didn't have to put up with the Colonel's constant censure. What would he think if she told him about the Colonel's insinuation this morning? She couldn't tell him, of course, for it would only grieve him that he was unable to protect her.

Tolley burst through the kitchen door, his black Sunday suit changed for a blue shirt and denim trousers. "I'm starved. How soon will dinner be ready?"

Susanna found his youthful brashness a welcome interruption to her unhappy thoughts, but she couldn't help but wish his oldest brother would come to the kitchen, too.

"If you set the table, it'll be ready a lot sooner." Mrs.

Northam put a pan of bread into the oven, then brushed strands of frizzy gray-brown hair from her face with the back of her hand.

"That's women's work." Tolley sauntered over to the sideboard and snatched up a leftover biscuit from breakfast.

Turning chicken over in the skillet, Rosamond snorted in a rather unladylike way.

"Humph." Mrs. Northam nudged her son with her elbow. "Then get out of my kitchen so we can finish our *women's work.*"

"What women's work?" Nate breezed through the door, and Susanna's heart did its usual somersault. "How can I help?" He gave Tolley a meaningful look. What a good example he set for his youngest brother. There went her heart again.

Tolley grimaced and put the half-eaten biscuit on the sideboard. "We can set the table." He moved to the cabinet where his mother kept her best china.

Soon to be second-best china, Susanna thought as a tiny bolt of happiness shot through her. How could she possibly leave before seeing this kind lady receive her extraordinary gift from her extraordinarily wicked husband? That meant Susanna would have to endure another three weeks in this house. Even then, how could she drag Daddy away when Zack and Angela took such good care of him? Unless he healed faster than he had in the past week, she would have to manage everything all by herself, an impossible task. She was stuck like a possum in a pot of tar, no question about it.

Once they'd prepared the food, Susanna found the tray Angela used to carry up Daddy's meals and loaded it with enough for two people. Laying a linen towel over the tray, she headed for the back stairs.

"Think your father can eat all of that?" Nate cut her off and peeked under the towel, then gave her a dubious grin. "May I carry it up for you?"

"My, you're full of questions, Nate Northam." As much as her silly emotions had improved when he'd come to the kitchen, she'd hoped to make her escape without attracting his notice. But he'd been entirely too helpful in the meal preparations, maybe enjoying her presence as much as she enjoyed his. "I can manage very well, thank you."

"I have no doubt you can." His gentle tone and soft gaze soothed her bruised soul like a healing balm. Did he realize she'd heard his father's cruel insinuations and want to make up for them? "But I'd still like to help."

Her eyes began to burn, so she clicked her tongue dramatically and shook her head. "Land sakes, do let me get on with it before the mashed potatoes get cold." If he didn't let her go right this second, she'd break down and cry. How could this man be so different from his father?

Nate stepped back to let Susanna pass, and she scurried out of the room almost as if she was afraid. Not of him, but of something. That confirmed his worst suspicions. He'd come to the kitchen on the pretext of helping so he could see how she was doing. While she still had a bit of sass in her, her crestfallen posture and overly bright comments to Mother and Rosamond had made it clear she'd heard the Colonel's remarks.

That tears it. This afternoon after Reverend Thomas left, Nate would confront the Colonel in his office and insist that he quit insulting Susanna and start treating her with proper respect. In the meantime, when they all sat down to dinner, he couldn't even look at his father, only stare at the empty chair across the table where Susanna should be sitting.

"A very fine sermon, Reverend." The Colonel sounded as if he was awarding a medal to one of his soldiers. At least that was how it sounded to Nate.

While Mother and Rosamond added their agreement, Rand and Tolley were busy stuffing their faces. Nate wished they would pay attention. Several things the preacher had said would apply to one or both of them. Yet when Nate looked at the Colonel, he was staring straight at him, as though he was some reprobate sinner. Not that he didn't struggle with his anger, but that wasn't what his father referred to. Yes, they'd have a talk this afternoon, and if he lost his temper, so be it.

"Thank you, sir." Like everyone else in the area, the preacher seemed to stand in awe of the Colonel, if his modest shrug was any indication. "I've been studying the Book of Proverbs for some time now and find its wisdom useful for the spiritual growth of an individual or a community."

"Hmm." The Colonel nodded thoughtfully. "An interesting insight. I look forward to seeing how you develop this series."

A whole series on Proverbs? How had Nate failed to hear that bit of information? Maybe instead of talking to the Colonel, he should take Rand aside, give him a firm shake and warn him to listen next Sunday instead of dozing off.

Or, maybe instead of doing either one, he would take Susanna out for a walk and try to make up for the way his father treated her. That would be a much better way to spend a Sunday afternoon.

"So *Alamosa* is Spanish for *grove of cottonwoods?*" Susanna walked with her arm looped through Nate's. Although she wasn't concerned about stumbling over the roots and rocks on the uneven path, she did enjoy holding on to his muscular forearm. The last time she'd walked arm in arm with a gentleman was last Christmas, when a would-be suitor tried to talk her out of coming west. Even though she hadn't wanted to leave her hometown, her promise to Mama that she would take care of Daddy defeated the arguments of every friend who wanted to keep her there. And now, of course, she found Nate's company far more enjoyable than that of any other man she'd ever met. Even though he was a Yankee.

"That's right." Nate looked up toward the cottonwood branches swaying in the warm summer breeze. "You've noticed we have lots of Spanish names around here."

"I recall you said so the day we met." Had it been only nine days since he'd saved Daddy and her on that mountain pass? It seemed a lifetime ago. "But your ranch's name isn't Spanish. How did your folks come up with Four Stones?" She guessed it had something to do with the family's four children.

Nate glanced at the house with obvious pride and affection. "The day we finished clearing this plot, the Colonel asked Mother how big she wanted her new home to be. She told each of us children to pick up a stone and mark out the four corners." He chuckled at the memory. "I don't think the Colonel expected us to make it so big because he walked away mumbling to himself. Of course, he eventually granted Mother's wishes, saying the ranch would be officially named Four Stones."

Susanna laughed with him, and it felt good deep inside. She needed to keep this conversation light before her foolish heart did something, well, foolish. "What do you think your town will be named?"

Nate shrugged one shoulder. "Don't have any idea." He stopped and gazed down at her, his green eyes bright in the daylight. "Don't know how to say this in Spanish, but I'd like to call it *the place where I hope Susanna settles down.*"

She should answer with something saucy. Should laugh and walk away. Instead, she breathed out, "Oh, Nate, what a lovely thing to say."

She had no idea how long they stood staring at each other. Yet she felt no embarrassment or awkwardness, just very much at home. Distant sounds reached her ears. Birds sang. Cattle bawled. Bess barked. None shattered the wrapped-in-cotton feeling that surrounded her. Against everything Mama had taught her, against her own sense of right and wrong, she longed for him to kiss her right here and now. She also hoped he would not. That was a bridge they must not cross, not now or ever.

"I just wanted you to know—" He hesitated, shook his head, then took her hand to resume their walk. After several moments, he added, "I'm getting used to having you around." The deep tremor of emotion in his voice said far more than his words.

Was he experiencing the same hopelessness about their...*friendship* as she was? Did he realize, as she did, that they had no hope of happiness together? If only she could forget that fact, maybe she could enjoy this day, this hour. Tomorrow a new week would begin and—

A happy little jolt reversed the downward spiral of her emotions and sent them bubbling upward. Tomorrow she would discover whether Angela would mind her using the ingredients for her special dessert. If she didn't mind, Susanna would give Nate a delicious treat he'd never forget.

Chapter Fifteen

Nate stood in a row with a dozen other men, each of them gripping a rope. At George Eberly's shout, they all pulled, and the wall frame of the barn slowly rose to an upright position. Other men scrambled to pound in nails to join this section to the adjacent raised wall, while more workers removed the ropes and attached them to the opposite frame. With each successful part of the work done, a cheer went up from the crew.

The needs of the Eberlys' livestock had outgrown the original barn, so George had torn it down to build the new one. The barn raising had begun before first light, with George's cook, Joe, providing breakfast to everyone who came early. By midmorning, close to fifty men, all of them the Colonel's handpicked settlers of the community, had joined in the work. The air was filled with the aroma of Joe's side of beef and a whole pig roasting over open pits, so everyone labored with enthusiasm as they looked forward to their reward at the end of the day.

Nate never felt more content than when he was working with his friends on a community project, whether it was a barn, the church, a home for a newcomer or a building to house a business. Each success inspired the next one and fostered a sense of community among the settlers. He had to admit the Colonel had a gift for gathering his troops, so to speak, and motivating them to do great things. Nate would be foolish to leave all of this, even though his father's constant criticism was hard to deal with, not to mention his groundless disapproval of Susanna and Mr. Anders.

Thoughts of Susanna drew his attention across the barnyard to where she and the other ladies were preparing the noon meal in the shade of several elm trees. To his surprise, she was looking his way, so he gave her a little wave. She was by far the prettiest girl there, even prettier than the five Eberly sisters, all of them too young for him. Rosamond wasn't bad-looking, but as his sister, she didn't count. Nor did any of the married ladies. No, Susanna had them all beat. For the past four days, she'd been holed up in the kitchen with Angela, and they'd refused to let him in. Since she'd accepted his challenge, he couldn't wait to see what she'd concocted for today. In fact, he'd better be close to the front of the line, or her dessert might be all gone by the time he reached it. Even if it didn't measure up to Angela's desserts, he would say it was the best he'd ever eaten.

"Watch out, Nate." Wes caught a board that had fallen from the frame and nearly hit Nate on the head. "What are you thinking about?" He glanced toward the ladies. "Never mind. It's obvious."

"Thanks, pal." Nate gave him a friendly shove. "But mind your own business."

And he'd better mind this business of building, or the next loose board might just knock him senseless. Not that he wasn't already senseless when it came to Susanna.

* * *

With a gasp, Susanna caught the empty platter before it hit the hard-packed ground. She'd been watching Nate and had seen his close call, so it took a moment to regain her composure. Thank the Lord one of the other men—Wes, if she wasn't mistaken—had caught that board just in time. When she started to return Nate's wave, he'd already gone back to work. Maybe it was best that he not look her way again.

"Here, honey, just lay these sandwiches out on that platter." Mrs. Eberly, a rounder version of Maisie and her four sisters, set a large basket on the cloth-covered plank table beside Susanna. "Do you think we'll have enough to feed everyone?"

Her question was aimed more toward the older ladies who'd busied themselves with food preparations. Several spoke up, some certain they'd have no trouble feeding this army, others just as certain they needed to go inside and cook more food.

Glad not to be in charge, Susanna arranged the square sandwiches in a random fashion so they would be easy to pick up, then spread a linen towel over the platter to keep the flies away. She looked around for another task, but the other ladies seemed to have everything in hand. Her dessert lay tucked away in the Northams' wagon, ready to be brought out when she was certain Nate would get a healthy serving. Because of all the time she'd spent in the kitchen, she'd had to tell Mrs. Northam her secret. Of course, she hadn't mentioned that Nate's teasing had motivated her, so her kind hostess kept complimenting her willingness to contribute to the feast.

With nothing to do, Susanna wandered in the shade watching the hum of activity. Countless workers buzzed about like a hive of bees, everyone seeming to know just what to do in building the massive barn. Even some of the children who were too young for such strenuous work carried water or lemonade to the men.

"Susanna, come over here," Rosamond called from the back porch of the large, two-story house. Beside her stood Maisie and two of her sisters.

Pleased to be included in whatever was happening, Susanna had to force herself not to run. Even in this informal setting, she could not forget Mrs. Sweetwater's teaching, *Ladies do not run. Ever.*

"What are you all doing?" Treasuring the generous way they'd accepted her, she climbed the two steps onto the wide, covered porch.

Rosamond giggled. "I just couldn't wait until this evening to give Maisie her present. Is that all right with you?"

"Oh, yes." Susanna had delighted in making the white shirtwaist, especially when Mrs. Northam had produced some lace from her sewing supplies.

Giggling as they went, the five girls scurried inside the house and upstairs to Maisie's bedroom, which she shared with one of her four sisters. On her bed lay the brown paper package tied with red grosgrain ribbon.

With no ceremony whatsoever, Maisie tore into the package and pulled out the shirtwaist. And stared at it as if she had no idea what it was. "Oh. How nice."

Susanna and Rosamond exchanged a worried look.

Maisie's sisters, on the other hand, squealed with delight and reached out to touch the cotton garment.

"It's beautiful. Can I borrow it?" Grace asked.

"Me, too," Beryl said.

"You don't like it." Rosamond seemed near to tears.

"Oh, no." Maisie flung her arms around her friend, squeezing the blouse between them. "It truly is beautiful. I really will wear it." Her eyes reddened, too. "Some-place."

"Maybe church," one sister volunteered.

"Yes. Of course." Maisie gave Rosamond a weak smile. "Church."

Susanna felt like backing out of the room and disap-pearing. She'd insisted on the lace and frills, and now she understood her mistake. Here in this very nice, very plain bedroom, she could not see a single other frilly item. Maisie was a cowgirl, not a debutante, and had no use for such fripperies. The shirts she and her sisters wore with their split skirts looked just like men's shirts, and they wore the same style to church with plain skirts. Even their boots didn't have a single feminine design etched into the leather. Having no sons, Mr. Eberly must be training his daughters to run the ranch.

"Well." Rosamond dabbed at her eyes with a hand-kerchief. "That's that. At least now we have one fancy shirtwaist among us, so if anyone needs something a bit more elegant than our usual clothes, they can borrow it."

The other girls laughed rather boisterously, as if they wanted to help her smooth over the awkward situation.

"It's about time to eat." Maisie tossed the shirtwaist onto her bed. "Let's see how we can help."

While the other girls dashed from the room and thun-dered down the staircase to the back door, Susanna sti-fled a sigh and descended the stairs at a more ladylike pace. To Rosamond's credit, she did not blame Susanna for the gift, and it would be pointless to claim responsi-bility now. Maybe later she could explain it all to Maisie. These girls were younger and less genteel than she was, but they had good hearts, and she despaired of ruining their budding friendship.

* * *

Nate lined up with the other men to clean up at the washtubs, then made his way to the food lines. After his near accident, he'd lost track of Susanna, but now saw her behind one of the tables serving food. He could always tell when she was sad or depressed. Although her posture never sagged, he could see the smallest difference in the tilt of her head or the turn of her shoulders. If the Colonel had said something to hurt her feelings, today of all days when she was working as hard as any of the ladies, he'd have to find a way to make it up to her when he reached her spot.

"Won't you have one of Mrs. Barkley's pickles?" She poked a fork into a Mason jar and pulled out a plump one that carried a powerful briny smell.

In the corner of his eye, he saw Mrs. Barkley nearby, so he smiled at Susanna. "Yes, thank you." With memories of how the older lady's pickles tasted, he decided he could bury it later when nobody was watching. "When do I get some of that dessert you made?" He waggled his eyebrows in the hope that she would give him one of her sassy responses.

She didn't even look directly at him, didn't even smile. "Mrs. Eberly said dessert will be served in the middle of the afternoon. That way nobody will get too full and not be able to go back to work."

"Good idea."

He touched the brim of his hat and moved on. Something had caused her sadness, and he intended to find out what it was. Once work resumed, he'd look for an opportunity to come back to ask her. But after he finished eating and returned to the rhythm of working on the walls side by side with the other men, no such opportunity arose.

In midafternoon, a one-horse buggy rolled onto the property. The driver, a youngish-looking man in a black suit, clearly wasn't looking to be a part of the work crew. When Nate noticed the Colonel and George Eberly striding toward the newcomer, curiosity got the better of him. He turned his job of toting siding boards over to another man and followed his father.

"Dr. Henshaw." The Colonel greeted him with an outstretched hand. "Welcome. Let's secure your horse away from the work area, and then I'll introduce you around. This is George Eberly."

While they talked, Nate ambled up as though just passing by. "Can I take care of your rig for you?" So this was the doctor the Colonel had summoned to serve their community, the son of the doctor who'd been his company's physician in the army.

"Why, thank you." He wrapped the reins around the brake and took great care in climbing down. Once on the ground, he straightened his jacket and bow tie.

Dandy. The word popped into Nate's mind before he could stop it. It wouldn't do to judge this man too hastily.

"Doc, this is my oldest boy, Nate." The Colonel jerked his head in Nate's direction. "How's your father?"

"He is well, thank you." The doctor removed leather gloves to reveal soft, pale hands. Even Preacher Thomas had a workingman's hands and had labored all day beside the others on the barn. "He said to give you his regards." The doc chuckled. "And his thanks for getting me out of his hair."

"Sounds just like him." The Colonel snorted out a laugh. "I guess he did all his bragging about you when he wrote to me." He clapped the other man on the shoulder. "Let me introduce you to the folks you'll be taking care of."

The three of them walked away while Nate led the horse to a corral by a shady stand of cottonwoods. There he unhitched him to graze with the other carriage horses. Nate would send one of the younger boys with water for all of the animals, but now he needed to get back to work.

Boy. That was what the Colonel had called him to this fellow who couldn't be more than a year or two older than Nate. And he'd shown more respect for the doctor than he'd ever shown Nate. He wouldn't fault the doc. That wouldn't do any good. But it soured in his belly like one of Mrs. Barkley's pickles to practically run Four Stones Ranch for his father and yet still be called a boy.

Would he get more respect if he became a doctor? A preacher? An army officer? He'd never know, because the Lord sure hadn't called him to any other profession than ranching. If his father had so little regard for that occupation, why on earth had he ever come west?

Susanna joined the other girls in washing dishes so the older ladies could rest before starting supper preparations. Several large washtubs were set on benches, and the stronger girls carried hot water from a cauldron over an open fire.

Despairing of ever having soft, white hands again, Susanna plunged into the task with all the energy she could muster. Before leaving home, she'd never had a callus on her palms or sunburn on the backs of her hands. But complaining or feeling sorry for herself wouldn't help, so she tried to join in the good humor of the other girls. All of them were as brown as berries and didn't seem to mind at all.

"Why, Miss Northam." Maisie held up a sopping dish-cloth and moved toward Rosamond. "I do believe you have a smudge on you cheek. Do allow me to get it off."

"Ha." Rosamond laughed. "I know your game." Before Maisie could reach her, Rosamond splashed a handful of water on her.

Maisie squealed and returned a similar gesture. Soon all the girls had joined the fray, and Susanna had to back away to avoid a soaking. Maisie's curly red hair fell out of its pins and down her back in a fiery cascade. Rosamond managed to keep her head dry, but her skirt was dripping. She lifted a cupful of water from the tub and started to fling it.

"Wait." Maisie froze, her eyes focused on something near the half-built barn. "*Who* is that?"

All the girls followed her gaze.

"Oh, my," Rosamond said. "That's one fine-looking gentleman."

Giggling, the other girls made similar remarks. Except Maisie. She just stared, and her jaw hung loose. Susanna had the urge to reach over and lift her friend's chin.

Colonel Northam had gathered the men around the newcomer, and although they were some distance away, his voice carried across the wide yard. Susanna had never seen him so enthusiastic, especially in the way he clapped the young man around the shoulders.

"You all know how much we appreciate Charlie Williams for taking care of our broken bones and sicknesses these past few years." He gave a nod in Charlie's direction, and everyone applauded. "To help him out a bit, I've brought John Henshaw from Boston. Now, he's a new doctor, so I'm sure Charlie will need to teach him a lot of things."

The crowd laughed, especially when Charlie declared his immediate retirement from doctoring. Susanna could see no one took the declaration seriously.

She searched for Nate among the men and found him

leaning against a corral railing, his hat tipped back and his arms crossed. His bemused expression wrung her heart. The Colonel was behaving like a proud father toward the newcomer, something she'd never seen in his treatment of Nate.

After several minutes, Colonel Northam and Mr. Eberly walked toward the ladies with the well-dressed younger man in tow. Maisie squeaked like a mouse and spun away, dashing toward the house.

Susanna touched Rosamond's arm. "Should we see if she's all right?"

Rosamond gave her a doubtful frown. "Well—"

"Rosamond." The Colonel beckoned to his daughter. "Come meet the son of an old friend."

Susanna had never even seen him smile, but this was more than a smile. More like when she and Daddy had set out from home. Daddy's face had been lit with hope and, for lack of a better word, joy. Anybody looking on could easily see that the Colonel planned to play matchmaker for his daughter and this handsome doctor.

To avoid any possible awkwardness, such as the Colonel not bothering to introduce her to the man, Susanna ducked away and hid among the other ladies. Still worried about Maisie, she decided it was best simply to pray for her. If her sisters or Rosamond weren't concerned, Susanna would let the matter rest.

Nate, on the other hand, was one person she could encourage. Making her way through the wagons and buggies parked in a nearby field, she found the Northams' wagon and retrieved her basket from under the driver's seat. When she returned to the tables, the other ladies were spreading out cakes, pies, cookies and other assorted desserts, and the men had lined up to partake. All except Nate. He still stood by the corral, arms crossed, staring down at the ground.

She had to dodge several men, Rand and Tolley in particular, who'd heard about her special dessert, but at last she reached Nate. His hangdog expression broke her heart. She'd refused to let him cheer her up earlier, so she owed him some teasing.

"Well, Mr. Nate Northam." She sauntered up next to him, hugging the basket like a treasure. "Here I thought you'd be storming the castle to get some of my dessert, but you don't even seem half-interested." She glanced over her shoulder. "Guess I'll just surrender it to Tolley. He almost snatched it right out of my hands."

Nate's gloomy expression slowly gave way to a smile, but she could see his heart wasn't in it. "Don't you dare give it to that boy. He'll eat it all in one sitting, then end up sick."

"All right, then." She held up the basket and opened the lid. "Help yourself." All of a sudden, her pulse sped up. What if he didn't like her best recipe?

He peered into the basket, then gave her a questioning look. "What is it?" His green eyes twinkled just a bit. "Is it edible?"

"The very idea!" She snapped the basket lid closed and spun away. "I'll offer it to someone who'll appreciate—"

Before she could take two steps, he gripped her arm and gently tugged her back.

"Oh, come on, now." He put on a pitying frown. "I'll save you from embarrassment and eat one."

"Don't do me any favors." She could hardly keep from laughing. This was her Nate, teasing in his lighthearted way. *Her* Nate? Not really. But hers to enjoy just for now.

He reached into the basket, lifted out one of the soft, light brown squares and bit into it. His eyes grew round, and he grinned as he chewed. "What are these? I like pecans a whole heap, but I've never tasted them done up this way. They're delicious." He made a grab for the basket, but she held on tight. "Can I have another one? Please?"

"They're pralines." She gave him a smug look. "And you'd better not eat any more. As you mentioned, too many sweets will make you sick."

"Oh, I doubt that." He gripped the basket. "Let's see how many I can tolerate."

"There are two kinds of pralines." Somehow she felt the need to explain. "Some are hard like candy. These are creamier because they're made with cream and molasses. The pecans are the best part." She permitted him to take one more, then firmly retrieved the container. Remembering the look on his face when she offered him Mrs. Barkley's pickles, she had a pinch of doubt about his sincerity. "Do you really like them?"

"Mmm-hmm." He nodded vigorously as he chewed. "Never tasted anything as good as these."

The glint in those green eyes convinced her that he spoke the truth. How good it felt to give this noble man a reward for all his kindnesses to her and Daddy.

"Well, I'd better go find Tolley. If I don't save him one of these, he'll never speak to me again." She turned to walk away.

Again, Nate caught her arm and tugged her back to stand in front of him. "Thank you, Susanna." His rich, warm voice, accompanied by his soulful, puppy-dog look, sent a pleasant feeling skittering through her insides. He wasn't talking about pralines.

"Thank you, Nate." Now she really had to walk away. If his father thought they were sparking, he'd make life impossible for both of them.

Sure enough, across the barnyard, the Colonel stood

staring at them, hands fisted at his waist, thunder riding on his brow. *Lord, have mercy.*

Because she had a feeling that if the Colonel set himself against either her or Nate, God's mercy was the only thing that would save them.

Chapter Sixteen

"**I** can't thank you enough for all your help." George Eberly stood in the center of his newly completed barn, with the entire community of workers standing around him or seated on bales of hay.

"We can't thank you enough for all that food," a man called from the crowd.

Nate joined in the laughter ringing to the rafters. He hadn't been this exhausted since the trail drive last year, but it was a good, rewarding tiredness. Both his spirits and his stomach were fully satisfied. Maybe even his heart. His short visit with Susanna had gone a long way to heal his bruised feelings about the Colonel's partiality toward the new doctor. She'd also introduced him to those remarkable pralines, his new favorite dessert. He'd have to make sure she knew he wasn't just being polite when he complimented her cooking.

"Well, with Colorado winters so harsh, our barns have to go up in the summer," George continued, "so I appreciate your generous gift of time when you all could be building on your own land. Just give me a holler if you need my help on anything." He surveyed the group.

"Today we made it through without too many injuries, and our new doc has taken care of those."

Even Nate had consulted the doctor about a splinter, one he could have removed himself. But he'd wanted to take the man's measure, and he found the doc to be a decent sort. Friendly, humble, glad to be part of the new community. Nate couldn't let the Colonel's partiality toward John Henshaw influence his own feelings about him.

George settled his gaze on Nate's parents. "Now, I've already apologized to Colonel and Mrs. Northam for stealing their thunder and having a big shindig just three weeks before their special anniversary party."

"Except ours will be a lot fancier, so wear your Sunday best," the Colonel called out. "And you won't have to work for your supper."

More laughter filled the barn.

"All right, all right." George waved a dismissive hand at the Colonel. "Folks, it's still early enough for us to have a little bit of dancing before our Independence Day fireworks. But we have one more thing to celebrate. Maisie, get on over here." He looked toward the door, where only four of the Eberly sisters stood with Susanna and Rosamond. "Where's Maisie?"

"Here, Pa." Maisie poked her head around the barn door, and several people gasped, Nate among them.

Was this the same little gal who'd engaged in mud and water fights with his sister and could outride most men he knew? Indeed it was, but the former tomboy had suddenly transformed into a lady. She wore a bright blue skirt instead of her usual riding getup. Pearl earrings dangled against her clean-scrubbed, freckled cheeks. Her bright red hair was piled up on her head in a tidy, fancy do, and she wore an equally fancy white shirtwaist. If Nate wasn't mistaken, that was the one Susanna and Rosamond had made for her. Across the way, the Colonel eyed him and tilted his head toward Maisie. Nate just shrugged. While he had to admit she made a fine picture, she still wasn't the girl for him.

George called his daughter over and announced that this was her eighteenth birthday. While everyone shouted birthday wishes, the Colonel motioned Nate toward Maisie. Nate's heart plummeted to his stomach. How could he make his father understand he had no desire to court Maisie, much less marry her? *Lord, help me, 'cause You know I won't marry that sweet little gal.* Not when Susanna stood right there beside Maisie, outshining her in every way, despite her wilted clothes and unkempt hair.

Fiddles, guitars and an accordion were brought out, and the musicians struck up "Old Dan Tucker." While couples took to the floor for a lively jig, Susanna moved closer to Rosamond and squeezed her hand. "Maisie looks beautiful, but is she just trying to make us feel better by wearing the shirtwaist?"

"I don't know for sure." Rosamond shook her head. "But I have a suspicion. Look."

Across the way, Maisie whispered something to her father, and he led her over to the new doctor. Instead of her usual boldness, she seemed almost demure. Almost. The dear girl obviously didn't know the meaning of the word, for she gripped his hand and shook it as if she was pumping water. Even so, Doc Henshaw gave her a big smile and waved his free hand toward the dance floor.

"Oh, my." Susanna laughed softly. "That's a surprise. A very nice surprise." She wasn't sure Maisie and the doctor would make a good match, but from the smile on Rosamond's face, jealousy over the newcomer would not come between the two friends. For her part, Susanna would look for the first opportunity to ask him to visit Daddy.

"Yes, a surprise indeed." Rosamond had just enough time to agree with her before Wes approached and asked her to dance. From the corner of her eye, Susanna saw Seamus, the Irishman, moving in her direction. Although her feet itched to be out there with the other merrymakers, she'd much prefer a different partner.

"Miss Anders." Seamus gave her an elaborate bow and a wink. "I'd be pleased and proud if you would honor me with this dance." If she wasn't mistaken, he was intensifying his Irish brogue for effect. Though he failed to charm her, she still couldn't turn him down. All these cowboys deserved a dance or two for all of their hard work.

"Thank you." She took his offered hand and walked with him to the center of the hard-packed barn floor. Too late she saw Nate headed in her direction. He waggled a scolding finger at her, but she stifled a laugh at his antics. No doubt he'd be waiting to claim the next dance with her.

Sure enough, when the fast-paced music ended, she managed to graciously decline Seamus's request for another dance and move right into Nate's waiting arms.

"I was about to get jealous." He put his hand at her waist as the three-four rhythm of "Sweet Betsy from Pike" began.

"And why would that be, Nate Northam?" Hadn't he seen his father's earlier scowl? "At best, you and I are just friends. Besides, Seamus, being Irish, outshines any other cowboy when it comes to a lively jig."

"Is that so?" Not missing a step in guiding her around the floor, he shrugged and laughed. "Anything else in particular that you prefer about him?"

"Well, you can't beat that brogue for charming." Susanna easily followed Nate as he raised their joined hands and guided her into a turn beneath his arm. Anyone watching might think they'd danced together for years. How good it felt to be on a dance floor again, even a hard-packed dirt one, with this particular partner.

"On the other hand, I did see him step on your toes more than once." He shrugged again. "Of course, I couldn't tell if it was your fault or his."

"His, of course." She gazed up at him, enjoying his firm grasp on her waist. Where had he learned to lead a dance partner so skillfully? Maybe that year he spent in Boston. "And you were watching us the whole time?"

"Only now and then." He looked particularly appealing when he put on his smug face. "With so many pretty girls here, it's hard to pay attention to just one." And yet his eyes hadn't left hers since they'd begun dancing.

"So remind me of why you were jealous when Seamus was my partner."

"Ha!" He tossed his head back. "You caught me." He guided her into another elaborate spin, perhaps to avoid saying more.

The music ended, and he led her to the refreshment table, somehow managing to politely rebuff several men who approached to ask her to dance. "You've been on your feet all day. Don't want you to get tired out."

"Tsk." She sniffed indignantly. "As if I can't keep up with the likes of you."

Handing her a glass of lemonade, he again gazed down at her with an intense look that sent her heart into a spin. "You can indeed, Miss Anders. That's one of the things I like about you."

The moment he used her false last name, her heart stopped spinning. How she longed to reveal her real one to him, to tell him she came from money, the same as he did. Daddy still insisted they keep quiet about their past. What would happen if Nate knew they were social equals and should be able to court if they felt so inclined? A quick glance beyond him answered that question. His Yankee colonel father stood across the barn glaring at the two of them as if they'd just shot Lincoln. For her part, if she surrendered her heart to Nate, she could never go home to Marietta. What would he risk if he fell in love with her?

Nate didn't have to look behind him to know why Susanna's smile disappeared. No doubt the Colonel was scowling at them the way he had this afternoon. And yet his father appeared not to have noticed that Rand had slipped out the back door about ten minutes ago, glass of punch in hand. If the Colonel expected this community to keep liquor out, he should start watching his own favorite son a bit more closely.

"Let's go out and get some fresh air." Nate set down his glass and started to guide her toward the door.

"Why, Nate Northam." She didn't move. "What kind of a girl do you think I am?"

"Uh-oh." Nate felt like a steer on locoweed. No lady would accept an invitation like that. "Should have thought it through a bit more." He grimaced. "Please excuse me, but I need to check on something."

"Never you mind, Nate." She gave him one of her saucy smiles. "I can take care of myself." She glanced around the barn as if looking for another partner.

Nate stewed on that for a moment, hating to leave her so some other man could stake a claim on her while he was tending to family business. Pretty selfish, considering he couldn't court her. Anyway, if she went with him, he'd be showing her the worst side of his family. She probably thought the Colonel was the worst.

Spying Tolley, he beckoned to him. When the boy arrived, he clapped a hand on his shoulder. "You see what a homely pup my little brother is," he said to Susanna. "Would you do us all a favor and dance with him?"

Tolley ignored Nate's insult. "Miss Susanna, would you do me the honor?"

"I'd be delighted."

She took his arm without a backward glance at Nate, but he didn't have time to worry about that now. As they lined up next to Rosamond and others for the Virginia reel, he headed out the back door.

He found Rand and Seamus, along with several other hands from various ranches, kneeling around a low plank, where playing cards and coins were spread, illuminated by lantern light. His back to Nate, Rand didn't see him approach.

A cowboy slapped his cards on the makeshift table, faceup. "Read 'em, boys. A full house." While he raked in the pot, the other men threw down their cards, grumbling.

"We'll do better next time, friends." Rand tossed a coin on the table. "I'm in."

Nate snorted. The gambler's eternal trap. Quickly forget the loss and believe he'd win the next time. "Say, little brother." He gripped Rand's shoulder. "There's a lot of pretty young ladies inside without partners. Why not join the dancing?" Never mind that the cowboys actually outnumbered the ladies. If he could get his brother to his feet, he could smell his breath for liquor.

"Maybe you're right." Rand stood and shoved the coin back into his pocket, blowing out a long sigh. "Sorry, boys. This just isn't my night."

Relief, not the stink of liquor, almost knocked Nate

over. Here he'd expected the worst, but all he could smell on Rand was lemonade and sweat. Not that gambling wasn't pure evil, but he'd tackle one of his brother's faults at a time.

While the Colonel drove, Mrs. Northam next to him on the driver's bench, Susanna sat beside Nate on a cushion in the back of the wagon as they wended their way home. Above them, thousands of stars sparkled against the black sky, while the moon was only a sliver of light. To keep the wagon safely on the rough road, Seamus and Wes rode ahead with lanterns held high. On the other side of the wagon bed, Tolley slept against Rosamond's shoulder while Rand shuffled a deck of cards.

After Nate had enticed his brother back inside the Eberlys' barn, he'd watched over him, as Edward had always watched over Susanna. She could see his affection for Rand and his worry about his bad habits. She didn't know why she was surprised to see such fraternal concern in a Yankee family. She supposed it was from a lifetime of prejudices being poured into her. As each day passed, she was learning that many of those prejudices were groundless when it came to a man like Nate. Now, his father was an entirely different story. The Colonel reinforced every one of her opinions about the North.

"Did you like the fireworks?" Nate leaned toward her to whisper, probably to keep his father from hearing him. As it was, a strong breeze blew from the east, so she doubted his words would reach the front bench. That didn't keep Nate's warm breath from sending a pleasant shiver down her spine.

"Yes, I did. They were a bit loud, but it was exciting to see the sky all lit up like that." Susanna felt a great deal of satisfaction over participating in the barn raising, but she almost hadn't been able to come. The Colonel hadn't been pleased to see her approach the wagon early this morning, but Mrs. Northam's gracious insistence that Susanna was needed to help the womenfolk had won out over her husband's objections. So naturally, every time Susanna turned around today, the Colonel was scowling at her. Didn't he have anything better to do?

"Did you have Independence Day fireworks back home?" As soon as Nate asked the question, he leaned back and seemed to frown, although she couldn't quite be sure in the dark.

How could she answer? Due to the war, many folks back home wanted no part in celebrating the signing of the Declaration of Independence. Others insisted the South had as much right to claim that great document as the North because it had set all of the former colonies free from England.

"Some." Daddy always hated the fireworks because they reminded him of being in the thick of battle. Every time a cannon thundered or a rocket exploded, he ducked, then got embarrassed. But Susanna couldn't very well say that to Nate. Although it could be her imagination, they both seemed to avoid talking about the war.

Nate nodded as if he understood her brief answer. "Well, I know one thing." His voice took on the teasing tone she loved so much. "You may have attended only one ball in your short life, but you did manage to learn how to dance fairly well. Why, you almost kept up with me."

Rosamond snickered. "Say, Nate, did you ever get around to dancing with Maisie?"

He didn't even look at his sister. "Who?" He leaned close to Susanna again, and his breath smelled of sugar and pecans. So he'd eaten that last praline she'd tucked away for a bedtime snack. He must like them as much as he'd claimed. "You hardly missed a dance. I'll be surprised if you can even walk tomorrow."

Maybe it was that sliver of moonlight shining in his green eyes. Maybe she was just too tired. But for some reason, Susanna couldn't think of a single sassy reply. She could only smile up at him and wish with all her heart he would kiss her.

"Go ahead, Nate." Rosamond stretched out her foot and kicked his boot. "Kiss her."

Susanna gasped softly as both she and Nate pulled away from each other and shot worried glances toward the Colonel.

Across the wagon, Rand and Rosamond laughed softly as if they were in on a great secret. A secret Susanna refused to admit to herself. She would not fall in love with Nate Northam. She would not!

Chapter Seventeen

"You can't take a girl for granted like that or some other man will snatch her up before you get your head on straight." The Colonel leaned back in his desk chair and eyed Nate. "Last night Maisie got all gussied up to show you how much she's grown up, and you didn't ask her to dance even once."

Nate couldn't remember the last time his father had invited him to sit on one of the expensive leather chairs in front of this desk, and he knew better than to sit without an invitation. That thought and his aching feet and back from yesterday's activities made him more than a little irritable.

"She seemed to be doing all right without me." He tried to keep the crossness out of his voice but could hear it nonetheless. "Your Doc Henshaw took to her right away." That wasn't the smartest thing to say.

The Colonel snorted. "John was just being polite because it was her birthday. He danced with Rosamond, too, and they make a fine-looking couple."

"You think so?" Nate couldn't keep the challenge from his voice.

"Yes, Mr. Knows-It-All, I think so." His father stood

and leaned forward with his knuckles on his desk, as he always did when he was about to give orders. "You think I didn't notice you hanging all over that Anders girl? And her looking at you all moon-eyed? She's not our sort, Nathaniel, and you would do well to remember that. I don't want to see you spending any more time with her. Is that understood?"

"What—" His father hadn't taken a minute to get acquainted with Susanna. How could he know what *sort* she was?

"Seems to me that lazy father of hers has had enough time to get back on his feet. You go upstairs this morning and tell him I want them gone as soon as he can put one foot in front of the other."

"But—" Nate's head felt as if it would explode. He would not send an injured man out to fend for himself with only his daughter to take care of him. If Mr. Anders and Susanna had to leave, Nate would go with them.

"And as soon as you do that, ride out and check the south fence again. George says somebody tried to break through a section of his fencing, so we may have some cattle rustlers trying to get in." The anger in the Colonel's tone sounded as if it was directed more at Nate than any rustlers.

"No, sir." Nate's right hand fisted almost as if it had a mind of its own. He needed to get out of this room before he did something he would regret for the rest of his life.

"What?" The Colonel's eyes blazed. "What did you say to me?"

"I said 'no, sir.' If you want to throw Mr. Anders and Susanna out, you'll do your own dirty work. If you want somebody to check that south fence, tell Rand to do it. He could do with having some responsibility around here."

"Now, you see here, boy." He thumped his fist on the desk.

"No." Nate shook from head to toe. "*You* see my back walking out the door." He spun around and strode from the room, with every step fighting the urge to go back and strike his father.

Snatching his hat from the front hall tree, he rushed down the center hallway toward the back door, ignoring Mother's call from the kitchen as he passed by. No one needed to see him like this. No one needed to hear the thoughts racing through his mind. *Anger* hardly seemed a strong enough word to describe his feelings. *Rage,* that was what it was.

Before he knew how he got there, he was on Victor and they were tearing up the road faster and harder than he'd ever ridden his stallion. With no idea where he was going, he just knew something in his life had to give way, had to break, or he wouldn't be able to go on.

At last his mount's labored breathing reached his awareness, and he gently tugged the reins, slowing Victor to a walk. The animal wheezed and snorted, tossing his head as if to ask what that had been all about.

"Sorry, boy." How foolish to punish Victor for his father's insufficiencies. Victor wasn't just any horse. He would sire Nate's string of cow ponies once he had his own place.

If he ever had his own place. Maybe after today the Colonel would disown him. In fact, maybe that would be best. One thing was certain. Nate needed to find a better way to deal with his anger before he did some real damage to some innocent person or beast. Riding a valuable horse into the ground was about the dumbest thing he'd ever done in his life. He'd always known that this strain of cow ponies wasn't bred for long, hard rides.

What would happen if he came right out and defied the Colonel, not just in the privacy of his office, but in front of everybody? Maybe his father was just waiting for him to do that. And what on earth had he meant by Mr. Knows-It-All? What a crazy thing to say.

Defiance, controlled defiance. That was the way to get out from under his father's thumb. Nate's first step would be to follow his heart and pursue a deeper relationship with Susanna. If everybody thought they were courting, so be it.

Anytime Susanna found herself in the kitchen with Mrs. Northam and Rosamond, she savored the easy camaraderie among them. It helped to ease the pain of missing her friends and family back home more than she could have imagined. How could she hate these Yankee ladies who treated her only with kindness? Or dear, warmhearted Angela, whose maternal ways reminded her of her childhood nurse. Did this wise woman know her own daughter rode into the settlement several times a week, days when the Colonel was also gone from the ranch house? If only Susanna could find a way to rescue Rita from his evil clutches. She stifled a sigh so the other ladies would not ask questions about her sudden depression.

Mercy, she'd done it again, dashed her own happy thoughts. She should be thinking about yesterday and how the whole community had come together to build that impressive barn. Should be thinking about dancing with Nate and the way he'd almost kissed her. Or the way she'd hoped he would, then been glad when he hadn't because of the trouble it could have caused. Oh, how she enjoyed his company. How she wished she were free to love him.

"Susanna, would you mind setting the table?" Mrs. Northam said. "We'll just be five for the noon meal."

"Yes, ma'am." As Susanna removed the mismatched everyday dishes from the cupboard, a happy thought silenced her concerns over eating with the Colonel. In a few weeks, Mrs. Northam would receive her Wedgwood china. What an exciting day that would be. Nate had told her other surprises awaited his mother, but she doubted he knew about the silver spurs for his father. Maybe that fine gift from his wife would shame the Colonel into improving his ways, spur him into good behavior, so to speak.

Chuckling at her own wordplay, she carried the plates and silverware to the dining room and set them around the linen-covered table. The Colonel always sat at the head, Mrs. Northam at the foot by the kitchen door, Rosamond to her left, Nate next to his sister and Susanna across from them. She retrieved freshly pressed linen napkins from the buffet just as the Colonel came through the door. He stared at her with his usual scowl. Her heart seemed to stop beating.

"We'll be only four at the table for dinner."

"Yes, sir." Barely giving him a glance, she put away one napkin and cleared one place setting, then made haste to return to the kitchen. She didn't need to be told twice that he didn't want her eating with the family. She, who had once dined with the governor of Georgia and attended balls at a senator's home, one of those plantation houses General Sherman had failed to burn down on his march to Atlanta.

Even if her own Southern heritage wasn't an impediment to her falling in love with Nate, the Colonel's rudeness toward her would always stand in the way of their happiness. She could not, must not surrender to her attraction to Nate.

* * *

Nate gave Victor his head, and the stallion trotted along the lane into the settlement right up to the hitching rail beneath the trees in front of the church.

"Whoa, boy." Nate leaned down to pat his neck. "This is Friday, not Sunday. What are we doing here?"

"Hello, Nate." Reverend Thomas came around the building, rolled-up shirtsleeves and dusty trousers indicating he'd been working in his garden. "Did you need to see me?"

Nate stared at him for a moment, then down at Victor. He grunted out a mirthless chuckle and dismounted. "I guess I do." Tying Victor's reins to the rail, he checked the horse's legs and breathing. After their hard run, he'd cooled him down with a long walk and given him a drink in the river, so he should be all right here in the shade.

"Come on into the house. We'll have some lemonade."

Nate followed him next door to the parsonage, a simple three-room edifice that would need to be enlarged if the young preacher married.

"Mrs. Eberly sent me home with some beef and pork, not to mention a whole basket load of other fine food." After washing his hands in a dishpan on the kitchen table, Reverend Thomas lifted the lid on his small icebox and pulled out a plate of sliced meat and other items. "This community not only builds fine barns for their neighbors, they know how to take care of their bachelors, too. Will you have dinner with me?"

The aroma of the beef started Nate's stomach growling, reminding him of his ill-timed departure from home. "Thank you. I will."

Soon they were seated at the table enjoying sandwiches and potato salad, washing it all down with tangy lemonade.

"How's everything out at the ranch?" Reverend Thomas had set some of Mrs. Barkley's pickles on a plate and now offered them to Nate. When Nate declined, the preacher took a big bite of one. "Mmm-mmm. That lady sure knows how to make fine pickles."

Being of a decidedly different opinion, Nate would not comment on them. But what should he say? Had the Lord led him here to seek counsel? Should he speak against his father to a man who owed the Colonel his current position, his very livelihood?

"You probably noticed when you were out there last Sunday how the crops are thriving. We finished digging the irrigation ditch to channel water from Cat Creek closer to the hay fields." He mentioned a few other improvements made around the place. "And I'm glad to say the new addition is almost completed. The carpenter from Denver arrived yesterday to do all the fancy woodwork in the ballroom."

"Very good. Everyone's talking about the anniversary party. It'll be quite an event." The minister ate the rest of his pickle, clearly enjoying it. But even the smell ruined Nate's appetite. "I don't have to tell you the Colonel not only has the respect of everyone hereabouts, he also has their affection. Very few of us would be here without his sponsorship."

Nate took a drink to avoid responding.

"Planning and building a community on biblical principles is nothing short of the Lord's work." Some of Reverend Thomas's Southern inflections reminded Nate of Susanna, but he wouldn't feel comfortable bringing her into the conversation, nor the Colonel's dislike of her and her father. "I'm not one to be a respecter of persons, but I believe the Lord's hand is surely on the Colonel."

Nate started. "You think so?"

The preacher blinked. "Why, yes."

If God was on the Colonel's side, where did that leave Nate? He stared at the lemon seeds in the bottom of his glass.

"In fact, I consider him a wise man." Reverend Thomas held out the plate of sandwiches, silently offering Nate another one, but he declined. "I wouldn't hesitate to seek his counsel if I needed it."

Nate's thoughts tumbled all over each other. The Colonel might be smart. But wise? "Now, that surprises me. You're the preacher here. People come to you for advice."

He chuckled ruefully. "They do. But unfortunately, a seminary degree only denotes knowledge, not wisdom." His words echoed Nate's thoughts. "That's why I've been studying the Book of Proverbs. That's why I look to older, godly men for guidance."

The preacher's humble attitude touched something deep inside Nate. What did this man see in the Colonel that Nate couldn't? Maybe it was a simple matter of perspective, like Mrs. Barkley's pickles. Some liked them and some didn't. Right now he didn't much like his father. But how would this man feel if the Colonel corrected everything he did? Criticized every sermon? Told him whom to marry? It was all well and good to admire a man who wasn't trying to control every minute of his life. Still, the near-reverence the minister exhibited toward the Colonel gave Nate something to consider. And to pray about.

"Well, I'd best be going." He stood and retrieved his hat. "Much obliged for the sandwich."

Reverend Thomas walked him to the door. "Did I miss something, Nate? Did you need to discuss anything?"

"Nope." Nate shook the preacher's hand. "I think we about covered it."

"Ah." Understanding crossed his face "The Lord works in mysterious ways."

Indeed He did. Nate headed home, pondering the deeper meaning behind their conversation. The preacher had been concerned that he'd missed something, but it was Nate who still could not comprehend why anyone would think the Colonel was wise. If that was the case, why did he refuse to give Susanna and her father a chance to prove themselves, as he had every other decent person who'd come to the community? If his father was so wise, why couldn't the two of them have a simple conversation to discuss their differences? If he'd just treat Nate with a little respect, Nate wouldn't have to constantly remind him that he knew a thing or two about running a ranch.

Chapter Eighteen

Susanna helped Daddy to a sitting position and put several pillows behind him on the bed, then tucked a napkin into his nightshirt collar. "Chicken and dumplings, dearest. One of your favorites." She brought the tray to him and made sure it sat firmly on his lap before taking her own bowl in hand. "Not as good as Minerva's, of course, but still tasty." Even though Angela was an excellent cook, Susanna often longed for their former housekeeper's delicious cuisine.

After they said grace, he dipped his spoon into the broth and brought out a small, round dumpling. "I don't know about that, daughter. Miss Angela's a mighty fine cook, too. I've enjoyed all her meals."

Something in his tone gave her pause, but she quickly dismissed it. Of course Daddy would become fond of the servant who took such good care of him.

"A new doctor arrived at the barn raising yesterday." She wouldn't mention that the Colonel had summoned the man from Boston to tend the community's health needs, for that would give their unwilling host too much credit. "I asked him to come see you today."

"Gracious, girl." Daddy coughed, as he often had since

being laid up. "I'll be fine. Why, Zack and Miss Angela are planning to get me on my feet this very afternoon."

"That's good news, but nevertheless, I want the doctor to look you over before you try to stand." Still stinging from the way the Colonel dismissed her from the dining room, she basked in Daddy's fond gaze. Poor Nate, having such a disagreeable father, who never showed such disapproval to his other children as he had to Nate all day at the Eberlys'. "Besides, that cough of yours worries me, so I want him to make sure you don't have pneumonia."

Securing his agreement to see the doctor, she went on to tell him about the barn raising, the food and the dance.

"Did he dance with you?" Daddy gave her a teasing grin.

"Who?" Had he guessed about her struggles not to become attached to Nate?

"Why, the doctor, of course." His eyes twinkled, but he was watching her closely. "Who else would I be talking about?"

"Oh, gracious, Daddy." She finished her dinner and set down her bowl. "That barn was overrun with cowboys. I danced until my feet ached." She brushed invisible lint from her borrowed skirt. "They still ache."

"I see."

Before he could further comment, a light tap sounded on the door. Susanna admitted Angela into the room.

"Eduardo," she began, then quickly added, "forgive me, Señor Anders, the doctor has arrived."

Susanna glanced between the two of them, but before she could question the housekeeper's use of the Spanish version of Daddy's first name, Zack and Dr. Henshaw entered.

Greetings were offered, introductions were made and then the doctor ushered Susanna and Angela out.

"The very idea! Why can't we stay?" Susanna huffed as they stood outside the closed door.

Angela frowned with equal displeasure, then shook her head. "He is in good hands."

"Yes, Dr. Henshaw does seem quite competent."

"No, *señorita,* it is the Lord's hands I speak of." She patted Susanna's shoulder. "Now I must prepare supper. With many people to feed, something must always be cooking, *sí?*"

"I'll be glad to help." Susanna followed her down the back stairs. Maybe she would see Nate, if he hadn't already left the house after eating dinner. What had he thought about her absence at the table? Had he guessed his father was responsible?

They found Rosamond washing dishes in the kitchen. "There you are, Susanna. Where've you been? With you and Nate gone, I was left to entertain my parents during dinner."

"Nate was gone?"

"Yep." Rosamond squeezed out her dishrag and wiped it across the wooden counter. "Father said he told you Nate wouldn't be there, and since you didn't plan to eat with us, you should have set only three places."

Her thoughts in a whirl, Susanna busied herself pulling potatoes from the wooden vegetable bin and placing them on the table to peel. The Colonel hadn't been dismissing her, simply informing her that Nate wouldn't be at dinner. But she hardly could have asked him to clarify his terse statement. Although she felt somewhat embarrassed, she was mostly annoyed. He'd turned a misunderstanding into a criticism of the way she set the table. What an impossible man!

* * *

Seeing a slow-moving wagon ahead, Nate urged Victor to a trot and soon pulled beside the large, canvas-covered conveyance. "Howdy." He touched his hat brim. "You men headed to Four Stones Ranch?"

"Yep." The driver and his rifle-toting partner offered guarded greetings.

"I'm Nate Northam. Follow me."

Thus assured he wasn't out to rob them, they responded with more enthusiasm, no doubt eager to deliver their heavy load. What had the Colonel ordered this time? Nate was privy to only a few of his father's secrets about the anniversary, mainly how fancy the ballroom would be once all the furnishings arrived. And of course, the china.

Every time he thought about the china, he thanked the good Lord for using it to introduce him to Susanna. Wasn't the way they met sufficient proof that God smiled on his feelings for her? Maybe he should have asked Reverend Thomas about that.

Riding slightly in front of the four-horse team, Nate guided the lead animals around the worst of the holes in the rutted road. When they got to Four Stones Lane, he'd ride on ahead and suggest to Mother that she might want to go upstairs and work on her quilt. Whatever was in the wagon, she'd play her game of pretending not to notice its arrival. He sure did look forward to seeing her face when the Colonel gave her all those surprises. And for all of Nate's anger toward the man, he knew his father would make a big fuss about what a fine quilt she'd made, saying it was exactly what he'd always wanted. A man had to admire a couple who still loved each other so dearly after twenty-five years of marriage.

Which only added to Nate's confusion about the Colonel's insistence that he marry Maisie. Couldn't the old man see how important it was to marry a woman he loved? Nobody submitted to arranged marriages anymore.

When he arrived at the house, Mother dutifully decided it was time to head upstairs to get busy with her quilting. Nate had directed the men to deliver the wagon's contents to the veranda outside the ballroom. The three of them started to unload the first wooden carton, but it proved too heavy. Nate rounded up several more hands, including the carpenter, who was staining the ballroom's mahogany balustrade. The two large boxes sat safely inside just as the Colonel entered, crowbar in hand.

Nate braced himself for a confrontation, but his father's mood was nothing short of jubilant.

"Let's take a look." He nodded to the driver. "It didn't have a scratch when I checked it in Alamosa last week." Not giving the other man a chance to respond, he began to pry open the slats.

Nate pitched in to help, and they soon had the packing removed. At last, the Colonel slid off the heavy quilted cotton protecting the object and ran a hand over his purchase for inspection.

"A grand piano," Nate said in hushed tones. He guessed this large, rectangular instrument was the finest piano in the entire San Luis Valley. The shiny mahogany surface matched the newly installed woodwork.

"Let's get the base unpacked. Bring it over here by the staircase." The Colonel directed the men, and they soon had the body secured on the base, which boasted four elegantly carved legs. "I see some scratches." His shoulders hunched up like a grizzly bear's, and he sent a dark look toward the driver.

"Do not vorry, Herr Northam." The carpenter scurried

over to inspect the damage, his toolbox in hand. "The damage, you vill never know it vas there."

The German craftsman proved true to his word. A bit of sandpaper, a touch of stain, and even a magnifying glass would not betray the spots. As he worked, Nate noticed the Colonel's shoulders relaxing. In those brief moments, he saw a side of his father he'd never before noticed. Or maybe hadn't given enough thought.

His generosity and protectiveness—to friends, to neighbors and especially to Mother—could not be denied. This was the better part of the man, the one people like Reverend Thomas saw and admired. Why did he not bestow any of those better feelings on Nate? Could he himself be the one in the wrong?

After paying the deliverymen and receiving their assurance that the rest of the furniture would be delivered the following week, the Colonel sent them on their way. Then he stood in the center of the room surveying every detail with a critical eye. "What do you think?"

Nate had to look around to be sure he was the person being addressed. "Looks good so far. With the rest of the furniture and the drapes Miss Anders is making, it'll be the finest ballroom in Colorado."

At the mention of Susanna's name, the Colonel cut him a sharp look. "What are you talking about? Rosamond is making the drapes."

Determined not to argue or even get angry, Nate shrugged. "Rosamond said she has trouble sewing velvet, but Susanna has a talent for keeping it from puckering."

The Colonel continued to glare at him as if it was his fault. "I'll be speaking to your sister about that." He stalked toward the interior door then turned back. "What are you doing for the rest of the day?" His tone was unusually genial, and his expression had softened.

Nate shrugged again. "Guess I'll ride out and check that south fencing."

The Colonel didn't turn away quite fast enough to hide his grin. For some odd reason, instead of irritating Nate, it stirred up a warm feeling in his chest. Maybe there was still hope for their relationship.

On Monday morning, Susanna made her way to Nate's room to check on Daddy. To her surprise, he and Nate stood beside the bed, with Daddy balancing himself with the crutch Zack had fashioned from a forked tree branch. A cushion, probably sewn on by Angela, covered the wood to spare his underarm. "Just look at you getting around on your own."

"Doc Henshaw gave his approval last Friday, and I've been practicing these past few days." He'd lost weight, but the color was returning to his cheeks. "It feels mighty good."

"And look at your new outfit." She sent a grateful glance toward Nate. Obviously, he'd loaned Daddy those denim trousers and that plaid shirt. If Mrs. Northam would sell her some of the material Nate had carted in with the china, Susanna could start sewing a new wardrobe for her father. "You look like a cowboy."

Daddy chuckled. "Maybe I'll go downstairs and take a turn around the property this afternoon."

"That's a good idea," Nate said. "I'll help you negotiate the stairs. In fact, why not come down for dinner?"

Daddy eyed him and frowned. "I don't want to put anybody out."

"Do you mean you don't want to run into the Colonel?" Nate gave him a rueful smile. "Never mind about that."

Daddy shrugged. "If you're certain, then I will. I'd enjoy sitting at a table again."

With the matter settled, they helped Daddy down the wide front staircase and out onto the shady front lawn. The effort tired him, so Susanna sat on a bench with him while Nate excused himself to do chores.

"The preacher asked about you yesterday." Susanna had thoroughly enjoyed the Sunday service, especially the singing. "He said he'll be out to visit you sometime this week."

"I'll be glad to see him again." Daddy gave her one of his long, speculative looks. "He's a real Southern gentleman and a handsome young man, don't you think?"

"Yes, he is." Susanna didn't try to hide her amusement. "I'd say between his looks and the doctor's, though, the doctor wins by a nose."

Daddy laughed, catching her joke about the doctor's most prominent facial feature. "But neither one can hold a candle to a certain cowboy."

Susanna released a long, weary sigh. No use trying to deny the obvious. Of course Daddy would have noticed her partiality for Nate, even tucked away in his bedroom all this time. In a way, though, it felt good to have her struggles out in the open. "Oh, well. He's a Yankee, so that's that." Her tone didn't sound as dismissive as she would have liked.

Daddy gazed out over the western field, where sunflowers towered above half-grown corn. "The heart is an untamed beast, daughter. Sometimes it tries to take us where we know we shouldn't go."

"I know." Her spirits sank at his pronouncement. "The heart is deceitful above all things, and desperately wicked. Who can know it?"

Daddy started. "Whoa, daughter. I believe that verse in

Jeremiah refers to matters of faith in the Lord, not a person you come to care about deeply." He ran a hand over
the smooth wooden bench. "I don't believe it's wicked to
love any person. It's what you do about it that matters."

"What if that person is a Yankee?" She held her breath
waiting for his answer. If he granted her permission to
care for Nate, she'd have no reason to deny her own
heart's longing. And truly, in spite of all she'd told herself, in spite of her dreams to marry a Southern gentleman, she did care for Nate. Cared enough to stay right
here in the San Luis Valley rather than return home to
Georgia.

"What if that person is a—" He shook his head. "Well,
look who's here."

Nate rounded the corner of the house, and Susanna's
emotions did their usual turn. She'd seen him only a few
minutes ago, yet one would think it had been a month
of Sundays. Daddy greeted Nate like a long-lost friend,
but she couldn't help but notice he'd failed to answer her
question.

"Let's eat." Nate helped Daddy back into the house
and down the center hallway to the dining room.

"Mr. Anders, I'm so pleased you're able to join us."
Mrs. Northam's warm welcome almost overcame the
chill emanating from the Colonel. Almost.

But Daddy, ever the Southern gentleman, comported
himself with dignity and grace that would have made
Mama proud.

That afternoon, after seeing Daddy safely back upstairs, Susanna joined Nate and Rosamond for an errand
into the settlement. Mrs. Northam, busy with arranging
food for the anniversary celebration, needed to know
what to expect from their neighbors. Although Rosamond

could have managed the errand alone, the Colonel sent Nate along, citing their run-in with the Utes two weeks ago. When they invited Susanna, she eagerly accepted.

As they neared the cluster of homes and businesses, she longed to direct Sadie down some of the lanes to see the varied architecture. Some of the houses appeared quite elegant, while others had a humbler look. Reining her horse nearer to Nate's, she asked, "Do you plan to name your town anytime soon?"

"That's a question I'd like answered myself. Seems like it's about time." He pointed to a lane, almost a street, which met their road at a right angle. "You can see the town's already been platted, but until we're incorporated, nobody wants to attach a name to it."

"When the railroad reaches us next year, we'll need to have a name." Rosamond gazed off thoughtfully. "I like Mountain View because whichever way you look, you can see mountains."

Susanna decided she could not improve on her friend's idea.

In the center of the settlement, they reached Miss Pam's café and dismounted.

"Now, you know she'll want us to have some pie," Nate said.

"That won't hurt my feelings." Susanna could just taste the delicious elderberry pie Miss Pam had served them when Nate had first brought her and Daddy through. Every time she saw the sweet lady, she thanked her again for the use of her boar-hair brush. One day she would repay her with more than words.

Soon the three of them were digging into their cream-covered pie and discussing what Miss Pam would bring to the anniversary party.

"My garden has an abundance of green beans," she said. "They'll be ripe for picking just in time."

Miss Pam also passed along several bits of benign gossip, such as the imminent arrival of a woman who would set up a mercantile next door to her café. "I've been waiting for a place nearby to go shopping since I left St. Louis nine years ago. I'm tired of getting my supplies over in Del Norte."

While they all enjoyed a good laugh over that, the news gave Susanna special delight. Not only would she be able to repay Miss Pam, but she would also be able to purchase material to replace Daddy's clothes that had been ruined by the thieves.

"Charlie's been hired to string the telegraph," Miss Pam said. "It'll be nice to have a faster way than letters to communicate with folks beyond the Valley."

Filled with pie and news, they took their leave and made the rounds of the town, gathering a list of food and beverages people would contribute to the party. Everyone seemed eager to participate.

Just beyond the church, Susanna noticed a pretty two-story Queen Anne home. "How lovely. Who lives there?" Outside the front fence, a vaguely familiar horse stood tied to a post under a shady elm.

"Mr. and Mrs. Foster," said Nate. "They knew the Colonel years ago, so when he invited them to be a part of this community, they couldn't resist. Mrs. Foster gives piano lessons and—" Strangely, he clamped his mouth shut. Maybe he'd come close to blurting out a secret about the party.

"If you haven't noticed—" Rosamond laughed "—our father has very strong persuasive powers."

Now Susanna clamped her mouth shut. She most certainly had noticed the Colonel's controlling ways. As they rode down the next street, she glanced back at the lovely home. To her shock, she saw Rita exiting the yard with an older lady. They embraced and shared a laugh, then Rita mounted the horse and rode away, while the lady went back inside.

"Do you mind?" Susanna turned Sadie around. "I haven't touched a piano since we left home." Never mind if they wondered how she could afford one. "Do you think Mrs. Foster would let me play just for a few minutes?"

Nate got that cute, surprised look on his face. "You play piano?" Why did he seem so happy about it?

"I think she'd love the company," Rosamond said. "Let's go."

As expected, the older woman graciously invited them in for a visit. When she learned Susanna played, she waved her to the piano stool. After a few arpeggios, with several missed notes due to a lack of practice, Susanna launched into "Brahms's Lullaby," then a few verses of "Amazing Grace," while the others joined in singing.

"How absolutely lovely. Another pianist in our community." Mrs. Foster, gray-haired and maternal, clasped her hands to her heart as if transported by the music. "And you play Brahms! I was just saying to young Rita that we must bring more classical music here. Colonel Northam was so wise to recognize her talent, and she's doing so well in her preparations for the anniversary party and— Oh, my." She put her hands to her cheeks in horror. "Have I spoiled the surprise? Surely not. You must know your father has arranged for Rita to learn how to play. She told me the piano arrived just the other day."

Rosamond smothered a laugh with her hand, while Nate cleared his throat. "Yes, ma'am. We know, but Mother doesn't. She's not allowed in the ballroom until their party. It's good of you to let Rita come and practice every day. She can't practice at home or Mother would hear her."

While they chattered away about the grand surprise, Susanna sat in stunned silence as the truth slammed into her. As sure as the sun did shine, God had arranged for her to see Rita leaving the piano teacher's house. The Lord, who knew every heart, knew she would seize the opportunity to find out what was going on. Which was not at all the evil she had imagined. Once again, the Colonel had found a way to please his wife. That was why he was so upset when Rita cut her hand. In the deepest part of her soul, Susanna knew not many Southern men would be so generous to a dark-skinned girl unless they had improper expectations.

Horrified, sickened even, by her own evil judgments against the man, Susanna could only offer a weak smile and thank-you as they left Mrs. Foster's parlor. Colonel Northam certainly had more than a few redeeming qualities. That still didn't answer why he hated her and Daddy so much, but she would pray for him and try very hard to excuse his bad manners.

As they headed back toward the ranch, Nate and Rosamond chatted about their visit. "Too bad you didn't get to meet Mr. Foster," Rosamond said to Susanna. "He's been Father's friend since the war, when they both rode with General Sherman."

Nate shot a worried glance at Susanna. "Yes, well..."

Susanna almost gave vent to a bitter laugh. So much for her guilty feelings. She may have misjudged the Colonel regarding Rita. But there was no misjudging any soldier who rode with Sherman. Nor was there enough forgiveness in any Southerner worth his or her salt to pardon Sherman's troops for what they did to the South. And to her family in particular.

Chapter Nineteen

Nate blamed himself. He should have had a frank discussion with Susanna regarding the Colonel's war service. Still, he gave her several days to recover from her obvious shock over hearing that his father rode with Sherman. He regretted his failure to alert Rosamond about how such a careless comment might upset their guests.

The whole family knew the Anderses were from Georgia, one of the states to suffer greatly during Sherman's march to the sea. He and his siblings had grown up accepting the general's brutal drive as necessary to end the war, which had killed over a half million men and nearly destroyed the United States. Of course, Southerners would view the matter differently. Not all of them were like Reverend Thomas, who had said in one of his sermons how much he welcomed the reunification of the North and South into one country.

Nate should sit Susanna down for a discussion on the matter and sort it out in a sensible way. It was madness for their generation to continue fighting the war that ended thirteen years ago. But until the anniversary party next week, he had too many responsibilities to complete. In the meantime, he admired the way she kept working around the house and taking care of her father. As for Mr. Anders, he began taking long walks around the property using the crutch Zack had made for him. He enjoyed visits from Doc Henshaw and Reverend Thomas. He even spent some time with Joe, the tanner, helping with his leatherwork. So much for the Colonel's assertion that Mr. Anders was a lazy Southerner.

On Thursday, the rest of the ballroom furniture arrived: four velvet chairs, two brocade settees, six mahogany side tables, four lampstands and an exquisite crystal chandelier. Susanna completed the drapes and sent Rosamond to fetch Nate to help hang them. The whole time he worked on nailing up the curtain rods over the four wide windows and adjusting the finished product, Susanna kept her eyes on the thick green drapes, pulling and picking at them to make sure they hung just right. Not once did she trade a glance with Nate or even Rosamond.

"Excellent." The Colonel's voice boomed behind them, and they all turned to see him standing on the steps leading down into the ballroom. He strode across the space and examined the drapes more closely. "Miss Anders, I understand you are responsible for this fine work. I insist upon paying you. Name your wages."

Her eyes blazing, she lifted her chin. "Why, no, indeed, Colonel Northam. Your *hospitality* while my father recuperates is more than sufficient payment." The iciness in her tone was enough to freeze the sunshine right out of the room. She spun around and marched away, head held high.

Only then did Nate realize how deeply she hated his father. But had he lost his own chance to win her affection? If she'd given him one look these past few days, one hint that she wanted to talk to him, he would go to her right now. Instead, Rosamond gave him a rueful frown and followed Susanna. That gave Nate a measure of peace. With the girls getting along so well, he had that one tiny thread of hope. It wasn't as though Susanna could go anyplace until her father was fully back on his feet.

"Very fine indeed." The Colonel acted as though nothing unpleasant had happened. Instead, he sauntered around the room inspecting every detail. From time to time, he sent an approving glance in Nate's direction.

Since the silent resolution of their argument last week, his father had been treating him with more respect. He'd even taken Nate's advice about giving Rand more responsibility in managing things around the ranch. Wanting to ensure their truce, Nate made a point of agreeing with— or at least deferring to—several of his father's decisions on things Nate usually handled.

"Mother will be overwhelmed." He moved up beside the Colonel as he studied the scalloped molding near the ceiling. "And happy."

His father gave him a curt nod, but he was smiling... almost. Nate's heart lifted unexpectedly. This was the way things had been when the two of them had shouldered the burden of moving the family across the country ten years ago. Somehow a bridge had been mended, and Nate couldn't be more pleased. Remembering Reverend Thomas's words, he tried to think of a way to reaffirm his trust in the Colonel's wisdom.

"Yessir, you sure do have some mighty fine ideas." Whether running a ranch, developing a community or honoring his wife.

His father eyed him with a hint of suspicion that quickly dissolved. He clapped Nate on the shoulder. "I'm glad to hear you say that, son."

Nate felt a foolish grin spread across his face. He'd

taken the first step to earning the right to persuade his father to accept Susanna. Now he had to find a way to convince Susanna they needed to forget the war and the Colonel's part in it and move on with their own lives.

Even as she longed to get out of this house, Susanna felt waves of nostalgia as she worked on various projects leading up to the party. At her parents' last anniversary together just over a year ago, Mama had been so beautiful in a rose-colored gown, and Daddy his most handsome in an elegant black suit. She would treasure those memories as long as she lived and would try to help make this anniversary as memorable for the Northams.

Despite loathing the Colonel, Susanna still could find no fault in Mrs. Northam. The lady had opened her home and provided for her and Daddy without a hint of reservation. What a stark contrast between her and her husband. Did the Colonel realize Susanna had it within her power to ruin all of his carefully planned surprises? That it was her Southern-bred honor that kept her mouth shut around those secrets? After the party, she would make sure he knew all about it.

Nor did she reveal to Daddy about the Colonel riding with Sherman. If she did, there was no telling what he'd do.

The week of the event arrived, and only a few more tasks required Susanna's assistance. Mrs. Northam instructed Nate to bring a large oak chest from the attic storeroom, and she opened it to reveal a tarnished silver tea service.

"Oh, my, these are exquisite, Mrs. Northam." She lifted out the creamer and sugar bowl to have a closer look at the etched designs. "Don't you think so?" Without thinking, she handed one of the pieces to Nate. At the touch of his hand on hers, a spark shot up her arm, and they shared a smile. He seemed particularly pleased to receive hers, if the sudden brightening of his green eyes was any indication. Oh, how she had missed their friendly banter, missed just being with him. Was it wrong to care so deeply for him when she could feel only loathing for his father?

"Bert gave me his secret baking-soda concoction to clean away the tarnish." Mrs. Northam rolled up her sleeves and lay a sheet out on the table. "Let's hope it works." From the sideboard, she took a small jar and several lengths of torn sheets.

"Please let me do it." Susanna would perform this one last kindness for her hostess. Right after the party, she and Daddy would be moving to a house Reverend Thomas had found for them, where they would stay until Daddy was able to travel to the silver fields. If he still wanted to go. "You have enough to do."

Mrs. Northam gave her a doubtful look. "Are you certain?"

"I can help." Nate removed the tea server from the box, then pulled out a large silver tray. The center boasted the monogram GEM in large script letters. The bottom of the piece was inscribed with the silversmith's name. "Paul Revere! Mother, why haven't I seen this before?"

She laughed. "I suppose because we haven't had a grand enough occasion."

"I'm duly impressed." Even living in the South, Susanna had learned of Revere's patriotic ride through Longfellow's 1861 poem.

"Well, your twenty-fifth anniversary is supposed to be the silver one," Nate said, "so I'd say that makes it grand enough. A Paul Revere silver service for a silver celebration."

"All right, then." Mrs. Northam eyed Susanna, then Nate. "I'll leave you to it. Don't have too much fun."

After she left, they sat at the table and began to work. Sure enough, Bert's secret formula, plus a strong dose of elbow grease, cut through the tarnish without scratching the silver.

"I've missed you." Nate kept his eyes on the creamer he was rubbing with a cloth.

She should say she'd been there all the time, eating with the family, answering when spoken to. But that wasn't what he meant. "I've—"

"Hey, Nate." Tolley burst through the door. "Seamus's got himself in a pickle with that mustang mare. Can you come help?"

Nate's shoulders slumped. "I'll be right there." He rubbed the black marks from his hand. "I'll come back as soon as I can."

After he left, the dining room felt more than empty. It felt bereft. Or maybe she was just thinking of how hard it would be to leave him behind.

She heard the thump of Daddy's crutch on the hallway floor. "Daddy? Come keep me company."

He poked his head through the open door. "I was just headed to the kitchen for a glass of water."

Susanna had noticed he made frequent such trips when Angela was busy cooking, but she wouldn't question him. "You can go through this way. Come see what I'm doing."

He limped toward the table, and his face contorted oddly.

"Daddy? What's wrong?"

"What do you have there, daughter?" His terse question was accompanied by eyes burning with anger.

"I-it's a silver tea service." What could be wrong? Daddy never got angry this way, even when the thieves had beaten and nearly killed him. "Paul Revere made it." Her words came out like an apology.

"I know who made it." He threw down his crutch and snatched up the half-cleaned tray. "Do you see this monogram?"

She nodded.

"GEM. Gabriel Edward MacAndrews." He traced the letters with a reverence that belied his rage. "Your great-great-grandfather."

"What?" Susanna scrambled to make sense of his words.

He pulled out the chair next to her and sat. "Listen, daughter." He ran a hand over his mouth, a nervous, angry gesture. "You thought I came to Colorado on a quest for silver, and you were right. But this—" he gently tapped the teapot "—this is the silver I've been searching for."

"Oh, Daddy." Tears filled her eyes, and she touched his arm. "This is Mama's silver service the Yankees took."

He nodded. "That's not all." He pulled on the chain around his neck and retrieved a locket from beneath his shirt. Inside was her parents' tiny tintype wedding portrait. "You know I wore this into battle, and you've seen the picture many times, but you've never asked about the necklace your mother is wearing."

She shook her head. Countless belongings had been stolen from their family during the war, but Mama had also sold some of her remaining valuables after the war to help Daddy start his business. Susanna had never wanted to bring up such a sensitive subject. "Tell me about it."

"Eleven sapphires, graduated in size and set in silver, an heirloom, like the tea service, this one from my mother's family." He winced when he mentioned Grandmama. Susanna knew he'd never quit grieving her death.

"You were just six years old, so maybe you don't recall when these were taken." He stared off, a dark frown creasing his forehead. "I was away fighting when those Yankee cowards came. Your brother was twelve." He drew in a ragged breath. "You may wonder why Edward Junior is such a cautious man. He wasn't always that way. Why, when he saw the Yankees storming onto our property, he started shooting and wounded a couple of them before they caught him." Daddy trembled at the memory, and Susanna gripped his forearm. He covered her hand with his.

"He was just a boy," Daddy's voice shook. "But they would have hanged him to set an example for any other Southerner who dared to defy them if your mother hadn't intervened. She promised a treasure to their commanding officer in return for Edward's life. She would have given them anything, everything, including her own life, to save either one of you. As it was, that officer was satisfied with this silver service and the sapphire necklace. She told them where she'd buried the items, and they helped themselves."

Daddy slumped wearily against the table. "In spite of that, the officer ordered your brother's guns, *my* guns, taken, too. He also ordered the house to be burned down with everything else in it. Then he ordered Edward's arms to be broken."

Bile rose into Susanna's throat. She vaguely remembered the grand plantation house and how her childhood nurse had hurried her away from the scene on Mama's orders. She knew the Yankees had hurt Edward, who'd never regained full use of his arms. And, as Daddy said, he'd become a cautious man. Almost fearful. As more memories flooded her mind, one currently familiar face came into focus. "Colonel Northam." She spat out the name.

"Colonel Northam." Daddy straightened. "Now you know everything. The Yankees recorded the names of every person who resisted them, so ours went on their list. That's why I changed our name when we came west. Why I didn't want them to know about our social standing back home. The best way to defeat an adversary is to keep him ignorant about who you are and what you plan to do."

"We have to go." Susanna rubbed tarnish from her hands and stood. "We have to leave this place right away."

Daddy gripped her arm and tugged her back down on the chair. "Don't be hasty, daughter."

She questioned him with a look.

"When I learned the name of the officer who brutalized and robbed my family, I knew I couldn't let it rest. I wrote letters and found out exactly where Frank Northam had settled. Before your mama died, I promised her I would settle the score, and the Lord led us here as surely as He led Moses to the Promised Land."

Susanna's hair seemed to stand on end. Was there more to Mama's dying plea for her to take care of Daddy? Had she thought Susanna could somehow stop his quest for revenge? As for his biblical reference, she would not remind him that Moses hadn't been permitted to enter Israel's new home because he'd failed to honor God in an important matter. But what would the Lord have her do in this situation?

"Only the Almighty could have arranged our meeting with Nate." Daddy chuckled. "Of course, I wish He'd found a less painful way. But then we wouldn't be in this house, wouldn't have had our silver put right into our hands."

Queasiness swept through Susanna. "What do you plan to do?"

His expression grew wily. "We don't have your mama's necklace, but we have this silver service, and it belongs to you. Go ahead and shine it with pride. When we leave, we'll take it with us."

"But that's stealing, Daddy. It would make us no better than the Colonel."

"That so?" Daddy gripped her shoulders. "Do you remember your grandmama's death? No, of course not. Your mama would have shielded you. *My* mama died of apoplexy right after that raid. Right out in the field as she watched the Yankees ride off and a fire destroy the home where she'd spent her entire married life and widowhood." His eyes shining with some undefinable emotion, he picked up a cloth and began to reverently rub away the tarnish from the silver platter.

While they worked in silence, Susanna considered all he'd said. Her conclusions came down to one question. How could she take these valuable items from this house when she and Daddy were beholden to Nate for their very lives and to Mrs. Northam for her extraordinary hospitality? Lying about their name and social standing was one thing; stealing, another.

On the other hand, all her life she'd heard friends and neighbors railing against the North for their invasion. Every person she knew considered it his or her duty to despise any and every Yankee. Had she betrayed her Southern heritage by falling in love with this family, with Nate? For indeed she did love him. There was no way she could deny it.

As Susanna was growing up, Mama hadn't talked much about the day when blue-coated soldiers invaded their home, had never discussed the way Grandmama died, preferring to help her family move on with their lives. But Susanna had heard frightening stories from other people. How far would Daddy go to take his re venge? Would he kill the Colonel and be hanged for it?

Voices sounded from the kitchen, meaning Angela and Mrs. Northam would soon need her help with supper. Before anyone else entered the room, she had to get the matter settled.

"Promise me one thing," she whispered.

He gave her a long look. "Depends on what it is."

She let out a long sigh. "Promise me you won't try to kill the Colonel, and I'll help you take the silver."

He didn't answer right away, then at last gave her a brief nod. But the hatred she saw in his eyes generated more than a little concern. Until this moment, her always-truthful father hadn't told her the real reason for their journey west. What made her think he wasn't still withholding the truth?

Chapter Twenty

Nate had one last strategy to try to recapture the friendship he and Susanna had forged before she knew about the Colonel and Sherman. Surely, by saving her father's life up on La Veta Pass, he'd won her trust, but he wouldn't try to manipulate her by bringing it up.

Instead, after breakfast the morning of the party, he asked her to take a look at the columbines to be sure they were presentable for their guests. With noticeable reluctance, she accompanied him out the back door, but refused his hand when descending the steps. Nor did she offer even a hint of a smile as they walked toward the flower bed.

"They'll look nicer if you trim off the wilted parts." She gave a dismissive wave of her hand and turned back to the house.

Disappointed that she hadn't teased him about such an obvious solution, he gently gripped her upper arm. "Wait. That's not all." The angry set of her jaw threatened to defeat him, but he wouldn't give up so easily. "Bess's pups are weaned. Do you still want that cute little runt?"

Surprise and a hint of joy spread over her face, reminding him of how beautiful she was. "W-well…" She stared down at the ground and bit her lip, as if thinking the matter over. At last she looked up at him with determination in those bright blue eyes. "Yes, but I plan to pay you for her."

He laughed. "Nobody pays for a dog. Not out here."

Her eyes narrowed, changing the brightness to ice. "I'll pay or not take her at all."

Take her? Did that mean she planned to leave? "Well, let's go give her the good news."

She glanced toward the barn, then back at the house. "I promised Mrs. Northam I would help in the kitchen."

"It'll just take a minute." He remembered the day they unpacked the china and addressed an obvious concern. "Wes is out there mucking out stalls, so we won't be alone."

Her eyes softened a bit. "All right."

Instead of the leisurely stroll he'd hoped for, she strode across the barnyard as if she was on a forced march. Once inside the barn, however, she stopped outside the stall where the puppies were sleeping one on top of another. All except the runt, who was curled up with one of the barn kittens, a tiny gray one just about the same age.

"Oh, how adorable." She sank down onto her knees beside them and began to stroke their fur. Awakened, both climbed into her lap and returned some of that affection. Susanna giggled like a child. "Oh, you silly things."

While she babbled cute little nonsense words to the animals, Nate felt a bittersweet pang in his chest. He hadn't heard her laugh in so many days, he couldn't count them. "Well, looks like you'll be adopting two critters instead of one."

She held up the kitten, its nose to her nose, and shushed its tiny mewing. "There, there, sweet thing. Don't cry. I'll take care of you."

Another pang struck deep in Nate's chest. How he longed to say *I'll take care of you* to Susanna. Yet until he made peace between the Colonel and Susanna, it was a promise he couldn't make. If he could never bring them together, even in an uneasy truce, would he have to choose his father over the woman he loved? He did love her, no doubt about it, and he believed she loved him. Why must a long-over war have to keep them from declaring what was in their hearts?

Susanna choked back tears, disguising her emotions by talking gibberish to the darling little animals she could soon call her own. With Nate so close beside her, she longed, *ached* to throw away all she'd ever known and tell him how deeply she cared for him. But to what end? They could never marry, for she refused to be a part of Colonel Northam's family. Imagine having children who would adore such an evil man and call him Grandpapa! She would never permit it.

Setting the puppy and kitten down with one last caress, she couldn't keep from looking straight into Nate's green eyes. She'd avoided his longing gazes for days, but now good manners obliged her to speak.

"Thank you. As you can see, I've fallen completely in love." She gasped. "With them, I mean."

"You can tell they return the sentiment." His eyes twinkled, and one side of his lips lifted in that heart-stopping grin.

"See you, boss." Pushing the filled wheelbarrow through the open barn door, Wes disappeared. How good of Nate to arrange for him to chaperone them for these few moments.

"I'd better go." Susanna couldn't stop staring into Nate's eyes.

"Right." He didn't seem in any hurry to leave, either. After an endless, agonizing moment, his gaze drifted to her lips, and he leaned toward her.

Longing welled up inside her to accept his kiss, her very first ever. But a memory flashed into her mind's eye. The scene of a raging fire her nurse had not been able to completely shield her from. Her family home deliberately destroyed by Nate's father. The fiery image consumed her tender yearning. She spun away from him and dashed from the barn back to the house. Finding Daddy resting in Nate's room, she flung herself into his arms, at last giving vent to her tears of hopelessness.

"Shh, daughter." He caressed her hair and placed a kiss on her forehead. "Everything will work out."

"How?" She moved back, pulled a handkerchief from her pocket and brushed away her foolish tears.

"The Lord hasn't brought us this far to leave us." His gaze hardened. "He'll show us what to do."

Vengeance is Mine; I will repay, saith the Lord. The verse from Romans sprang to the tip of her tongue, but Daddy shushed her.

"You get all dressed up fancy and enjoy the party tonight. I'll be there sitting in a corner. I'm not in any hurry to make my plans."

Susanna dutifully obeyed, completing the chores she'd promised to do for Mrs. Northam and then going to Rosamond's room to prepare for the evening. With all the enthusiasm she could muster, she helped the dear girl dress and arrange her hair, and accepted the same help in return. Flowers in their hair and fans at their wrists, they were ready to go.

"We're quite the picture, aren't we?" Rosamond looped her arm in Susanna's and directed her gaze into the dressing-table mirror. "You're so beautiful. You should always wear pink."

Susanna nodded. "Permit me to return the compliment." She could not despise this generous girl, who'd shared everything with her, even her clothes, since she'd arrived. This was the sister she'd always longed for.

Rosamond gripped Susanna's shoulders and stared into her eyes. "Listen, I don't know what happened between you and Nate, but I want you to fix it."

Susanna choked out a soft laugh. Like Maisie, Rosamond had no idea about subtlety. She shook her head. "Some things can't be fixed."

"Humph. Is my brother being stubborn about something? He can be pretty pigheaded, you know."

Susanna grasped her friend's hands. "I believe the Lord has it all under control."

"Oh." Rosamond blinked. "Of course. Well, then, let's go down to the party."

Pleased to be free of her questioning, Susanna lifted a silent prayer for the day when this precious girl fell in love, entreating the Lord that no complications would threaten her happiness.

Arm in arm, they descended the front staircase. They waved to Pedro, a relative of Angela's hired to serve at the party, whose job was to greet guests at the front door and direct them to the parlor. There, dressed in their Sunday best, Nate and Tolley stood as sentinels outside the ballroom's closed double doors.

The look in Nate's eyes and his enthusiastic "Wow" confirmed Rosamond's compliment about Susanna's appearance. Yet what good did it do? She had no plans to dance with him or even to accept a glass of punch from him. If her feet betrayed her and insisted upon dancing, she would ask Tolley to be her partner.

But that wasn't likely to happen. Ever since Daddy told her about the day their valuables had been stolen, dark memories had emerged from the distant past, things her nurse and Mama had tried to shield her from, tried to make her forget. But she'd been six years of age, old enough to comprehend the terrifying events. And she would never let herself forget them again.

"Ladies, please step this way." The brothers slid open the double doors and waved them inside.

"Allow me." Nate offered his arm to Susanna, but she pulled up her fan and waved it before her face.

"Thank you. I can manage." She slid past him and stepped through the doorway, taking hold of the mahogany banister as she descended the five steps into the ballroom. As he'd promised, Daddy sat in the corner on a settee, and he waved her over. "I don't think I can do this," she whispered.

He squeezed her hand. "Yes, you can. Just sit here with me. The evening will pass quickly enough."

Rita entered, along with the three musicians who had played at the barn raising, and they formed an orchestra beside the piano. As the others played, Rita joined in softly so their instruments would cover the sound. Across the room, a photographer had set up his camera in front of one window, closing the drapes for a background for the pictures he would take.

Despite her reservations, Susanna found the fully decorated ballroom enchanting. The scent of roses wafted down from floral garlands hung from the scalloped molding some eight inches from the ceiling. The oak flooring had been polished to a sheen, then lightly dusted with chalk to keep dancers from slipping. Rosamond had stationed herself beside the silver tea service, which sat on a table. Susanna didn't see the china anywhere in the room. If she'd planned the party, she would have it all set out so Mrs. Northam would see it right away. Maybe the Colonel was afraid some of it would break during the dancing. But why on earth did she bother to think about his concerns?

The room filled with neighbors Susanna had met at the barn raising and church, and each one came to meet Daddy and welcome him to the community. When he didn't correct them and say he was a prospector, Susanna experienced no little relief. Reverend Thomas and Dr. Henshaw paid their respects to him and Susanna, with the doctor asking her to save him a dance. Pedro's two brothers passed among the guests offering refreshments from wooden trays.

"Good evening and welcome, everyone." The Colonel's voice boomed throughout the room as he and Mrs. Northam made a grand entrance and stood at the top of the staircase. The entire assembly applauded, and numerous whistles sounded above the noise. The sight of the Colonel, handsome to a fault in his blue army uniform, medals gleaming on his chest, caused Susanna to gasp in horror. Even Daddy jolted beside her, and a deep growl emanated from his throat. But Susanna's eyes quickly moved to Mrs. Northam, resplendent in a blue satin gown, with Mama's brilliant sapphire necklace sparkling around her neck. In an instant, every good or kind or admiring thought Susanna had toward Mrs. Northam vanished.

If Daddy hadn't held Susanna's hand in a vise grip, she would have dashed across the room and snatched the heirloom jewels right off the woman. How could she not know they belonged to another lady? How could she boldly wear the spoils of war? Susanna's gaze darted to the silver set, and a terrible truth dawned in her mind.

With the monogram clearly etched on that silver tray, Mrs. Northam had to know these were stolen vessels. How could she serve beverages to these other church friends, knowing another lady was bereft of her valuable heirlooms? Did this Yankee woman have no shame?

Apparently not, for she stood gazing about the room, laughing and exclaiming over every beautiful adornment, especially the piano. The crowd laughed with her, as did her pompous husband. How clever he must feel, Susanna thought. Giving his wife gifts that cost another woman so dearly.

"Mrs. Northam, may I have this dance?" The Colonel sketched an elaborate bow before his wife.

Rita launched into a Strauss waltz, and the anniversary couple took to the floor. After they made a few turns, others joined in. Seated beside Daddy, Susanna declined each gentleman who invited her to dance. When Nate approached, she focused on her father and refused to look at him.

"I couldn't bear to be in his arms, Daddy," she whispered after he indicated Nate had gone.

Daddy nodded his understanding. His own gaze hadn't left Mrs. Northam since she entered the room. Was he thinking about the last time Mama wore that lovely necklace so many years ago?

Across the room, Nate spoke to Tolley and pointed his chin in her direction. Tolley questioned him, then shrugged. He fetched two glasses of punch and, with his usual puppy-dog eyes, ambled their way. "Thought you might be thirsty." He set the cups in their hands, then moved away before they could object.

"Thank you," Susanna said too late for him to hear her. Her eyes stung, both over his kindness and her own bad manners, which would shame Mama.

"Nate keeps looking out for us, doesn't he?" Daddy's eyes were a bit moist, too.

The party went on and on, yet even the lively accordion music did not tempt Susanna to stand up with any of the gentlemen who continued to approach her. She did take some pleasure in watching Maisie and Dr. Henshaw dance together. If she wasn't mistaken, they already had a romance under way. In church last Sunday, they had sat together and shared a hymnal, along with many warm smiles. Apparently, he found her tomboy ways a part of her charm.

At last a buffet supper was announced, and Reverend Thomas offered grace. Guests took turns wandering into the dining room to retrieve plates of beef, chicken and pork, with countless side dishes and fixings. Susanna managed to sneak full plates for herself and Daddy without any unpleasant encounters, but her lack of appetite caused her to leave half of hers uneaten.

When everyone reassembled in the ballroom, the Colonel took his wife's elbow and gave Nate a nod. Nate in turn signaled to his brothers, who stood just inside the door. Like a line of marching soldiers, they and their cowhands carried in wooden boxes and set them on a table hastily moved to the center of the room. The few children not outside playing were warned to stay with their parents, then a hush came over the assembly.

"Charlotte," the Colonel said, "in honor of the best twenty-five years of my life, a life that just keeps getting better and better because you are my wife, I'd like to present you with a small token of my affection."

Mrs. Northam began to open the boxes and exclaimed over and over how beautiful the china was, how clever and good her husband was, how she'd thought this beautiful ballroom was her gift, which was far more than she'd hoped for, and on and on. She then surprised him with the exquisite silver spurs. Everyone in the crowd laughed at the Colonel's genuine shock and his artificial disappointment over not receiving the quilt he'd been expecting. George Eberly quipped that it was about time somebody outwitted the Colonel. Again the crowd erupted in laughter until Susanna's ears began to hurt from the sound of it.

The couple's mutual adoration stung her heart. Daddy and Mama had also loved each other with the same kind of deep devotion. What would these evil people think if some man stole this china and gave it to another woman? But Susanna did like Mr. Eberly's remark. Soon she and Daddy would also be *outwitting* the Colonel, and she could hardly wait for that day.

After many toasts and speeches by neighbors proclaiming all that the Colonel and Mrs. Northam had done to create a wonderful, vibrant community, Mr. Eberly announced that a vote had been taken. Everyone agreed the best name for their growing town was Northam City, or just plain Northam.

As if he already knew about their scheme, the Colonel modestly accepted the honor, declaring that he would prefer the name Mountain View, or the Spanish version, Monte Vista. "But who am I to argue with popular opinion?"

With that matter settled, he beckoned to Nate and Maisie. "Come on over, you two."

Nate's face turned a darker shade of tan, and Maisie glanced up at Dr. Henshaw with nothing short of bewilderment. They slowly approached the Colonel, and he took his place between them, imprisoning them with his long arms around their shoulders.

"I'm sure this young couple has been hiding their good news so as not to overshadow tonight's little celebration."

His face now a deep red, Nate tried to pull back from his father, but the Colonel held on tight. "Ever since George and I settled this land side by side, we've looked forward to the day when we could expand our holdings to benefit both of us. Now that Maisie is all grown up—" he gave her a tighter hug "—it's time to announce the joining of our properties through her marriage to Nate. As my eldest son, he will inherit..."

He continued talking, but Susanna no longer heard his words. Wide-eyed, she stared at Daddy while her heart twisted inside her chest. So all this time, Nate had only been flirting with her. He'd never intended to court her. Never intended to do anything other than play with her emotions with all of his sweet talk and outward courtesies. He was just like the rest of his family. A Yankee through and through, with every bad quality that name indicated.

"Well, that settles that." Daddy squeezed her hand. "I'm sorry, daughter. In spite of everything, I hoped you and Nate—"

She couldn't listen to another word. She hastily wended her way through the crowd and up the stairs to the parlor. There she collided with Dr. Henshaw, who was claiming his hat from Pedro.

"It seems I'm not the only one shocked by the news." He tipped the hat to her and strode toward the front hall and out the door.

Turning the other way, Susanna ran up the stairs to Rosamond's room, where she slammed and locked the door. Facedown on the bed, she sobbed bitterly. To think this very afternoon Nate had tried to steal a kiss from her. He was more like his father than she'd ever imagined.

* * *

"But, Colonel." Maisie twisted free of his hold and almost shouted her protest. "I don't want to marry Nate. He's like a brother to me." She fisted her hands at her waist. "Didn't you know I'm sweet on the doc? And he's sweet on me?" She cast a look of exasperation toward the door he'd just exited.

Even as relief flooded Nate, he saw the color rising up the Colonel's neck. Maisie's short speech may have set him free from his father's plan, but it also threatened to shame the Colonel before the entire community, maybe beyond repair. No matter how angry his father had made him, he couldn't let that happen. "Yep, Colonel, I should have told you." He let his posture droop with apparent disappointment. "Once you brought that Harvard-educated doctor to the community, I lost out."

The Colonel's confusion quickly cleared, and he grasped the lifeline Nate offered. "Well, I'll be a Christmas goose. How's a man supposed to keep up with such goings-on?"

Maisie seemed to catch on, because she patted the Colonel's shoulder in a comforting gesture. "It's not your fault, sir. You know how fickle we women can be. I took one look at Doc, and all these cowpokes disappeared." She cast an apologetic grin over the assembly, and everyone laughed.

At that moment, Nate wanted to give her a big, brotherly kiss, but that would ruin everything. Across the room, George Eberly scratched his head in confusion. For the first time, Nate doubted Maisie's father had even been aware of the Colonel's plans.

"Well, time's a-wasting." Maisie strode toward the steps. "I got me a doctor to catch." More boisterous laughter rang throughout the room.

Nate made a split-second decision, not caring how it looked. "Hang on, Maisie. I'll help you catch him." Behind him, the good-natured laughter continued in the ballroom as he followed her all the way to the front door. "Do you need me?"

"Naw." She thumped her fist against his shoulder. "I expect you need to do some catching yourself." With that, she dashed outside.

"*Señor,* if it is the other young lady you seek." Pedro pointed toward the staircase.

"*Gracias.*" Nate took the steps three at a time. Hearing Susanna's sobs through the door of Rosamond's room, he knocked softly. "Susanna, open up. Please let me explain." How he ached to comfort her and explain it all away. Yet in an odd way, he also felt a bit encouraged. She wouldn't be crying about his supposed engagement if she didn't care for him.

Chapter Twenty-One

"That was some party." Nate lingered in the kitchen after breakfast in hopes of seeing Susanna, but only Rosamond joined him at the kitchen table. It was still dark outside, but he'd already done his early chores, then came back for some of Angela's griddle cakes.

"Yes, it was." Rosamond wore an uncharacteristic frown, which put Nate on alert. "Mother's sleeping. When she gets up, we're going to take some of the leftover food from last night to needy folks in the neighborhood."

"Good." Nate took a sip of coffee. "Maybe Susanna can go with you." If he didn't have work to do that couldn't be postponed, including helping Tolley break his first mustang, he'd spend the day wooing her like a lovesick Romeo. Restless all night, he'd fallen asleep only after deciding to tell the Colonel of his feelings for her and face whatever came after that.

But life on a ranch didn't wait on either courting or confrontation, so he'd have to bide his time and wait until he was free to take care of both matters. He assumed Rosamond's downcast mood concerned Susanna. If she'd just come downstairs, he could at least see whether he had a chance with her or whether he should resign himself to being miserable for the rest of his life.

He finished his griddle cakes and carried his empty plate to Rita, who was up to her elbows in the dishpan. "That was some fine music last night, Rita. I hope you'll keep up your playing."

"*Sí,* Señor Nate. Señor Colonel says I must learn everything Mrs. Foster can teach me." Beside her, Angela beamed with maternal pride.

He headed toward the back door, considering his strategy for teaching his youngest brother the fine art of taming a wild horse. Before he could put his hand on the doorknob, the Colonel burst in looking oddly wild-eyed. Nate hadn't spoken with him since the embarrassing incident at the party, so a wave of apprehension surged through him.

"Where's Rand?" Desperation colored his father's tone, something Nate had only seen once before when his middle brother had suffered a bad fall from the roof.

"Rand? I don't know."

"What do you mean you don't know?" This was the old Colonel, worried about his favorite son.

"I mean—" Nate forced the rancor from his voice "—well, he was up before me, so I assumed he rode out with the boys to cut the calves for branding." He couldn't keep from adding, "Like you ordered him to do."

"Did you see him after the party last night? See him in bed?"

Nate frowned. "Now that you mention it, no, sir. I didn't see him. Maybe he slept in the bunkhouse."

The Colonel slammed his hand against the doorjamb. "Just as I suspected. He and that no-good Seamus have ridden over to Del Norte on a gambling binge. Saddle up. We're going after him."

An odd feeling washed through Nate. The Colonel usually let Rand get over his binges himself, after which his brother, like the biblical Prodigal Son, dragged himself home, where his sins were never even mentioned. Never before had the Colonel chased after him. Maybe he'd shake some sense into Rand. *Maybe* Nate's prayers were getting through at last.

Susanna stayed in bed as long as she could, but hunger finally drove her to get up and dress. After checking on Daddy, she descended the back stairs fully aware that she would have to face Rosamond. She'd rebuffed the younger girl's attempts at conversation both at bedtime and early this morning. Rosamond's wounded tone of voice had revealed her hurt, and now Susanna tried without success to dismiss her guilty feelings. It wasn't Rosamond's fault her parents had stolen Mama's valuables. Not Rand's nor Tolley's and certainly not Nate's. She constantly had to remind herself that Nate had saved Daddy's life, and hers, too. Of course, that didn't obligate him to love her, not when he'd been promised to Maisie.

Mama always said there was no excuse for bad manners, and Susanna wouldn't excuse herself this time. The only way to apologize would be to put on a cheerful face and continue to help around the house. Only now she would assume the attitude of a servant, maybe even stop taking meals with the family so she didn't have to sit down with the Colonel and Mrs. Northam. If Daddy still wanted to eat with them, that was his business.

"Good morning." She entered the kitchen only to find Rosamond wasn't there. Nevertheless, she gave the room's sole occupant a bright smile, despite the disturbance it caused in her stomach.

"Susanna." Mrs. Northam rose from the table and embraced her. "Good morning. I'm so glad to see you. Did you sleep well?"

Susanna couldn't keep from stiffening, but she kept her artificial smile in place. "Why, yes, indeed, I did, thank you. Did you sleep well after all that celebrating last night?" She almost gagged on the question. After the plantation house burned, had Mama lain awake at night fearing the Yankees would return?

Mrs. Northam laughed as she returned to her seat. "After all the months of planning, I have to confess it's a relief to have it all over and done with."

"My, my." Susanna knew she needed to keep her mouth shut before some of her bitterness leaked out. With no choice but to sit down with this woman, she went to the stove and served herself some bacon, eggs and griddle cakes. What she wouldn't give for a bowl of grits and molasses right about now.

"I will confess, however," Mrs. Northam said, "it will be hard to get back to normal, whatever normal is on a ranch. Seems like something out of the ordinary is always happening."

"Mmm." Now seated, Susanna busied herself with devouring her breakfast. Once she convinced Daddy they needed to leave, she would cut several five-dollar gold pieces from her old petticoat to pay for the food they'd eaten and the two animals Nate had sold her. Of course, they'd need horses, too, so maybe Nate would sell them a team. She hadn't worn the petticoat since arriving, hiding it in the back of a drawer and using Rosamond's outgrown clothes instead. Maybe she would buy some of those to wear until she could make her own.

Biting into a crisp piece of bacon, she looked up to see Mrs. Northam watching her thoughtfully. She questioned the woman with a single raised eyebrow, although

Mama would not approve of such a gesture, especially when Susanna's mouth was full.

"Is something wrong, dear?"

Susanna swallowed. "No, ma'am. Everything's fine." A wild thought crossed her mind. "I heard you tell Colonel Northam you're working on a new shirt for him. Can I help you do that today?"

"Why, thank you. You're a gifted seamstress. Rosamond tells me you made the ballroom drapes. I've never had success sewing with velvet. You must teach us how to do it."

"I'd be pleased to. Why don't we start right after breakfast?"

"Oh, didn't Rosamond tell you? Today we wanted you to go with us while we take some leftover food to our needy neighbors."

Susanna scrambled for a reason to stay home and settled on Daddy. "My father didn't look particularly well this morning, so I'd best stay home with him. I'd love to make use of my time and work on that shirt while you're gone."

Mrs. Northam opened her mouth, probably to object, then nodded. "That would be lovely. After you finish eating, we'll go up to my room and I'll show you what I've done so far."

"Oh, my." Susanna almost laughed. Going to the master bedroom was exactly what she'd hoped to do. Only one problem presented itself. "Why, Miz Northam—" she poured on her thickest Southern pronunciations "—I would be mortified if the Colonel showed up and I was in your bedroom. Why, what would he think of me?" Not that she cared.

Mrs. Northam had the grace to look abashed. "You're right, of course. I hadn't thought of that. But my husband isn't home today. He and Nate had to…" She frowned and released a weary sigh. "They had to ride over to Del Norte." She tilted her head toward the west. "Rand and his friend Seamus may have gotten into a little mischief. They may need some help getting out of it." She let out another sigh. "In any event, they won't be home until late this afternoon."

Susanna could see the woman's embarrassment, and her heart softened. From what she'd seen, Rand wasn't wicked, just prone to tomfoolery. "I'll pray they bring him safely home." The words were out before she could stop them, but she would keep the promise for Rand's *and* Nate's sakes.

Mrs. Northam's eyes reddened. "Thank you, Susanna. I pray without ceasing for each of my children, but Rand's always needed a double dose." She laughed softly. "We mothers want only to see our children happy and healthy." After dabbing her eyes with her napkin, she stood. "Shall we go up?"

"I should wash my dishes first."

"You go," Rita said. "As you can see, I am washing dishes again. The Colonel, he says it is permissible after the anniversary playing."

With that, Susanna and her hostess made their way to the upstairs chamber. The room was grandly decorated with wallpaper, brass sconces, draperies, a stone fireplace with brass andirons and elegant mahogany furniture. Under the west window sat the sewing machine.

"You can work right here. Then, if you see the men returning up the lane, you can leave." She tapped her chin thoughtfully. "In fact, why don't we bring your father in to keep you company, maybe read you the latest newspaper from back east as you work? He'll be comfortable on the chaise longue, don't you think?"

"Yes, ma'am." Everything was working out just as Susanna had hoped. Beside the tall mahogany wardrobe stood a matching dressing table. On it, next to the usual hand mirror and brush, lay a black velvet jewel box, maybe containing Mama's sapphires. Her heart skipped a beat. "That will be just fine."

After Mrs. Northam showed her the half-completed shirt, she sat comfortably before the Singer and began to pin and sew the sleeves to the rest of the shirt. When Rosamond entered the room, Susanna managed a cheery greeting she really meant. It would be nothing short of wickedness to blame the children for their father's sins. Besides, sewing always relaxed her, so this would be a good day.

Before leaving on their charitable mission, the two ladies escorted Daddy from Nate's room and settled him on the chaise, a blanket, a newspaper and *Bleak House* on his lap.

"Angela or Rita will be up to check on you from time to time," Mrs. Northam said as they exited the bedroom.

When Susanna saw their carriage driving up the lane, she huffed out a sigh. "I thought they'd never leave." She dashed to the dressing table and picked up the faded black velvet box. Although it had been brushed to clean the fabric, she could still see some deeply embedded gray soil. Her heart ached to think of Mama having to bury this box, only to have those Yankees dig it up and steal it.

"What do you have there, daughter?" Daddy peered at her over the edge of the *Boston Globe*.

Not opening the box, she moved to the edge of the chaise. "What do you think?"

He took it reverently in hand as though he, too, noticed the imbedded soil from home. Slowly lifting the lid to reveal the glimmering silver and sparkling sapphires, he blinked as tears rolled down his cheeks. "Oh, Belle," he choked out. "What I wouldn't give to see you wear these again."

Susanna swallowed her own tears. Mama had never desired jewels or fancy clothes. Despite her frightening experiences during the war, or maybe because of them, all she'd ever wanted was for her family to be happy and healthy. Like Mrs. Northam. The thought came unbidden, and Susanna thrust it away, along with the guilt that tried to seize her. This was Mama's necklace, and it was high time to reclaim it and the other valuables. "I know where the tea service is kept."

Daddy's eyes brightened. "And?"

"We need to take our belongings and leave. Today." She studied his face and reassured herself that his color was good. He could travel without a relapse. "The Northams are away and won't be home until evening. We can buy another team of horses right here. Nate's told me they always have some for sale, and Wes or one of the other hands would know which ones are best for pulling the prairie schooner." Mentioning Nate's name brought a sharp pain to her heart, but she would not dwell on it. "The wagon is in the barn, and when I checked the other day, no one had opened the secret compartment. Our gold is still there."

"Today?" Daddy stared off thoughtfully, but she could see he liked the idea.

"Yes, today." As her excitement mounted, she laughed and cried at the same time. "This is what you came for." She took the open jewel box in hand, seeing for the first time the countless number of tiny diamonds circling each sapphire. "Forget living in this community. Now we can go back home to Marietta."

He drew back with a frown. "Marietta?"

She stared at him. "What ails you, Daddy? Yes, Marietta. You know, that finest of Southern cities in the state where we were both born and bred? Where our family and friends will welcome us back with open arms and scold us for ever leaving?" She punctuated her speech with a laugh, but when he continued to frown, she closed and set down the jewel box and gripped his hands. "What is it, Daddy?"

His expression was a study in cautious happiness. "I can't go back to Marietta. Can't go back to anyplace in Georgia."

"What? What are you talking about?" Clearly, the thought did not dismay him as it did her.

He pulled one hand from her grip and touched her cheek. "Please listen to me with an open heart, daughter." At her nod, he continued, "You know I loved your mama. Still do. But she's with the Lord now, and I'm still here." He grimaced, as if he feared to continue. Susanna squeezed his hand to encourage him. "All these weeks we've been here, Miss Angela has taken mighty good care of me. It was always proper, mind you, with Zack always around to help with things she shouldn't do. We've had some wonderful talks and, well, I've fallen in love with her, daughter. I plan to marry her."

"You've fallen in love with Angela?" Susanna liked the woman very much, but—

"Now, I know what you're going to say. She's a Mexican." He breathed out a long sigh. "I no longer care about such things. She's a good, sweet Christian lady. But you know as well as I do that the folks back home will never accept her as my wife, no matter how strong a Christian she is. I won't leave her behind, and I won't dishonor her by asking her to go with me under any arrangement other than marriage."

"But—" Susanna couldn't quite sort it out. Daddy falling in love again? At his age? "I can't stay here loving Nate as I do and knowing he's obligated to marry Maisie."

"Marry Maisie?" Daddy chuckled. "I forgot to tell you—"

"Ah, there you are, Señor Anders." Angela entered the room, her face aglow. Did that mean she loved Daddy in return? "May I bring dinner up for you and Señorita Susanna, or would you like to go down to the dining room?"

Daddy reached out a hand and tugged her down to the nearby chair. "I've told her, sweetheart."

Angela gasped and turned a hopeful look in Susanna's direction. "You are not angry?"

Susanna's bothersome tears started again. "Not in the least. I'm thankful to you for bringing joy to my father. I wish you both great happiness." Now that Angela would be taking care of him, Susanna would no longer need to keep her promise to Mama. "I-is there some way I can go back home?" Oddly, the thought of returning to Marietta without him seemed painfully unacceptable. The thought of never seeing Nate again pained her even more. But why? Even if he wasn't promised to Maisie, she would never consider marrying into his family.

"But no, *señorita*." Angela glanced at Daddy. "You must stay and live with us. Many people here love you." She exchanged another look with Daddy. "Tell her."

Stunned, Susanna could only stare at them. Finally, she lightly smacked Daddy's hand. "Where was I when all of this was going on?"

"Why, if I'm not mistaken, you were involved with affairs of the heart yourself."

She snorted in a most unladylike way. "And you saw last night how well that turned out."

"Ah," Angela said. "She does not know this."

"What else don't I know?" Susanna had experienced just about all the surprises she needed for a while.

"Why," Daddy said, "that fool of a Colonel thought he could force Nate to marry Maisie, but she told the whole community she's in love with the doc, and he with her." Daddy threw back his head and laughed. "You should have seen what a fool that man made of himself. And Nate rescued him by claiming he was disappointed in Maisie's choice."

"Yes, well, he's pretty good at rescuing people, isn't he?" Relief poured over Susanna. Nate was free to marry whom he chose. An odd bit of hope skittered through her, but she quickly dashed it. She refused to be a part of the Colonel's family, so seeing Nate again would only cause her grief. A sense of urgency filled her. "We need to get the silver and leave while they're gone. Now."

"Eduardo?" Angela gave Daddy a chiding frown.

"Now, honey, I've told you all about that. Those things belong to us. The Colonel stole them from my wife during the war."

The older woman sighed and bowed her head. "Oh, Dios, what is Your will? Give us guidance that we might not sin against You." She looked at Daddy. "All my life, many of my belongings have been stolen by bandits until I come here. I would like to have my things back again, but that will never be. I will go with you, and we will take your stolen things. But please remember, no matter what they did to you, the Northams have been kind and protected my daughter and me."

He gave her a decisive nod. "I understand."

"And!" She held up a scolding forefinger, and he smothered a grin. "You will not seek any other revenge against the Colonel. I have already seen one husband hanged by our enemies. This Colonel Northam is too powerful to cross. You will promise, or I will not marry you."

Daddy considered her words for a moment, then nodded. "I don't want to see you grieved again, Miss Angela, so I'll do as you say." He brushed a hand over her cheek. "But I'll never forgive him, never forget what he and the North did to my family." Carefully moving his injured leg over the side of the couch, he positioned his crutch so he could stand. "All right, let's get packed up."

"Yes, sir." Susanna's heart leaped into her throat as she and Angela helped him to his feet. "Instead of taking the house the preacher found for us, let's go back toward Alamosa or down south to Angela's relatives."

Daddy chuckled. "Daughter, do you think you're the only one who's been making plans? I've already sent the money to Reverend Thomas to buy that plot of land where the three of us can live in peace."

Susanna's jaw dropped. "What? You want to stay in a community named for Colonel Northam?"

He shrugged. "What better place to settle? Here I can be a burr in the saddle of that arrogant Yankee."

"Why, you rascal." This was her old daddy, and she couldn't be more pleased. "And you did all of that without me?"

He shrugged. "A man's got to make plans, daughter. Now, you go find Zack or Wes and see about those horses. If they'll sell them to us, have them bring out the wagon."

Susanna traded a look with Angela.

"You best do as he says." The amusement in Angela's eyes tickled Susanna's insides.

Now, if they could just make their escape before any of the Northam family came back home. Angela assured them the family wouldn't miss the silver items because they would assume she'd stored them. But if they did realize they were gone, Susanna knew Nate would be terribly disappointed in her, perhaps even hate her.

And maybe that was best.

Chapter Twenty-Two

Nate followed the Colonel into the Shady Lady saloon north of Del Norte. In the middle of the day, even a Saturday, he hadn't expected to see so many patrons gambling and imbibing. To his surprise, nearly every table was filled, and the rank smell of liquor hung in the air. He couldn't see Rand, but when a couple of the women called out to him, Nate quit searching and focused on his father. If one of those foolish girls got friendly with him, he'd just tell her to go to church and make friends with God.

"Good morning, Colonel Northam." The bartender no doubt made it his business to know the important people in the surrounding area. "Come for your son?"

The Colonel stormed up to the bar, casting an uneasy glance toward the steps leading upstairs. "Where is he?"

The man had the audacity to laugh, but his tone held no mockery. "Why, over at the jail, of course. He—"

The Colonel spun on his heel and marched back through the swinging doors. They rode in silence to the center of town, where the sheriff's office was located. Leaving their horses at the hitching rail, they entered the two-story wood-frame building.

"Dad!" Rand broke from a group of men near the jail cells and strode across the wide room. "Am I glad to see you. Wait till you hear—"

"I don't need to hear anything you have to say." The Colonel brushed past him and approached the sheriff. "What do I owe you for his bail?"

"Owe me?" The sheriff gave him a long look. "It's what we owe him we need to talk about."

"What?" The Colonel barked out the question in a way that usually made two of his sons cower.

As usual, Rand just laughed. "Wait till you hear this, Dad. Tell him, Sheriff."

Nate swallowed his disgust at Rand's brashness. Once again his brother would get off without punishment.

"Why, these two boys—" the sheriff beckoned to Seamus, who sheepishly joined the group "—these two *men* are responsible for rounding up a couple of the mangiest, lowdown horse thieves I've ever seen. Outdrew them and shot one in the leg. The other one's over at the undertaker's."

In a flash, pride in his brother's heroism cooled Nate's anger, and he sent Rand an approving glance. Then he peered around the sheriff to see a dark-suited man, probably a doctor, tending a scruffy fellow in the cell. A chill went up his spine. The scar-faced wounded man fit the description Mr. Anders had given of one of the thieves who'd beaten him. If Susanna hadn't been fetching water, Nate shuddered to think what the surly thief would have done to her. As it was, he wanted to pummel the man who'd nearly killed her father. His old temper threatened to carry him over to the cell to do just that, so he turned his attention back to the sheriff.

"I've been trying to catch those two varmints for over a year. They had gold from the sale of the horses they've stolen, and they were loco enough to go over to the Shady Lady to gamble it away. That's where they encountered your son and Seamus." The middle-aged sheriff beamed at them with paternal approval. "He was just telling me how he came to know they were thieves."

Rand shuffled his feet and stared down at the floor. "It didn't take much. After a few drinks, they were bragging about killing some old man up on La Veta Pass and making off with his horses. That one—" he jerked a thumb toward the cell "—even bragged about giving his girlfriend some fancy duds he found in the prairie schooner." He grimaced as he looked at Nate. "I knew right away he was talking about Mr. Anders and Susanna. Thank the Lord the old man didn't die, or this one would be up for hanging."

"Horse stealing's a hanging offense, too," the sheriff said. "The circuit judge will be riding through soon. Then we'll see this one's taken care of." He seemed to relish the idea. "Now, what am I gonna do for you boys? O'course the money you won from 'em at cards is yours, but there's also a reward for their capture, dead or alive."

"Aw, I don't care about the money." Rand stared down at his feet. "In fact, I feel a little sick to my stomach over the whole matter. I've got a lot to sort out." He traded a look with Seamus, who gave him a firm nod. "One thing's for sure. I'm done with gambling. Give the money to charity."

Seamus echoed his vow, and Nate could see by the relief in his eyes that he meant it. He also had a suspicion that Rand had been dragging Seamus along on his escapades just to have some company.

Rand looked at the Colonel. "Dad, I can't say I'm proud to have killed a man, but they gave us no choice. Once I called them on the robbery, they went for their guns. Please forgive me for shaming your name by consorting with such evil men."

Nate started to protest that he'd done the right thing, but the Colonel beat him to it. "Son, I had to do some things during the war that still eat at my soul. But just as God helped David kill Goliath, this was a righteous killing. You can check with Reverend Thomas, but I believe God's forgiven you for it. As for the gambling, I have. Any shame connected with it will be canceled out by righteous living from now on. But—" he held a finger up to Rand's face "—I expect you to be accountable to me from now on for everything you do."

"Thanks, Dad." Rand's eyes reddened. "I'll do that."

Nate could feel a bit of dust in his own eyes. "Colonel?" He wished he could feel comfortable calling him Dad. "Some of that money ought to go to Mr. Anders for the sale of his horses and for the other stolen things. I know they could use it." He wouldn't even think about reclaiming Susanna's dresses after some saloon girl had worn them.

Rand chimed in with his agreement, and they settled on three hundred dollars, sixty for each horse and sixty for the other belongings. The sheriff insisted that Rand and Seamus should split the five-hundred-dollar reward, and at the Colonel's urging, they accepted it.

As they rode back home, Nate felt a strange mixture of emotions. Most of all he felt pride in Rand's courage and, best of all, his repentance. But he was also disappointed when their jubilant chatter as they traveled kept him from telling his father he planned to court Susanna. A smidgen of anxiety also colored his thoughts. What if she didn't accept his courtship?

Anyway, this was Rand's day and a time to celebrate. Of course, most days were Rand's days, but somehow that awareness didn't depress Nate as it usually did. He was just glad his brother was all right. Further, he couldn't deny his relationship with the Colonel had greatly improved. Just the fact that his father had insisted he come along to rescue Rand bolstered Nate's confidence that one day soon he'd feel comfortable addressing the man as Dad.

"Oh, Mamá," Rita cried. "I am happy for you, but I am not yet ready to manage the kitchen by myself."

"Of course you are, my little one. When I was your age, I alone managed my father's house because *madre mia* was with the Lord." Angela embraced her daughter while Susanna and Daddy finished packing the prairie schooner. "You know we would be pleased if you went with us, but as we decided, Colonel and Mrs. Northam have been so good to you and me, *si?* We must not leave them without a cook. Just remember all I have taught you. If you have *problema,* you come to my new home on the day of your piano lessons." The pride in her voice when mentioning her *new home* moved Susanna almost to tears. Every woman, no matter what her culture, longed for a place to call her own.

Zack had chosen four sturdy horses from those available for sale and hitched them to the wagon. Once he'd driven it around to the front of the house, Susanna surreptitiously checked the stash of gold and found it still safely tucked into the secret compartment. What a wonder that the thieves hadn't found it. Perhaps they were too busy beating Daddy and destroying their supplies and clothing to search too diligently. How wise of Daddy to insist that they wear rough clothing and use only paper money so no one would suspect they had gold.

She'd decided not to take a single item from Rosamond's wardrobe, for that truly would be stealing. Instead, she now wore her old brown wool skirt and mended shirtwaist. She missed the pleasant feeling of being nicely dressed.

"Come along, daughter." Daddy scurried around with such excitement, Susanna began to worry about his health. Angela reassured her that he would be all right.

"Will you come with us?" Daddy placed a hand on Zack's shoulder. "I could use your help, and I'll pay you well."

Zack tipped his hat back and scratched at his forehead. "Well, sir, you give me something to think about. Since Nate's been the foreman, he hasn't let me do what I used to on account of a few broken bones over the years. Treats me like an old man." He studied Daddy up and down. "Tell you what. If you put me to work and let me decide how much I can do, I'll feel worth my salt more than I do here."

"It's a bargain." Daddy held out his hand, and they shook on it.

As glad as Susanna was that Daddy would have a man to help him, she couldn't help but admire the way Nate had looked out for Zack, just as he had her and Daddy. Swallowing the tears that kept threatening to slow her down, she busied herself arranging the contents of the wagon.

With the last of their few possessions packed and the retrieved valuables safely hidden beneath Angela's clothes and blankets, the party began to climb aboard. Taking one last look around, Susanna saw Bess and two of her pups near the barn.

"Wait. I forgot Lazy Daisy and Shadow."

"What on earth?" Daddy called from the driver's bench. "Daughter, we need to leave."

"I'll just be a moment." She dashed across the wide barnyard and into the structure. "Come, my little ones." Already weaned, neither seemed to mind being taken from its mother. At least she hoped not.

She hurried back across the yard just in time to see the Northam men turn down the lane. Breathless now, she paused at the back of the wagon and handed the tiny pets to Angela, who was already settled inside.

"Here, Rita." She pulled a gold piece from her pocket and handed it to the girl. "Tell Colonel Northam this is for the animals. Nate said I could have them."

Before she could climb in, the men arrived in a cloud of dust. Nate was the first one to dismount, with the others right behind him. Seeing the Colonel's hunched-up shoulders, Susanna swallowed a lump of fear. His posture had been just like that when they'd arrived. Surely, now he should be glad to see them gone.

"You're leaving?" Nate's wounded tone cut deep into her heart. "But I wanted—"

"Let 'em go."

For once, the Colonel's snapped response didn't silence Nate.

"Look." Standing by the wagon, he pulled from his pocket a leather bag that jingled as he held it up to Daddy. "Rand and Seamus found the thieves. I'm sorry to say your horses were already sold, but here's the money for them." His brief explanation of their trip to Del Norte astounded Susanna, and she could see Daddy's shock, as well. "Don't you want to stay until the trial so you can be a witness? The circuit judge will be here in the next month or so."

"Oh, we'll still be around." Daddy spoke to Nate in a loud enough voice for the Colonel to hear. "Got me a little place up on the Rio Grande." He accepted the bag from Nate. "This'll help pay expenses, Thank you Nate. Not just for this but for all you've done."

Susanna hated that he wanted to maintain their pose of poverty. Why couldn't they just tell them all who they were and be done with it?

"Zack." The Colonel was the only one who hadn't dismounted. Susanna suspected he wanted to maintain a more intimidating position. "I'm assuming you'll be returning my horses once you park these people some-place far away from here."

Zack started to answer, but Daddy held up a hand to silence him.

"Colonel Northam." His voice cut through the air like a steel rapier, something Susanna had rarely heard from her mellow father. "I paid for these horses, a fact to which both your man Wes and my man Zack will attest. You'll find your money in young Rita's care, and I have the bill of sale right here." He patted his tattered jacket right above the pocket.

Thunder rode across the Colonel's brow. "*Your* man Zack?"

Zack cleared his throat. "Um, yessir. I've decided to go to work for Mr. Anders."

Colonel Northam snorted out his disgust. "So much for your loyalty to me."

His arrogant remark must have stung Zack because he spat over the side of the wagon and pulled his hat lower on his forehead.

"But where will you go?" Nate reached for Susanna's hand, and a pleasant shiver went up her arm. Oh, they really must leave before his protectiveness undid her.

"As Daddy said, we have a place." She refused to look into his eyes, even when he tugged on her hand.

"Where? When can I come see you?" He looked up at Daddy, then briefly at the Colonel.

"Let them go, son." The Colonel dismounted and handed his horse off to Rand, then gripped Nate's shoulder. "We're well rid of them."

"No, we're not. I—"

Puppy yips from inside the wagon interrupted him, and he gave her his lopsided grin.

"I'm glad you didn't forget her. Did you take the kitten, too?" His sweet look tore at Susanna's heart. It was all she could do not to throw herself into his arms.

"I told you," the Colonel barked, "she can't have that dog." He marched to the back of the wagon and lowered the tailgate. "Angela, what are you doing here? Are you deserting us, too?"

Nate started. "What's going on?" This time he spoke to Daddy.

"Well, son, Miss Angela and I have decided to get married."

Susanna broke away from Nate and hurried to the Colonel. "This puppy is the runt of the litter and has a bum leg, so she won't do you any good for herding cattle. And I paid for her. Ask Rita." She waved a hand toward the girl, whose round eyes revealed her anxiety and who quickly held up the gold coin.

"What else did you *buy?*" The Colonel began to fling aside the blankets. "Well, well, well. Nate, get over here, boy. Take a look at what your sweetheart and her thieving father decided to carry off along with some of my employees."

Nate heard Mother's buggy arrive, but Tolley had just come over from the barn. He'd have to take care of helping her down. Nate walked to the back of the prairie schooner on wooden legs, terrified of what he would see. Casting a glance at Susanna, he noted that her chin jutted out and defiance blazed in her eyes.

"Now, don't those boxes look familiar?" The Colonel reached in and pulled one crate onto the lowered tailgate. He lifted the lid to reveal Mother's silver tea service. "See anything amiss here, son?"

Nate couldn't speak for the sick feeling clogging his throat. Nor could he look at Susanna. What a fool he'd been. While Mr. Anders's injuries had been real, everything else Nate had believed about the two of them was surely a lie.

"What's happening here?" Mother joined them, with Rosamond and Rand right behind her. She first saw Angela and started to address her. Then, seeing the silver set, she gasped. "Susanna, what have you done?" Mother reached out to touch Susanna, but Susanna jerked away.

"What have I done?" She moved toward the front of the wagon. "Why don't you ask your husband what he has done?"

"Now, wait just a minute." Nate could feel his temper rising at her angry tone of voice. Standing here with his family, he knew where his loyalties lay.

"No. *You* wait just a minute." Susanna glanced up at her father. "Am I going to tell them, or are you?"

"Well, daughter, you were there when it happened, so you go right ahead."

At the old man's smug look, Nate wanted to plant his fist on his jaw. "Dad, why don't we just send for the sheriff and be done with it?" He was gratified to see his father didn't correct the way he addressed him.

"You can do what you like, Nate." The curl of Susanna's lips shouted her disgust. "But first you and your whole family will hear what I have to say." She pointed an accusing finger at the Colonel. "This fine, upstanding leader of your community is nothing but a thief and a murderer."

"Now, just a minute," Nate repeated. Every good thing he'd ever thought about her now made him sick to his stomach.

"Quiet, son." The Colonel crossed his arms and narrowed his eyes. "Go on, girl."

She faltered for a moment and, oddly, Nate wanted to help her. What a foolish, lovesick puppy he was. No wonder his father had wanted him to listen to Reverend Thomas's sermon on Proverbs. This truly was one deceitful woman in front of him now.

"First of all, our name isn't Anders. It's MacAndrews." She gave the Colonel a piercing look. "Does that sound familiar, Colonel? You should know it seeing as how you tried to wipe it off the face of this earth."

His glare softened, replaced by a look Nate couldn't identify. Worry? Shame?

"Y'all are so proud that Colonel Northam rode with General Sherman," Susanna said. "Well, I'm going to tell you something you don't know about that little excursion. On November 29, 1864, he and his troops rode onto my father's plantation. Daddy was away fighting, so of course those coward Yankees took great pleasure in terrifying the women and children he'd left behind. When my brother, just twelve years old, tried to stop them, this *heroic* soldier ordered him hanged. Hang a twelve-year-old! If my mama hadn't given him the buried silver tea service and her own sapphire necklace—*our* family heirlooms—he would have murdered a mere boy who was just trying to protect his mama and baby sister." She went to the back of the wagon and returned with a black jewel box, then held it in front of Mother. "Look. You can still see Georgia soil imbedded deep in the velvet."

"Oh, Frank." Mother held a hand up to her lips, and her eyes filled with tears.

Nate still felt sick to his stomach, but for a different reason. Why wasn't the Colonel denying these charges? Instead, his face had gone pale, almost ashen, and his arms dropped to his sides.

"As if that wasn't enough." Susanna's eyes also filled, "this brave officer ordered my brother's arms broken and the house burned down with everything in it. His men killed our livestock and even our pets." Her voice shook, but she seemed to force herself to continue, "My sweet old widowed grandmama died of apoplexy right out in the field while those coward Yankees rode away laughing." She looked around at each member of Nate's family, her accusing gaze settling at last on him.

He quickly turned to his father, whose face bore no denial of her charges.

"Frank, is this true?" Mother dabbed at her tears with a handkerchief.

"MacAndrews. Yes, I remember the place." The Colonel eyed Susanna's father and studied him briefly. "I remember." His shoulders slumped, and he walked to his horse, mounted and rode south.

As the hoofbeats died away, quiet settled over the front yard. The rest of the family stared around at each other.

Mother stood to her full height of five feet nothing and marched to the wagon. "Mr. Anders, I should say, Mr. MacAndrews, I never would have worn that necklace or used that lovely tea service if I'd known they were spoils of war. I thought my husband bought them in New York on his way home from the war." The pain in her voice sent shards of remorse through Nate for the way he'd spoken to brave Susanna. "Please keep your heirlooms with my blessings. You will have no trouble from anyone named Northam on this account." She looked at Nate, Rand, Rosamond and Tolley, silently ordering each of them to obey as only Mother could.

Mr. MacAndrews tipped his hat to her. "Ma'am, I can see you're entirely innocent in this matter. And now, please accept my humble gratitude for taking such good care of my daughter and me in our ill fortune. I don't know what we would have done if Nate hadn't come along." He spared Nate a smile and a nod. "We'll be eternally grateful."

Thumbs hooked on his gun belt, Nate shrugged and scuffed the toe of his boot across a piece of driveway gravel. He noticed Susanna struggling to lift the tailgate and hurried over to help her. Just brushing his arm against hers sent a bittersweet pang through his chest. Wordlessly, he helped her into the wagon beside Angela, then secured the gate. Through no fault of their own, their love was doomed never to blossom. This must be the way Romeo and Juliet felt when their families' feud kept them apart.

With no little difficulty, he walked around to the front of the wagon. "Ready to go, sir."

"Thank you, my boy." Mr. MacAndrews touched the brim of his hat. "Shall we go, Miss Angela?" he said over his shoulder. "We have an appointment with the preacher, and we don't want to keep him waiting."

As they drove away, Susanna peered out at Nate just as she had weeks ago while they'd crossed the Valley in their separate wagons. Only now, instead of her cheerful smiles and friendly waves, her lovely face exuded the same sense of desolation weighing on his chest like a one-ton bull. And with her went every hope he'd ever had for happiness.

Chapter Twenty-Three

Susanna and Zack stood up with Daddy and Angela for their wedding ceremony in the church. Afterward, as they all sat in Reverend Thomas's small parlor sipping coffee and eating the cake Angela had cleverly brought along, Daddy retold their story.

The minister listened with great interest. "As a Southerner, I understand how you must feel, Mr. MacAndrews. My father fought for the Confederacy, but his brother chose the Union. They still don't speak to each other. Some of that same animosity still runs deep in the South, especially with the failure of Reconstruction." He accepted Angela's offer of more cake and dug into it before continuing.

"Like everyone else growing up in a divided family, I've had to sort out my own opinions about the war. In truth, I'm glad the Confederacy failed. I'm thankful to the Lord for bringing us back together as a country. After growing up in Virginia, then attending seminary in Massachusetts, I just couldn't go back to a town where President Lincoln's assassination is still celebrated. That's why I accepted Colonel Northam's invitation to serve this community as their pastor. Maybe out here in the West, we can put all of that behind us and start doing the Lord's work in earnest."

He smiled at the newlyweds, then focused on Daddy. "I can see you've already set aside some of your old ideas."

"Reverend, we will say no more about those old ideas." Daddy took Angela's hand and gazed at her fondly. "Miss Angela is a gift from the Almighty, a light in my dark, lonely world."

Susanna watched them through tear-filled eyes. The minister was right, of course. They needed to leave the past behind and find out what the Lord wanted for their future. While Susanna had no hope of ever marrying Nate, she couldn't help but be happy for Daddy. Even Mama wouldn't want Daddy to be alone the rest of his life, but what would she think of his marriage to a Mexican lady? Then again, Mama was in heaven, so it didn't matter. That thought shocked Susanna, but it also rang true deep in her soul.

Now she had to figure out her own opinions. She already liked Angela and had enjoyed working side by side with her in the kitchen. Her generosity and faith in God set an example, especially considering all that she'd suffered. And although she'd been a servant, she knew how to manage Daddy. That alone was an admirable feat.

"Daughter?" Daddy touched her hand and winked. He must have noticed her preoccupation. "What have you decided to call your new stepmama?"

Susanna saw the lady's apprehensive smile, and her heart warmed with the desire to reassure her. For a Southerner, that meant only one thing.

"Why, if it's all right with both of you, I believe I'd like to call her *Miss* Angela."

Nate settled uneasily back into his old room. Oddly, not a trace of Mr. Anders—MacAndrews—remained, not a single gray hair or scent of liniment. Either Angela had cleaned it before they left, or Rita was eager to show the family she could manage all of the housekeeping chores. Still, Nate missed sitting at the bedside chatting with the old man. He'd felt closer to him than he ever had the Colonel.

That wasn't true. During those long months ten years ago as the family had traveled across the country, first by train, then by wagon train, he and his father had worked side by side taking care of the others. He'd been only thirteen years old when they started out, but the Colonel had treated him with respect and depended on him as if he were a grown man. Sometime after they arrived in the San Luis Valley and began to build their ranch, his father changed. He gave Rand his head, ignored Tolley, doted on Rosamond and just barked orders at Nate. Nate still had no idea what had happened to bring about that change.

Now the Colonel had changed again. He did his work and showed up for supper every evening, but his eyes bore a haunted look, and he took no interest in conversation. That was the final proof Nate needed to believe everything Susanna had said. No wonder she hated his father.

Although Nate had been shocked to learn of the connection between his family and hers, he couldn't condemn the Colonel. He and Sherman and Grant had done what they had to do to end the war and preserve the Union. From the way the Colonel had reacted to Susanna's story, he no doubt felt a hefty measure of guilt for some of his actions. Nate just hoped his father took up the matter with the Lord before his guilty feelings made him sick. He also hoped never to go to war himself, but a man had to go when duty called.

Nate already felt pretty sick about losing Susanna. As much as he wanted to ride up to the settlement and find where she lived, maybe go see how she and her father were doing, he had responsibilities on the ranch that couldn't be put off. In the next week, he and some of the hands would ride up into the hills where the largest part of their cattle herd had grazed all summer. They'd round them up, drive them down to the ranch, check them for disease and injuries, brand any calves that had been born and then send the healthy ones off to market before winter snows closed all of the passes.

All that was left to him was to pray for Susanna to find peace. And maybe remember him from time to time. He knew he'd never forget her. Only one bright thought cheered him. Her father had bought property and wouldn't be likely to leave it. When Nate came home from roundup, he couldn't think of a single thing to prevent him from going to see her. Whether she wanted to see him was an entirely different matter.

"You silly puppy." Susanna removed Lazy Daisy from the burlap bag beside her on the ground. The pesky pup seemed determined to dig out every potato Susanna placed in it. With Shadow, the dog's favorite playmate, back at the house, she was doing her best to get into mischief while Susanna worked.

Bending over to retrieve the scattered potatoes, Susanna straightened carefully, holding one hand against her aching back. Several yards away, Miss Angela hummed as she plunged a pitchfork into the ground beside a withered plant, pressed down on the handle and pushed the round, red potatoes to the surface. No matter how much she watched her stepmother, Susanna could not figure out how she could work so hard without hurting her back or complaining. With her example and Mama's before her, Susanna tried to maintain a cheerful attitude, even as her heart cried for Nate. If he'd truly cared for her, wouldn't he come see her? Or had his father forbidden him?

The season's first hard frost had come early, setting the sugars in the fruit and berries, and signaling harvest time for the potatoes and other produce. Today Zack had driven them in the prairie schooner to a farm north of their new home, just across the Rio Grande, where for a small fee the farmers allowed people to dig their own supply of potatoes. These vegetables were not Susanna's favorite, but they were an important staple to keep on hand. She did look forward to enjoying the corn they'd already picked and dried. The widow who'd sold Daddy the property left behind some chickens and a hog, and Zack located a milk cow. These provisions, along with what they could purchase at Winsted's General Store, just opened beside Williams's Café, would see them through the winter.

Like the Northams' house, the foundation, fireplaces and chimneys of her new home were built of stones gathered from the surrounding fields. Zack explained that the man who'd built the house had wisely chosen a rocky bluff above the flood plain to lay his foundation. There in the shade of cottonwood, elm and pine trees, they could enjoy the river flowing beside their property without worrying about spring floods washing them away. They could also add to their larder all the trout Daddy and Zack could catch. Susanna and Angela put up elderberry and chokecherry preserves and dried slices of the plump green apples from the tree beside the house.

While they worked, Susanna questioned Miss Angela about her life. What began as a means of forgetting Nate ended up as an education.

"In 1840, the government of Mexico gave my father a land grant north of Mount Blanca. After the war between Mexico and the United States, the Treaty of Guadalupe Hidalgo said we must leave. My father had been a wealthy man, and he put all of his money into his ranch. When his land was taken without payment, he would not leave my mother's grave. He stayed in the San Luis Valley, working as a horse trainer for the American man who was given our land."

Susanna felt a chill go up her spine. Miss Angela's family had suffered at the hands of a conqueror just as hers had. "How can you speak so casually about it? Seems as if you would despise all Americans."

Miss Angela shrugged. "The Indians, whose land was stolen in the first place, have tried to drive us all out since the days of the *conquistadores,* but they, too, fight among themselves. Even now the Utes try to intimidate the whites into leaving. But there are too many for them to drive out. If they go to war, what good will it do? No good at all, only death, only grief for everyone. To have peace in here—" she tapped her chest above her heart "—it is better to forgive. Better to see others through the eyes of Dios." She tightened the cord around the mouth of the bag of potatoes she'd just filled. "Better to find the place where Dios wants you to be, better to become the person He wants you to be. That alone brings true peace inside you."

Peace. How Susanna longed for it. Forgiveness did seem a better path to finding it, a better attitude than bitterness, so she would try to follow Miss Angela's example in regards to Colonel Northam. The entire North, in fact. She'd seen Daddy struggle with it, and now he seemed at peace. Miss Angela was a good influence on him, and maybe having Mama's valuables had helped to settle the matter for him. At least now Susanna and Miss Angela didn't have to worry about his taking revenge and possibly getting hanged.

"Dios wants us to have joy," Miss Angela said. "Sometimes He wants us to be with a special person." She gave Susanna a teasing grin. "I know this one young *vaquero guapo,* very kind, very strong, very handsome. Maybe Dios wants you to be with him?"

While Susanna appreciated her wise advice, her frequent hints about Nate didn't help in the slightest. Yes, he was all the things she said, but if he wasn't willing to go against his father, they had no future together.

Shading her eyes, she surveyed the section of field they'd just harvested for any missed potatoes. Lazy Daisy scampered across the field, and Susanna chased after her, catching her before she reached the edge. In the distance, across the river, she saw a familiar form of man on a horse, and her heart skipped. Nate! Before she could wave, he turned his horse southward and rode away. Had he been watching over her all this time? Maybe he was working up the courage to visit her.

In the days that followed, however, he didn't come. Nor did she encounter any of the other Northam family members in the burgeoning settlement. On Sundays, to avoid possible unpleasantness, Daddy took his household to the community church in Del Norte.

With each passing week, Susanna grew more and more resigned to her loss. Maybe when spring arrived, she should return to Marietta as she'd planned, marry a Southern gentleman and forget all about a certain cowboy.

But that thought no longer satisfied her daydreams. In fact, it didn't sit well with her at all.

Chapter Twenty-Four

Even though Nate had only seen Susanna at a distance, he relished the memory of watching her in the field. He'd laughed at the puppy's antics as Susanna tried to work, but he hadn't had time to cross the river and talk to her. In a hurry to get back home from doing an errand for Mother, he'd consoled himself that he would see her at church on his last Sunday before roundup. When the MacAndrewses hadn't shown up, he had a hard time listening to Reverend Thomas's sermon. Every time he heard feet shuffling behind him, he'd turned to see if they were coming through the door.

On the ranch, once the Colonel had returned, no one spoke of the incident with the MacAndrewses. Thus, nothing much had changed for the Northam family, except for the gaping hole Nate felt without Susanna in the house. He sort of suspected Rosamond and Mother missed her, too, and of course they all missed Angela.

Now up in the hills to bring down the herd, Nate lingered by the chuck wagon to eat his supper to avoid joining the Colonel, Rand and the other boys around the campfire. Why his father had felt it necessary to come on this roundup was beyond him. Once again the Colonel was managing everything. He seemed so pleased with Rand's repentance over his gambling and his staying awake in church that he barely noticed Nate's constancy. Nor did he spend any time with Tolley. At fifteen, the boy had no friends his own age with whom to release his boyish foolishness, so one of these days he might do something rash to get the Colonel's attention. Nate tried to commend his youngest brother at every opportunity, but the boy's hangdog glances at their father showed whose approval he really wanted. Nate understood how he felt.

After turning his tin plate and fork over to Cookie after supper, he sat on his bedroll and leaned back against his saddle to gaze at the sky, just as he and Susanna had done the first night after they met back in June. The countless number of stars strewn across the night sky reminded him of the tiny diamonds on the necklace Susanna had reclaimed. Of course, everything reminded him of something about Susanna. Further, he still missed his chats with Mr. MacAndrews. Now, there was an attentive father, a man who set an example Nate wanted to follow when and if he ever had children of his own. Not that the old man was perfect. Nate would never drag a daughter halfway across the continent just to reclaim some stolen valuables. Of course, if Mr. MacAndrews hadn't done so, Nate never would have met Susanna, a depressing thought.

Words from Reverend Thomas's Sunday sermon came to mind. Speaking on the story of the Prodigal Son, he'd said, *Only God can be the perfect Father.* Nate couldn't argue with that.

He eyed the Colonel, whom he'd not called Dad again since that fateful day weeks ago in Del Norte. His father's face, never in the least bit fleshy, now had a thin, haggard look. Did he struggle with guilt over the incident at the MacAndrews plantation? If not that, something was eating at him, and for once Nate felt sorry for him. Too bad he didn't have a close friend to confide in, somebody like Mr. Foster, who'd served with him in the war and would understand his struggles.

One thing Nate was sure about. He was tired of being angry and bitter. The preacher's sermon had spoken to him, and he'd vowed that day he wouldn't be like the Prodigal Son's bitter older brother. Holding on to a grudge was like holding a rattler to his chest, just waiting for it to bite. *Lord, I'm letting go. You take over.*

No matter what the Colonel did or didn't do, he would show him respect, real, honest respect. As for Rand, Nate would keep on praying he'd never go back to gambling. And Tolley? Well, he'd watch over the kid like the Colonel should be doing. In only one matter would Nate stand up to his father. When they returned to the ranch, he would announce his plans to ask Mr. MacAndrews if he could court Susanna. If the Colonel said no, Nate would seek the Lord's guidance for the next step. If God told him to move out and move on, he'd do that.

"I sent Rand out to see about those calves we branded today." The Colonel eased himself down beside Nate.

Lost in thought, he hadn't noticed his father's approach. Here was his first chance to keep his vow. "Good idea." Any one of the men could have done it. Maybe his father wanted to give Rand more responsibility, as Nate had suggested.

"You doing all right?" his father said.

Where had that come from? It was a question his father never asked him.

"Yessir." He had the strange notion he was being tested, but whether by God or the Colonel, he didn't know. He sent up a quick prayer for wisdom.

"I've been thinking." His father looked up at the sky and released a long, weary sigh. "A man who steals from helpless women and children is no better than those thieves who stole MacAndrews's horses."

Nate's spine tingled. Yes, this was a test, but not what he'd expected. The Colonel was confiding in him, something he'd never anticipated. Could he be the friend his father needed? He searched for a response to the Colonel's declaration, but no words would come.

"We did what we had to do. We got the job done. We scorched the South and won the war. The slaves were freed, the Union saved."

Right about now, Nate thought he should say, *Praise the Lord,* but he couldn't speak. So he continued his silent prayer.

"But that doesn't stop the guilt."

Nate longed to tell his father he had no cause to feel guilty, but the words stuck in his throat. He didn't believe it, anyway. War or not, he'd done wrong.

"I've been burying my memories all these years. It feels good to have them out in the open. Now I can face what I did and confess it to the Lord."

Nate nodded, still unable to speak. By now he was pretty sure he wasn't supposed to.

"That boy, Rand." The Colonel grunted. "He reminds me of my little brother, the one who ran away to join the army and died at Gettysburg. Our father was always pretty harsh with him. I think that's why he ran away. I never wanted to make that mistake with Rand."

Nate swallowed hard. So all this time, the Colonel had been acting out of fear, not favoritism for his middle son. Now that Nate thought on it, the favoritism had begun after Rand disobeyed their father's orders while they were building the ranch house and suffered that bad fall from the roof.

"Not like you." The Colonel clapped Nate on the shoulder. "I could always trust you to do the right thing." He chuckled. "Of course, you've always been Mr. Knows-It-All, but I'm glad to see you've listened to the preacher's talk on Proverbs. Knowledge isn't worth much if it's not accompanied by wisdom." He grunted again. "But your attitude isn't a surprise. You remind me of a young lieutenant I used to know."

From his rueful grin, Nate guessed he was talking about himself. Still, the knows-it-all charge was valid. Nate had always been proud of his ability to tackle any job and do it well. He was good at figuring things out, sometimes even better than his father. However, such talents were gifts from the Lord and didn't give him the right to be boastful. He'd be wise to keep thinking on that.

"Get some sleep." The Colonel stood and ambled toward his own bedroll. "You have the next watch."

Nate started to say, *I know that.* He caught the words just in time. "Good night, Dad."

The Colonel looked his way and gave him a slight smile. "Good night, son."

Nate couldn't begin to describe the feeling of peace flooding his soul. He knew only that his relationship with his father would be all right from now on. And now he realized his father hadn't been referring to Susanna as the strange woman in Proverbs, hadn't been thinking about her at all. So maybe, just maybe, he could persuade Dad to revise his opinion of Susanna, who'd never done him any harm.

Susanna double-checked the contents of the prairie schooner. Miss Angela's special corn bread, potato salad, ham sandwiches, green beans, one plain cake for serving right away, a second fancier cake for a cakewalk prize. And, of course, Susanna's pralines. Trepidation and excitement vied for control of her emotions as the family packed for their journey into the settlement. The entire community would be meeting for their annual Harvest Home in the field next to the church and across the road from Williams's Café and Winsted's General Store. They would have speeches, horse races, games for grown-ups, games for the children, singing, dancing and far more food than all of them put together could consume.

She would see Nate today, and the thought made her insides flutter. After learning two weeks ago he'd gone on a roundup, she'd realized he hadn't been ignoring her. Even so, she had no idea how she would behave when she saw him. If Miss Angela was right, Nate would be eager to see her, but Susanna wouldn't count on it. If his loyalties lay with his father, he'd probably done his best to forget her.

As for her view of the Colonel, she'd taken Miss Angela's advice to heart and concentrated on forgiving him. His plundering of the plantation hadn't been a personal attack against her family. Even Daddy admitted to being troubled by his own actions during the war, so how could she hate a Yankee officer who was doing his duty, however evil that duty might be? She'd probably never like the Colonel, but she could show him God's love, just as Miss Angela had taught her. On the other hand, if she and Nate did mend their fences and marry, she would resign herself to his father's dislike. Back home, her poor brother, Edward, never did anything right, according to his mother-in-law.

The five-mile trip to the settlement seemed to take forever. At last, the church spire came into view, then the larger homes and, last of all, the two-story general store. Zack drove the wagon into the field and found a spot where the horses could graze. Susanna jumped down from the driver's bench and helped Miss Angela and Daddy carry their food to plank tables set up beneath the cottonwoods.

Their arrival was noticed right away by the other ladies. While many called out greetings, Mrs. Northam offered a wary smile. Rosamond hurried around the table and pulled Susanna into a tight embrace, nearly knocking her over. "I've missed you so much."

"I've missed you, too." Susanna's voice broke, and tears sprang to her eyes. *Oh, bother.* She had promised herself she wouldn't cry.

To cover their heightened emotions, both girls began to rearrange various bowls and plates on the table, chattering along with the other ladies about the abundant harvest. Across the way, Susanna caught sight of the Colonel and gasped softly to herself. In the few short weeks since she'd last seen him, he appeared to have aged ten years. The lines of his face had deepened considerably, and his dark brown hair was streaked with gray. Even his posture, always military straight, was now slightly bowed. To her surprise, he approached Daddy.

"MacAndrews, may I have a minute of your time?" His voice lacked its usual booming authority. "Will you accompany me to a more private location?" He waved a hand toward the church.

For a moment, Daddy stared up at the taller man with a calm regard. Then he gave a curt nod. When Miss Angela tried to follow, Daddy whispered something to her, and she let them go.

Susanna tried to busy herself, but her hands were shaking.

"They'll be all right." Nate's words, spoken softly near her ear, sent a shiver of surprise and happiness down her neck.

She looked up to see his charming, lopsided grin and those bright green eyes. Her heart did a dozen somersaults, and she found it hard to breathe. With some difficulty, she managed to say, "La-di-da, Mr. Nate Northam, I'm sure they *will* be just fine." But it all came out on a sigh, not at all the saucy tone she'd intended.

His gaze intensified, and his smile disappeared. "May I speak to you privately over by your wagon?" Worry lines appeared on his forehead and around his eyes.

"Yes." Rosamond gave Susanna a shove. "Go."

Even Miss Angela tilted her head in that direction, granting both permission and her blessing.

"Very well." Susanna took Nate's offered arm and walked with him to the site.

When they arrived, he lifted her up onto the lowered tailgate and leaned against its side. "We have a lot of things to sort out." He gave her a doubtful look. "That is, if you're interested."

Every pert answer she might have given him fled from her mind. "I'm interested. Go on."

"Your father—" He looked out across the field and chewed his lower lip. "I mean, my father…"

"Nate." She set a hand on his arm. "This isn't about their quarrel or about the war or about anything else. This is about you and me."

"You're right. It is." His worried expression cleared. "I've already told Dad I'm going to ask your father if I can court you, but considering the circumstances, I thought I'd—"

"Wait." She held up one hand to punctuate her interruption. "You're asking me whether you can ask my father to ask me whether I want to court." She burst into an uncontrollable giggle that almost pitched her off the tailgate. Surely, her giddiness came from relief and joy.

Nate laughed, too. Then he guffawed, a sound that lifted Susanna's heart clear up to the top of the nearby cottonwoods. "Yep. That's about right."

As soon as she could control herself, she forced a sober tone into her voice. "Well, I don't know, Nate Northam. If you'll kindly recall, you did call me a thief." She challenged him with a hard stare.

He blinked and frowned. "Yes, I guess I did." He crossed his arms and gave her a sidelong look. "I still say you're a thief."

Her jaw fell open, and she had a hard time closing it. "Why, Nate Northam. How dare you?" All her hopes exploded in a painful burst.

She started to jump to the ground, but he swung around in front of her and placed his hands on the tailgate on either side of her.

"Now, don't deny it." There went that grin again. "You stole my heart."

"Oh, you!" She smacked his hand while joy and relief flooded back into her chest. "Yes, I want you to speak to Daddy. Yes, you may court me." She shook a scolding finger in his face. "Just don't plan on a long courtship, you hear me?"

He offered a mock salute. "Yes, ma'am. Whatever you say."

"Oh, Nate." She touched his cheek, enjoying the gentle scratch of his late-morning stubble.

"Oh, Susanna," he sang in his slightly off-pitch way. "Oh, won't you marry me?"

Her heart still giddy with joy, she giggled again. Mama

would be appalled at her lack of self-control. No, under the circumstances, Mama would be laughing, too.

"Young man." Daddy marched toward the wagon, followed by the Colonel. "You have not asked my permission to court my daughter."

Not doubting his approval for a moment, Susanna gave Nate a mock-worried frown. "Oh, my. What are you going to do now?"

"Mr. MacAndrews, sir." Nate straightened and stepped over to Daddy. "May I court your daughter?"

"You may." His eyes dancing, Daddy shook Nate's hand. Then he glanced over his shoulder at the Colonel. "I assume you have no objections."

The Colonel's expression was less than cheerful, but he shook his head. "None that I can think of right off."

"Well, I do." Susanna jumped down from the wagon and marched to the center of the little group. "I object to you two being enemies. I want to see you shake hands right now." They traded a look but made no move to mind her.

Somewhere in the back of her mind, she became aware of a crowd gathering around them, but she persisted in her mission.

"You'd better listen to me." She shook a schoolmarm finger in each of their faces. "If you two don't put aside the past, as Nate and I have done, I'll never let either of you see your grandchildren. I won't have the war refought on my front porch for the rest of your lives."

"That's the way to tell 'em, Susanna," Miss Pam called from the crowd.

"The war's over," someone else cried. "No more fighting."

"That's why we came out west," Reverend Thomas added.

Other folks chimed in with their agreement.

"Well, Colonel," Daddy said, "seems like the residents of Northamville, or Northam Town or Northampton or whatever you plan to call this place, have spoken. I'll go along with them. What do you say?"

The Colonel wiped a hand down the side of his face. "I had a short speech prepared for later, but I may as well deliver it now, since you're all right here." He cleared his throat and surveyed the gathering. "We can't change what happened in the past or our opinions about the war, but we can move forward and make a better future for our children and grandchildren. As to the name of our town, I'm honored that you voted to name it for my family, for me. But I'm declining that honor."

Groans and protests arose from the crowd, but he lifted his hands in a placating gesture. "Let's choose something that shows just what we've been talking about. We've all come west in hopes of making a new life, a new *way* of life. Does anyone object to New Hope?"

"Or—" Daddy moved in front of the Colonel and faced the crowd "—in keeping with the local custom of using Spanish names, how about the Spanish word for *hope, Esperanza?*" He sent Miss Angela a smile. "Esperanza, Colorado."

"I like it," Miss Pam called out.

To a person, all agreed. With that matter settled, everyone returned to their activities.

Nate pulled Susanna aside into the shadow of the prairie schooner. Holding her in a gentle embrace, he caressed her cheek. "I love you, Susanna. I have since that moment on La Veta Pass when I looked up to see you holding a Winchester on me. You're brave and beautiful and sweet and sassy. I admire the fact that you know your own mind and, most of all, that you're a woman of faith. Will you marry me?"

"La-di-da, Mr. Nate Northam." She couldn't resist teasing him. With all, or most, of their problems solved, she could now relax and have some fun with this Yankee boy. Yankee *gentleman,* she amended. "When I said I wanted a short courtship, I didn't mean only fifteen minutes."

He threw back his head and laughed. "Well, how about if I ask you again after dinner?" He pointed his chin to the tables, where folks had lined up to fill their plates.

"That might do just fine."

Without so much as a by-your-leave, Nate bent and kissed her. Just a quick peck, so she couldn't object too much, although she noticed one older lady watching them with a scowl.

On the other hand, there stood Daddy and the Colonel talking quietly like old friends, although Susanna noticed a familiar gleam in her father's eyes. Just as he'd overrode the Colonel's will in naming the town, she was certain he had every intention of challenging everything the Colonel did from here on out.

Chapter Twenty-Five

Back home in Georgia, September and October weather could be counted on for warm, sunny days and gradually cooler nights. Nonetheless, Susanna found the frosty autumn weather of the San Luis Valley very much to her liking. Of course, part of her happy sentiments were due to her upcoming wedding.

After conferring with Miss Angela and Mrs. Northam, she decided to make a white wedding dress, no matter how impractical it seemed for a dress worn only once. However, such a gown could be made with wide seams and a deep hem so it could be passed down to future Northam brides who might grow taller and wider than Susanna. Mrs. Winsted must have expected to supply just such needs, for her new general store stocked several large bolts of white silk and plenty of lace.

While the ladies split their time between wedding preparations and preserving the winter's supply of food, the men had their own duties. The Colonel had chosen Rand as his trail boss, and most of the cowhands had gone with him to drive the cattle to market. That meant Nate had to shoulder much of the responsibility around the ranch, so Susanna didn't see him often enough to suit her. He did continue the Northam family custom of resting on Sundays, only now he spent those days at the MacAndrews house.

"Angela, I've missed your cooking something fierce," he said over dinner one Sunday after church. "Maybe after the wedding, I'll just move up here to live with you folks."

Daddy and Miss Angela laughed, while Zack shook his head.

"Why, Nate Northam." Susanna sniffed with artificial displeasure. "I'll have you know I'll be doing the cooking for you and me." Not only was Miss Angela a gifted cook, she was also an excellent teacher. Susanna had perfected many dishes under her guidance. But she wouldn't undermine Rita and insist upon cooking for the rest of the Northams, for she doubted she could ever please the Colonel.

"But, darlin'." Nate leaned back in his chair and mimicked Zack's cowboy dialect. "As tasty as your pralines are, a man can't live on 'em."

She shook her fork at him. "Just for that, no dessert for you today."

Of course, Miss Angela served him two slices of apple pie with a heavy dose of cream poured over them. Only after he'd praised the flavor did Susanna admit she'd made it.

"Well, then, I guess you'll do." He shoveled in the last bite with a flourish and gave her a wink. "At least when it comes to desserts."

Later, after Susanna and Miss Angela cleaned up the kitchen and he'd had his weekly chat with Daddy, they walked hand in hand down to the river.

"I can't imagine what takes all of your time." Susanna couldn't bear being parted from him for another week. "Now that the herd's off to market, what on earth do you do out there on the ranch all day?"

His bright green eyes sparkled in the sunshine, and he puckered away a smile. "Oh, you have no idea. Got horses to tend, fences to mend, hay to harvest and store."

She got the feeling he was hiding something from her, but Mama, and now Miss Angela, had warned her against being a nag.

Instead, they talked about their future, about both of them wanting a large family, about the day they'd have their own house and, most of all, about the extraordinary way the Lord had brought them together.

"Say, did you and your father ever finish reading *Bleak House?*"

"We did." She sat on a fallen pine tree beside the river. "It was long and sometimes tedious, but there's a lesson to be learned about being honest and not keeping secrets from those we love. I also liked the ending. Even though the lawsuit destroyed several lives, good, sweet Esther ended up the happy mistress of her own house, married to a wonderful man who loved her."

"Hmm." He sat beside her and put an arm around her waist. She leaned against his sturdy shoulder, relishing his strength. "It occurs to me that our fathers could have gone to court over your silver. Some people regard spoils of war an honest way to acquire property. It would all depend upon the judge how it would turn out."

She shuddered. "Thank the Lord for their reconciliation."

He chuckled "And thank Him for my mother's interference. After finding out how my father got those things, she wouldn't have kept them even if Mr. Lincoln himself had handed them to her."

She gazed up at him, her heart bursting with joy and love. "Like Esther, now I get to be the happy mistress of my own home. But with all the teasing we like to do, it will be anything but a *bleak* house."

Now he laughed out loud, a sound she dearly loved. Unlike his singing, his laughter was decidedly musical. She could listen to it all day, and soon she would be able to.

Nate stood beside Dad and Reverend Thomas at the front of the church. The ladies had been keeping secrets lately, so he had an idea Susanna's wedding getup was something to behold. Rita started playing the "Wedding March" on the small pump organ, and Rosamond walked slowly down the aisle. When she reached the front of the church, Susanna entered on her father's arm, and sure enough, she was a vision like nothing Nate had ever seen.

"Steady, son." Dad put a hand on Nate's shoulder. "Breathe."

Nate did as he was told, gasping in a breath.

Mr. MacAndrews still limped a little, so it was hard to tell who was leaning on whom as they moved toward the front. Before Nate knew what had happened, he was saying "I do," and Reverend Thomas gave him permission to kiss the bride.

Mindful of the watching crowd, he bent down and placed a quick peck on Susanna's pretty pink lips. To his surprise, she gave him one of her cute little scolding looks.

"Is that all I get?" She grabbed the front of his shirt,

stood on her tiptoes and taught him a thing or two about kissing.

Goose bumps shot through his entire body, and he was all but certain his toes curled up right inside his boots.

"There." Susanna put on her smug look. "Now we're honestly and truly married."

Before Nate could answer, Dad cleared his throat. "Son, may I speak to your bride?"

All humor left her face, but here in front of the entire community, how could he say no? He gave a quick nod.

"Susanna," Dad said, "we got off on the wrong foot, and I'm entirely to blame. You are a lovely young woman, and I'm proud you've chosen to marry my son. Welcome to the Northam family."

Nate held his breath. Every time he'd brought up his father's inhospitality or his actions against her family during the war, she'd changed the subject. Did she realize how much was riding on her response?

Susanna's eyes burned as she blinked away tears. What would Mama have her do? In the past weeks, she'd had more memories of that last fateful day on the plantation. She saw brave Mama facing this same man, who'd never had the courtesy to even dismount from his horse while ordering the livestock killed and the house set on fire. Susanna blinked again, and the tears rushed down her cheeks. She cast a pleading glance at Miss Angela, who tapped her chest above her heart, and the answer came clear and fast. She had to make peace with this man before moving back into his house, this time permanently.

She stepped past Nate and reached up to place a kiss on her father-in-law's cheek. "Thank you, Father Northam. I'm pleased as punch to be a member of your family."

Applause erupted from the congregation, along with a few cheers.

"Let's eat," somebody called out.

They all adjourned to the field next door, where linen-covered plank tables held a grand wedding feast. For over an hour as folks ate and danced, Susanna and Nate suffered the usual teasing about newlyweds. She overheard Zack and another cowboy whispering about a shivaree, and she cast a worried glance at Nate.

Grabbing her hand, he put one finger to his lips. "Shh. Let's go."

He led her around to the back of the church, where Mother Northam's buggy stood hitched and ready to go. "Let's hope nobody misses us."

Taking a long road around the settlement to avoid being seen, Nate drove them at last down the long road to the ranch. But when they came to the stone archway, he kept on going.

"Mr. Nate Northam, just where do you think you're taking me?"

"Just wait and see." A quarter mile from the Four Stones archway, he turned down a newly smoothed road and up to a pretty white house with a stone foundation and chimney.

"What do you think?" Filled with a worried look, Nate's green eyes had never been so appealing. "Would you like to live here?"

For a moment she couldn't speak. All this time, he hadn't been neglecting her. He'd been building their own home. She wouldn't have to live with her in-laws after all. "Oh, Nate, it's beautiful."

He jumped down from the buggy, lifted her in his arms and carried her right through the front door. "Welcome home, Mrs. Nate Northam." He set her down and waved one arm to take in the sizable parlor, a hallway on one side no doubt leading to the bedrooms, and the dining room and kitchen off to the other side. "Make yourself at home."

"Why, *Mr.* Nate Northam." She flung herself into his arms. "I believe I'll do just that."

* * * * *

Dear Reader,

Thank you for choosing *Cowboy to the Rescue,* the first book in my Four Stones Ranch series. I hope you enjoyed the adventures of my heroine, Susanna MacAndrews, and my hero, Nathaniel Northam. For many years I have wanted to write a series of stories set in the beautiful San Luis Valley of Colorado, and now I'm doing just that.

I moved to the Valley as a teenager, graduated from Alamosa High School and attended Adams State College. Later my husband and I settled in Monte Vista, where my parents owned and operated a photography business, Stanger Studios. Three of our children were born in Monte Vista, and one was born in Alamosa. Even though we moved to Florida in 1980, my heart remained attached to my former home in Colorado. Writing this book has been a sweet, nostalgic trip for me.

Those familiar with the history of this area of Colorado may recognize a little bit of Monte Vista in my fictional town, Esperanza. I could have used the real town, but then I would have shortchanged the true pioneers of Monte Vista, who deserve accolades for their courage and foresight in building such a fine community. Any resemblance between my characters and those who actually settled in this area is strictly coincidental.

If you enjoyed Susanna and Nate's story, I hope you'll look for Book Two in my series to see whether Rand Northam finds romance in the San Luis Valley. I love to hear from my readers, so if you have a comment, please contact me through my website: blog.louisemgouge.com.

Blessings,
Louise M. Gouge

Questions for Discussion

1. As the story begins, Susanna is so fearful for her father's life that she welcomes help from Nate, even though he's a Yankee. What is Susanna's strongest reason for not wanting to fall in love with Nate? What keeps Nate from permitting himself to fall in love with Susanna? Is the greatest barrier to their love internal or external?

2. How have both Susanna and Nate kept their parents' prejudices alive? Why did both of them avoid discussions of the war? Would their relationship have grown or faltered if they had brought it out into the open soon after they met?

3. At twenty-three years old, why is Nate still seeking his father's approval? What are the Colonel's expectations from Nate? Given their circumstances (running a ranch together), are those expectations reasonable? Are there people in your life whose approval you are seeking? Why or why not? What is the solution?

4. The Colonel and Mr. Anders seem very different in their parenting methods, but are they actually very much alike? How does this affect their children? What is your view of God? Do you see Him as a loving, gentle Father or a demanding parent whom you can never please?

5. Mr. Anders was adept at keeping secrets, not only from his enemy but also from his own daughter. Do

you think Susanna would have accompanied him to Colorado if she had known his real purpose? The Colonel also has some secrets. Would knowing those secrets have helped Nate react differently to his father?

6. Susanna tries not to let the Colonel's rudeness and hostility affect her, even as she struggles not to let her hatred for all Yankees color her feelings toward the rest of the family. Have you ever found yourself in a situation in which someone dislikes you for no apparent reason? How did you feel? How did you react?

7. Susanna and Nate fall in love with each other before they know the deeper issues that might divide them. When the truth is revealed, both Susanna and Nate stick with their own families. What does this reveal about their character? How do they resolve their issues?

8. Susanna left her life of ease in Marietta, Georgia, to accompany her father on an arduous journey. Why was she willing not only to go with him but also to make the best of it? Whose example did she try to follow? Although we never "meet" her mother, what do we learn about her through Susanna's memories?

9. Several times in the story, Nate makes decisions based on Scriptural examples. Which ones are they? What choices did he make based on those examples? Do you think Nate is a strong hero? What is your definition of a hero?

10. How might this story have turned out differently if Mr. Anders refused to forgive the Colonel? If Susanna refused to forgive Nate for siding with his father?

11. At the end of the story, what does Nate do to show his understanding of Susanna's need not to live with his family? What does this reveal about his character?

12. Which character changes the most in the story? Susanna? Nate? In what ways did each one mature and become stronger?

13. The overarching themes of this story are revenge and forgiveness, two sides of the same coin. How did Susanna and Nate work through their own issues? How could each one of them have taken an easier path to resolving their issues?

14. Will the people of Esperanza be able to keep their resolve not to let the war affect their community? Why or why not?

SPECIAL EXCERPT FROM

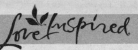

*Get ready for a Big Sky wedding…or fifty! Here's a
sneak peek at
HIS MONTANA BRIDE by Brenda Minton,
part of the BIG SKY CENTENNIAL miniseries:*

"Bad news," Cord said. "That was the wedding coordinator. She's quitting."

"Ouch. So now what?"

"I'm not sure."

"With no coordinator to help, will you call off the wedding?" Katie asked.

"No." There was too much at stake. The town needed this wedding and the money it would bring in. They had a bridge in need of repairs and a museum they couldn't finish without more funds. "I'll just figure out how to pull off a wedding for fifty couples, maybe get some media attention for Jasper Gulch and hopefully not mess up anyone's life."

"I think you'll do just fine. Remember, it's all about the dress."

"How long are you going to be in town, Katie?" He placed a hand on her back and guided her up the sidewalk.

"I'm not sure. I'm supposed to be helping my sister, but she seems to have escaped and left me here." She sighed and glanced at him.

"Do you think that as long as you're here…"

They were standing in front of the massive wooden doors that led to the church. She had a slightly red nose from the cool morning air and her lips were tinted with pink gloss. As long as she was there, she could be a friend. That wasn't what he'd planned to say, but the thought framed itself as a question in his mind.

She was studying his face, waiting for him to finish.

"Maybe you could help me with this wedding?"

"I thought maybe you wanted me to run interference and keep the single women at bay. 'Hands off Cord Shaw,' that kind of thing." As she said it, somehow her palm came to rest on his shoulder as if they'd been friends forever.

It was the strangest and maybe one of the best feelings. It tangled him up and made him lose track of the reality that he was standing in front of the church. The door could open at any moment. And for the first time in years, a woman had made him feel at ease.

Can rancher Cord Shaw and Katie Archer pull off Jasper Gulch's latest centennial event without getting their hearts involved? Find out in
HIS MONTANA BRIDE by Brenda Minton,
available October 2014 from Love Inspired.

SPECIAL EXCERPT FROM

Danger and love go hand in hand in the small town
of Wrangler's Corner. Read on for a sneak preview of
THE LAWMAN RETURNS by Lynette Eason,
the first book in this exciting new series from
Love Inspired Suspense.

Sheriff's deputy Clay Starke wheeled to a stop in front of
the beat-up trailer. He heard the sharp crack, and the side
of the trailer spit metal.

A shooter.

The woman on the porch careened down the steps and
bolted toward him. Terror radiated from her. He shoved
open the door to the passenger side. "Get in!"

Breathless, she landed in the passenger seat and slammed
the door. Eyes wide, she lifted shaking hands to push her
blond hair out of her eyes.

Clay got on his radio and reported shots fired.

He cranked the car and started to back out of the drive.

"No! We can't leave!"

"What?" He stepped on the brake. "Lady, if someone's
shooting, I'm getting you out of here."

"But I think Jordan's in there, and I can't leave without
him."

"Jordan?"

"A boy I work with. He called me for help. I'm worried
he might be hurt."

Clay put the car back in Park. "Then stay down and let
me check it out."

LISEXP0914

"But if you get out, he might shoot you."

He waited. No more shots. "Stay put. I think he might be gone."

"Or waiting for one of us to get out of the car."

True. He could feel her gaze on him, studying him, dissecting him. He frowned. "What is it?"

"You."

He shot a glance behind them, then let his gaze rove the area until he'd gone in a full circle and was once again looking into her pretty face. "What about me?"

Red crept into her cheeks. "You look so much like Steven. Are you related?"

He stilled, focusing in on her. "I'm Clay Starke. You knew my brother?"

"Clay? I'm Sabrina Mayfield."

Oh, wow. Sabrina Mayfield. "Are you saying the kid in there knows something about Steven's death?"

"I don't know what he's doing here, but he called me and said he thought he knew who killed Steven and he needed me to come get him."

A tingle of shock raced through Clay. Finally. After weeks with nothing, this could be the break he'd been looking for. "Then I want to know what he knows."

Pick up THE LAWMAN RETURNS, available
October 2014 wherever
Love Inspired Suspense books are sold.